PERFECT
Enemies

Perfect Enemies is a work of fiction. Names, characters, places, and incidents are the products of the author's imagination or are used fictitiously. Any resemblance to actual events, locales, or persons, living or dead, is entirely coincidental.

Copyright © 2021 Jill Ramsower

All rights reserved. In accordance with the U.S. Copyright Act of 1976, the scanning, uploading, and electronic sharing of any part of this book without the permission of the publisher is unlawful piracy and theft of the author's intellectual property. Thank you for your support of the author's rights.

Cover Model: Sergio Carvajal
Photographer: Miguel Anxo
Edited by Editing4Indies

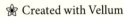 Created with Vellum

Books by Jill Ramsower

The Five Families Series
Forever Lies
Never Truth
Blood Always
Where Loyalties Lie
Impossible Odds
Absolute Silence
Perfect Enemies

The Savage Pride Duet
Savage Pride
Silent Prejudice

The Byrne Brothers Series
Silent Vows

The Of Myth & Man Series
Curse & Craving
Venom & Vice
Blood & Breath
Siege & Seduction

PERFECT ENEMIES

JILL RAMSOWER

CHAPTER 1
Valentina

NIGHT HAD LEACHED THE CITY OF COLOR, BUT I COULD STILL see the heavy purple bruising blossoming around Reyna's left eye as if an inky shadow from the trees above had cast her face in splotchy darkness. That would have been far less sinister than the truth. The mark wasn't a magical trick of the moonlight, much to my horror. Someone had hurt my friend.

"Reyna, honey. What happened?" I wrapped her in my arms, the arctic December air forgotten. Reyna had sent me a cryptic message to meet her halfway between our houses. I'd been so worried that I'd snuck out of the house in a hurry, only realizing I'd left my coat at home once I was two houses away. I'd debated running back, but now I was glad I hadn't wasted another second.

My friend shook in my arms as violent sobs wracked her entire body. I gave her time for the emotion to work its way through her system. Only once her jerky, turbulent breaths evened did I pull back to search her face for answers.

In the months we'd spent getting to know one another, Reyna had never been forthcoming about her background, but I'd never imagined she was in danger. I'd gathered that her family situation wasn't great. It was relatively common for students at an elite private school to experience a bit of neglect or have unrealistic expectations placed upon them. Still, it never occurred to me that someone might be hurting her.

Shock and horror hollowed out my insides. Remorse over not figuring it out earlier made my lungs burn with every shallow breath.

Reyna refused to meet my gaze. "There's something I should have told you months ago, but I ... I didn't know how."

"You can tell me anything, Rey. You know that."

I adored my best friend. Reyna Vargas was the most genuine, kindhearted person I'd ever met. I'd felt an urgent need to take her under my wing the first day she joined our school at the start of senior year. She was so soft-spoken and delicate that she would need protection if she was going to survive the hallways of Xavier Catholic School, where privilege was the backbone of the curriculum and the air itself was infused with the fresh leather scent of entitlement. The kids at my school were carbon copies of their CEO fathers and corporate counsel mothers. They'd been trained since birth to smell blood in the water from a mile away.

Xavier bullies could teach the CIA innovative new torture tactics.

Reyna had been a brand-new shiny target in a plaid pleated skirt until I took her in my arms and claimed her. No one at school had dared touch her after that. As one of the students who'd been at Xavier since preschool, I'd had plenty of time over the years to ensure everyone understood that messing with me would have consequences. I had acquired dirt on all my classmates and had earned sainthood in the eyes of the faculty. By means of our new friendship, my status extended to Reyna for the most part.

Life slipped into the comfortable embrace of routine as our senior year unfolded. Despite knowing my other friends most of my life, Reyna became my closest confidant. She was loyal with a dry sense of humor that most people missed entirely. I saw past her shyness to her incredible insightfulness and found a lasting friendship I'd never expected. I hated to think she was scared to ask me for help.

Rey shook her head, her face scrunching as if caving to another onset of sobs, but she took a deep breath and reined in the wayward emotion. "No, this is different." Her watery eyes finally lifted to mine. "My dad is part of the Sonora Cartel—the head of it, now that my uncle is dead." The words were whispered into the darkness as if the wind might carry them away and spread her shameful secret.

My body went rigid. The impact of her admission invited the bitter cold to seep deep into my bones.

Reyna's family was cartel.

My family was at war with her family.

My eldest sister, Giada, had been kidnapped by the cartel and had only escaped home the night before last. We'd spent weeks terrified we'd never get her back.

I cocked my head and tried to make sense of the information—of how my heart could mislead me so terribly. How could someone I'd protected and called my closest friend also be my enemy?

"Did you know? Did you know who my father was?" My face contorted along with my heart, horrified at the possible implications. I tried to pull back, but Reyna clasped my hands.

"Please, give me a chance to explain." More tears trickled down her cheeks. "I knew who you were. My dad told me to befriend you in order to feed him information, but I swear on my life that I never once gave him anything. They're wretched, awful people, Valentina. That's why I never talk about them. Please—" Her breathing hitched. "Please don't push me away. Not now. Not when I need you more than ever."

Reyna's Latina genes had gifted her with flawless olive skin, full lips most girls would kill for, and mesmerizing dark eyes that tilted up to give her an exotic vibe. While she was different from most girls at school, her uniqueness was its own source of beauty. Her looks and shy demeanor were precisely what made her such an attractive target at school. But nothing was pretty about her brutal honesty. No beauty in the gruesome nature of her swelling eyelids or the brutally raw depths of her remorse.

Seeing her so distraught sent a wave of uncertainty crashing over me.

I trusted my instincts, and they'd never once detected that Reyna meant me harm. Her plea was dripping with sincerity. Literally. A stray tear splattered on my hand where she clasped it between us.

I looked at my friend, trying desperately to seek the truth.

Maybe it was the bruising around her eye that tore at my heart, but I couldn't paint her as a villain. She could have continued the charade without ever telling me who she was. If she'd meant me harm, she could have done it at any time. Her confession was purely for my benefit. In fact, her honesty was entirely counterproductive to any ulterior motives.

"Why tell me now?"

"Because I wanted you to know. And because I need your help. You're all I have."

I stared deep into her chestnut eyes, nearly black beneath the shadows of an old oak tree, and felt the tendrils of friendship solidify between us. Reyna was my friend. The identity of our parents changed nothing. She needed me, and I would always help her.

Tears welled in my own eyes as I pulled her into a hug. "I'm not going anywhere, Rey. You're stuck with me."

Her chest shuddered against mine, arms clasping me tightly as though I might run at any moment. When her breathing settled, she pulled back and began to explain.

"Your family ordered my father and his men back to Mexico. They showed up at the house yesterday, and Dad was so angry," she whispered that last part, fear palpable in her broken words.

"Is he going to leave?" I asked softly, pulling back to meet her worried gaze. My sister was safely back home, but my parents didn't share details about anything else they might have known. We'd only recently learned my father was in the mafia, so I certainly wasn't privy to information about his secret life.

"He was making plans to go back for my uncle's funeral." She shook her head back and forth adamantly. "I can't go back there, Valentina. I can't go back to Mexico. If I do, I'll never be free of him."

"When you turn eighteen in May, you'll be an adult. Then you can live wherever you want."

"No, you don't understand. He'll *never* let me leave. The only reason I was allowed to come with him to New York was *you*. I'm just a pawn to him. Something to use for his gain. He'll have me marry one of his associates to secure a business alliance. My life will never be my own."

What was it about men that made them think they could own people? The actions of the male sex made me wish I wasn't attracted to them. Life would be so much simpler without testosterone-fueled egomaniacal power trips. Men could be so damn annoying. And the worst thing we could do as women was to let them get away with that shit. Not me. I believed in holding people accountable. I believed in standing up for myself and for those around me.

Whether it was feminism or just plain old human decency, I didn't know and didn't care. I wasn't the type of girl to give someone else control over me or my friends and family just because that person was born with a dick between their legs. Not only that, but I was hella persistent. Reyna's dad might have given her his DNA, but that didn't give him the right to dictate the rest of her life. Nor did it give him the right to lay hands on her.

My conviction to help my friend grew deep roots and stiffened my spine, preparing for the battle ahead. Saving Reyna from her father wouldn't be easy, but she was worth the fight. She was my best friend. An attack on her was an attack on me, and I was the type of girl who fought back.

"Juan Carlos Vargas may be your father, and he may be powerful, but he's not God. He has weaknesses, and he can definitely be outsmarted." A man like him with an ego bursting at the seams would easily underestimate the abilities of a teenage girl. "If you can convince him to let you stay until graduation, I'll find a way to keep you here for good."

Reyna flung her arms around me. "Thank you, Val. You're the one good thing my father's ever done for me. Even if none of this works, your friendship alone has been a gift I'll always cherish."

I would have burst into tears if my mind wasn't already half occupied with brainstorming ways to give Reyna a fresh start. I had an impressive history of success when I set my mind to a goal, and freeing Reyna was now my top priority. I refused to let her down.

CHRISTMAS BREAK LASTED AN ETERNITY. Now that I knew who Reyna's father was, I was extra careful not to mention her to my parents. There were no holiday sleepovers, and we kept all text conversations superficial. Reyna had already limited our time together away from school in an attempt to protect me, so my parents had only heard me mention her a few times in passing. I'd never been to her house, and she'd always refused my invitations to mine.

Now, it was even more crucial we kept both our fathers in the dark for any chance of success planning Reyna's escape. That meant I had to keep her identity a secret from my family, and she had to keep our conversations mundane since her father monitored her phone.

I debated whether it would be more prudent to tell one of my sisters about Reyna or to keep her a complete secret. It would be helpful if I wasn't totally on my own, but bringing anyone else into the loop would increase the risk of my father finding out. Giada would be the one most likely to take a risk on my behalf but was also the biggest threat of leaking information. Get a glass of wine in her, and she had no filter at all. Giada was entirely too risky, and Camilla was a world-class Goody Two-shoes. I highly doubted she'd agree to help Reyna. The small chance I was wrong wasn't worth the risk of asking.

I was close to my cousins, but none of them was suited as a confidant. Maria, the eldest, lived and breathed the mafia, so she'd never help anyone from the cartel. Alessia worried about everything. Her anxiety would lead her to rat me out, even if I wasn't in any direct danger. There was no way she could be trusted. My youngest cousin, Sofia, was my best bet. She had kept a surprising number of secrets that had recently come to light, so she could be trusted to keep quiet. However, she had just gone through a hellish situation of her own, so I hated to drag her into more drama. I would keep her in mind if time wore on and I had no other option, but for now, I would see if I could manage on my own. I had faith in my abilities, and now that Reyna had successfully convinced her father to let her stay here with her mom, we had some time to work on a solution.

His acquiescence was an enormous relief. Doubtless, his concession was rooted in a selfish desire to have her spy on me, but I didn't care about his reasons. All that mattered was she got to stay. No amount of planning would have helped if her father had snatched her back to Mexico over the break.

We had five months to find Reyna a way out—and by we, I meant me.

No pressure.

The first day back at school, I searched for her the second I was dropped off on that cold January morning. Hurrying through the front doors, I made a beeline straight to the library. Rey liked to get out of her house as early as possible, so she had her driver take her an hour before the first bell when the assistant principal first unlocked the school. While the building was still dark and footsteps echoed off the locker-lined hallways, she slinked to the library and hid until I arrived. She wasn't necessarily afraid of the other kids; she just liked to be alone. It seemed lonely to me, but she swore she enjoyed the solace. I guess if I'd had a drunk mother and a tyrannical father, I would have preferred to be alone too.

Regardless, my arrival each morning signaled the end of her reprieve.

"Aren't you looking lovely this morning," I greeted her as I plopped down in the chair next to hers.

Rey slammed her book shut and jumped up to hug me. "It's so good to see you! I thought the break would never end."

"I'm sure mine wasn't as rough as yours, but I've been anxious to get back so we could talk again. Not being able to communicate sucked." We released one another and settled into the chairs at her table. I was pleased to see that her bruise had healed, and she bore no other obvious signs of abuse. I had assumed that would be the case with her father gone but wasn't entirely sure.

"Have you come up with any ideas on how to hide me away?" Her face was so hopeful that I had trouble maintaining eye contact.

"Not exactly, but it's nothing to worry about," I assured her. I was a little nervous about what to do, but I would never tell her that. I didn't want her to worry. "I considered petitioning for your emancipation before you're eighteen in May, but that would be difficult and wouldn't necessarily keep your father from stealing you away. Our best bet is to get some money together and hide you." She wouldn't be able to work anywhere without paperwork, so she'd need enough money to survive until I could find a way to get fake documents. I'd watched enough movies to know that stuff existed. I just needed to figure out where to get them.

The other problem? Money. Something I'd never thought much about. Her father didn't let her have any of her own, of course. That would have given her a certain degree of freedom and power, and an asshole like him could never allow that. I had a trust fund and would gladly give her some of my money, but as a minor, I still needed my father's permission to withdraw funds until I turned eighteen. I didn't think he'd be willing to support the escape of the cartel leader's daughter. Our families were already at odds. Helping Reyna disappear might stir up an even greater war than they were already facing.

My birthday was in March. If we could make it until then, I could get to my money and help her. My dad would know I'd taken the money, but only after the fact. That would get Reyna to freedom, but to have any chance of long-term success, she needed a new identity—a driver's license and social security number at the very least. Where the hell was I supposed to find those?

That was the wall I kept running into. Anyone with shady connections who might be able to help me was also connected to my father and would likely rat me out. I'd gone round and round over the limited options. So far, blackmail seemed my best bet. If I could leverage a secret over someone, I could keep them from telling my father. It wasn't my best plan ever, but it was all I had at the moment.

"I do have a little money," Reyna confessed. "But it wouldn't support me for long."

"I'll get it all sorted out," I assured her. "You just keep your father at bay and try not to worry. Come on, bell's about to ring."

She rolled her eyes but followed me. We walked to first period English, which was one of three classes we had together. Our school was small compared to city public schools but decently large for a private K-12. I could guarantee I'd know most of the faces in any given class but having classes with friends wasn't a given. The four classes Reyna and I had shared during the first semester had dropped to three, which would have to do. At least we got to start our day together.

We slid into the front-row seats we'd occupied the first semester and got ready for class. I hardly paid any attention to the other students filtering into the room. Most were still sipping their mochaccinos and waking up, uninterested in conversation so early in the morning. I vaguely took notice of a rumbling masculine voice but snapped to attention when the words *new student* drifted to my ears.

I casually shifted my gaze to peer at the newcomer, only to find him staring straight at me. Unapologetic. Demanding and utterly mouthwatering. He wasn't just attractive; he was the personification of unattainable perfection. The ideal beauty standard every Instagram model promotes but has to use filters to achieve. His broad, square shoulders and chiseled jaw gave him an edgy look that warned against messing with him like thorns on a rose. Sandy-blond hair flopped down close to his eyes but left just enough room to allow his penetrating gold stare to pierce through beneath. His irises weren't brown or hazel. I'd never seen anything like them. It was almost as though they were lit from behind like the incandescent glow of a harvest moon.

With that kind of natural beauty, this guy had probably never been told no in his whole life. No doubt he believed he was God's gift to women. No matter how pretty he might be, that kind of drama was never worth it. He was trouble incarnate, and his calculating stare flicked with interest from me to Reyna.

Oh, hell no.

I could handle myself, but Reyna was different. She was sensitive and had way too much to deal with to add a womanizing playboy to the list. He could take that hypnotic stare and focus it somewhere else—anywhere else besides my sweet, innocent friend.

Most of the seats in class had been filled except for a couple near the back. He never even considered them. Instead, he approached the girl sitting in the desk behind me and squatted down so he was eye level with her. I refused to turn and watch him lest he interpreted my attention as encouragement. All I could do was sit, spine tall and ears pricked for the slightest sound.

"Hey, my name's Kane," he offered in a sultry murmur. "This is my first day, and I guess I'm a little late to get a seat at the front. I hate not to see the board, and since I misplaced my glasses while we were unpacking, would you be a sweetheart and let me have your seat?" He spoke to her intimately as though they were longtime friends making a deeply personal arrangement.

It was pure manipulation.

He was a master con artist who painted his way through

life with strokes of flattery and flashes of his perfect smile. It made me sick.

"Oh, of course. Yeah ... here." The girl slid from her desk and gathered her bag. "I'm Paisley ... um, yeah, okay." She stumbled over her words as she retreated to the back of the room, drunk off the gift of his attention.

You have got to be kidding me.

I couldn't help myself. I glanced over my shoulder at him, shooting him a scathing glare.

"Ouch," he murmured. "Not sure what I did to deserve that."

I ignored him, but his comment drew Reyna's attention. He pounced on the opportunity.

"Hey, I'm Kane."

I could hear the smarmy grin in his words. Just as I feared, Reyna's cheeks were flushed bright pink when I peered over at her.

"I'm Reyna," she said shyly.

"What lunch do you have? I don't know anyone yet, and I hate to sit alone if I don't have to."

Oh, brother. This master manipulator would chew up my sweet friend and spit her out the moment something better came along. There was no way in hell I was letting that happen.

"All seniors have lunch at the same time," I cut in. "You'll be able to sit with whoever you want. I'm sure you'll be welcome at any number of tables."

"That's great, but maybe I don't want to sit with just anyone."

I slowly swiveled in my seat to face the newest member of Xavier High, my glare so arctic that Elsa would have been impressed. "I don't think either of us wants to sit with you. We've got enough friends, thanks."

Kane relaxed back in his chair, a lazy smirk gracing his full lips. He wasn't at all intimidated by my rebuff. Those amber eyes sparked at a challenge. I'd just waved a red flag in front of the bull, and he was ready to charge.

His eyes flicked to Reyna. "You say that, but I don't think she feels the same."

"I think I know my best friend a little better than you, thanks."

"How about we let her speak for herself?" His eyes drifted back to Rey, and I had no choice but to follow.

Both of us stared at her, waiting for her reply as she withdrew behind a curtain of silky black hair. "Um, it's fine. You can sit with us, Kane." Her eyes shot back to me, brows drawn with uncertainty and apology. As if I could be mad at her. She was too intimidated to send him away. That's precisely why I'd tried to do it myself.

"There you go," Kane purred from behind me. "I'll see you ladies at lunch."

Smug bastard. A ragged sigh slipped out as I turned back to face the board.

As if escaping a cartel wasn't bad enough, my second semester of senior year just got even more complicated.

CHAPTER 2
Kane

EVERYTHING ABOUT THIS PLACE MADE MY SKIN CRAWL. THE power plays and posturing. The snobbish cliques and haughty entitlement. I'd had an idea how things would be when I arrived, but living it was another story. Walking into the school cafeteria, I felt like I was cast in an over-the-top coming-of-age movie where each character had its very own stereotype to portray and not a single person was multidimensional. I'd only ever been to public school before, where kids bought square slices of generic pizza or brought brown paper sack lunches of PB&J and a bag of chips. Not at Xavier. There was a fucking sushi station, for Christ's sake.

How could any of these people be substantive when they'd never even stepped foot in the real world?

In a way, it made being there easier. All I had to do was play my role until I could get out. There would be no attachments or complications when the people around me were as deep as a parking lot puddle. Pretty faces and nothing more.

Eyes the shade of tempered steel floated in the back of my mind, still shooting glacial daggers at me. The queen "B". I never asked for her name, but it wasn't necessary to know she was school royalty. That kind of confidence always came with a crown. The question was, why had she deigned to wield her power against me? I rarely faced that kind of blatant rejection. What did she have against me? Poor Reyna looked like a deer in headlights when forced to choose between us. Was she a mindless minion, powerless to go against her ruthless monarch? I was endlessly curious in the same way people scan for bodies as they pass a car wreck. If I pushed to befriend Reyna, could I get past her vigilant watchdog, or would the silver-eyed cynic prove to be an insurmountable challenge?

There was only one way to find out.

I'd had second period with Reyna but didn't have a single chance to talk to her. She was good at avoiding people. I didn't push the issue because it was only my first day. Given a little time, I would work my way under their skin and learn what made each of them tick. And while the cafeteria ensemble cast may have been a joke, the scene was still an opportunity to talk more with the girls. I spotted them sitting with a small group in a far corner of the cafeteria. My calzone in hand, I wedged myself between Reyna and her overzealous bestie on the wooden bench seat.

"I'd ask if I could join, but I know your answer." I flashed my opposition a grin and added a wink just to piss her off.

Those silver eyes blazed. "Why ask if you're just going to ignore the answer?"

"Exactly." I ripped off a chunk of calzone and placed it in my mouth, all while staring at my new sparring partner.

"Just ignore her, Kane," said the redhead girl across from me. "Val's been a little salty all year."

Her friends call her Val. Good to know.

"Nice, Chloe," Val shot back.

The girl just grinned a saccharine smile. "I'm Chloe. We had chem two together this morning, but you were too busy chatting up Harper the Hoover for me to introduce myself." This girl was clearly another alpha. I was intrigued by her friendship with Val. In my experience, girl groups imposed a one-alpha hard limit. Otherwise, it was like putting two beta fish in a tank together—they tore each other apart.

"Harper the Hoover?" I asked.

"She'll suck out your soul right after she sucks your dick. Don't take the bait, trust me," said a big guy next to Chloe. Uniforms made it a bit harder to tell who belonged to what stereotype, but if the guy's neck girth was any indication, he had to be a jock.

"And you are?"

"Bryson," he spoke through a bite of apple.

I nodded, taking a sip from my water bottle, then turned a fraction to the ice queen beside me. "And you're Val. I didn't get your name earlier."

"Valentina," she corrected.

I smirked. Her irritation shouldn't have amused me as much as it did, but I couldn't help myself. I should have been winning her over—it would have made life a hell of a lot easier—but her anger was infinitely more entertaining. I turned to my silent neighbor on the other side. "Reyna is a lovely name. Spanish, right?"

She nodded. "I'm from Mexico originally."

"Really? You hardly have any accent."

The corners of her lips twitched with a small smile. "My father hired a tutor when I was young. He was insistent that I learn perfect English."

"Damn, and I thought my dad was hard on me."

"So, where are you from, Kane?" Valentina cut in, directing everyone's attention my way.

"Texas." I loosened the ridiculous tie and unbuttoned the collar of my uniform dress shirt.

"You're going to want to leave that on, or you'll get a dress code violation. Three strikes, and you get suspended."

My wannabe nemesis giving me advice? Interesting.

I grinned and took a big bite of my calzone.

Val's eyes took another trip around the inside of her skull. "Whatever. Get in trouble, see if I care," she muttered under her breath.

Laughter stirred in my chest, but I kept it locked down.

"Hey, Kane." The voice behind me was a sultry purr I recognized immediately from chemistry class. "You should have come sit with me, silly. This crowd doesn't know how to have any fun at all." Harper placed a hand on my back, then motioned to a table of fake blondes, all watching raptly.

"By all means," Val encouraged. "I'm sure Harper can show you all sorts of fun."

A tiny flare of temper had me casting a glare at her. "Maybe tomorrow, Harper." I turned my attention back to the girl behind me and painted on my most charming smile. "But thanks for the invitation. I'm good right here."

"Well, you know where to find me when you get bored." She flung her mane of fake sun-kissed hair over her shoulder and strutted back to her minions.

Everyone at the table chuckled and went back to their own conversations along with the rest of the cafeteria, which had grown suspiciously quiet during our exchange.

"You should have gone," Valentina whispered so that only I could hear.

When I looked over, our eyes collided and locked in a wordless battle. A cacophony of veiled threats and murderous promises. Why was she so resistant to me? Was she so accustomed to getting her way that she couldn't stand me refusing to concede? That wasn't it. She'd set herself against me before we'd ever said a single word to each other.

"Like I said," I murmured back just for her ears. "I'm happy right where I am." Without taking my eyes from hers, I snagged one of the strawberries from her fruit salad and sucked it between my lips.

The muscles of her throat flexed as she swallowed.

Bingo. Miss Valentina wasn't so impervious as she insisted. Now we were getting somewhere.

I turned slowly back to Reyna. "What class do you have next?"

Val shot to her feet beside me. "Rey, we need to get going. I told Mr. Halcomb we'd stop by the office before the end of lunch." She threw her half-eaten lunch back in an insulated designer bag and withdrew herself from the bench seat.

Reyna hurried to comply, collecting her things with an apologetic glance.

"Have a good afternoon if I don't see you," I said to her, earning a small smile as she paused to look at me before trailing behind the commander in chief.

"Looks like we have yet another class together." I lowered myself into the seat next to Reyna.

She gave me a shy smile. "You'll like sociology. Mrs. Wentz is a really great teacher."

"Good to hear. So far, everyone seems pretty intense."

"That's Xavier."

"Have you gone to school here long?" I studied her discreetly, curious about the girl who was just a little different from everyone else. Was that simply my own projections or maybe a product of her introverted nature?

"Only since the start of this school year."

"Is that when you moved from Mexico?"

Reyna's eyes flicked to the teacher. "Yeah."

"That had to be quite the adjustment," I prodded.

"You have no idea."

"Tell me about it. You said you had tutors?"

Again, her eyes slid to the front of the room. When the teacher called our attention to start class, Reyna's shoulders seem to sink in relief. She shot me a thin smile as though she were remiss to end our conversation, but I got the sense she felt quite the opposite.

Had I come on too strong? Had her friend warned her away from me? Whatever the cause, I'd have some work to do if I was going to befriend her. I smirked when I envisioned Valentina worrying over what classes her friend and I might have together. Girls like her had to control everyone around them, and she'd hate that she was powerless to intervene during those class periods.

I started to think my afternoon would be Val free until I walked into my final class of the day. Valentina sat in the back row next to the only vacant seat in the room, her dark wavy hair cascading down around her shoulders as she scrolled on her phone.

I wasn't surprised when no one sat beside her. The others were probably too terrified to go near her. Even though I wasn't remotely intimidated, I also had no desire to intensify the headache I'd already been nursing after a full day of forced smiles and repeated conversations.

Yes, I'm new. Moved from Texas. No sports.

I started to squat and oust someone from their seat near the front like I had during first period, but our no-nonsense poli-sci teacher ordered me back to the vacant desk next to Valentina. I dropped down into the seat with more protest than I should have. I preferred not to give her or anyone else a window into my thoughts, but my patience had run thin.

I wondered how she'd interpret my irritation. Maybe it would give her something to think about. She had probably assumed I got off on giving her a hard time, and while that wasn't totally wrong, it also wasn't entirely true either. My motives were my own, and for the moment, I wasn't interested in arguing with her.

I never once glanced in her direction. I could feel the weight of her stare periodically, but I didn't give in to its tempting lure.

"Who can tell me the source of this quote?" Mr. Barnard asked the class, pointing at the whiteboard.

Tell me and I forget, teach me and I remember, involve me and I learn.

My hand was up before I'd even considered the attention I might draw.

"Mr. Easton?"

"Benjamin Franklin," I said without hesitation. I'd read that quote so many times, I could recite it in my sleep.

"Very good! It sounds like you won't have any trouble adjusting to our rigorous curriculum. Now, the point is, we'll be doing a number of projects in class because hands-on learning is far more effective than listening to me blather on." He continued to outline our semester, but I tuned him out.

When he turned his back to write on the board, Valentina slipped me a small scrap of paper. I unfolded it and read her message.

I thought you had trouble reading the board from the back of the room.

The corners of my mouth fish-hooked upward. It didn't surprise me that she'd been paying attention first period or that she'd call me out on the fib. I took the cap off my pen and jotted two words before passing back the note.

I lied.

Her response was swift. *Stay away from Reyna.*

I studied her for a moment before penning my reply. *You two an item?* It was a joke ... mostly. A tiny part of me wondered what it was between them that explained Val's odd behavior toward me.

Her eyes shot from the paper to me then back down. *Would you leave her alone if we were?*

Nice try. I grinned.

She crumpled the note in her fist and refused to look my way again.

CHAPTER 3
Valentina

I'D BEEN ABLE TO SEE REYNA TODAY, BUT THAT WAS THE ONLY good thing to come of our first day back. Just the thought of Kane Easton sent angry flames licking up my neck as we walked to the front of the school.

"Did you end up having any other classes with him?" I asked Reyna, eyes trained on the path ahead of me so I didn't smack into anyone in the throng of people exiting the school.

"Who?"

"Kane. Don't fall for his bullshit, Rey. He's a total player."

"I appreciate you looking out for me, Val, but dating is the last thing on my mind. If that's what you're worried about, you can lay off him. You know you're only egging him on." She wasn't wrong, but how could I ignore him when he pressed every one of my buttons?

I groaned as we stepped outside. "I know. I'm just worried about you."

"I may be quiet, but I've survived seventeen years in my family. I'm not totally helpless," she chided me playfully, bumping my shoulder with her own.

"You're right, I'm sorry. I'll try to chill." I'd spent months looking out for Reyna, so it wasn't easy to just push those protective instincts aside. Maybe she was tough beneath the surface, but her quiet nature made her seem vulnerable. I didn't want her to latch on to a guy who would only hurt her.

We took our places on the sidewalk out front, where we usually waited for our rides, which were always some of the last to arrive. While we watched students slip into cars in the circle drive, I noticed a pair of blondes approaching us from the corner of my eye. Not every blonde in the senior class belonged to Harper, but there were enough of them that it was a safe bet to assume this could be trouble.

Addison and Penelope. Not just part of Harper's cheerleader crowd; they were Thing 1 and Thing 2—her closest co-conspirators. In sixth grade, the popular kids in our class separated into two groups after Principal Hale, our principal at the time, announced a new ambassador's program. One student from each grade for sixth through twelfth would be selected as a part of a committee on a new inclusiveness initiative. Not only would members work collectively but each would also spend time with Hale individually as he mentored them on team building. I'd been ambitious early on and knew that kind of experience would be great for getting into college. I applied for the sixth-grade representative position and was selected. That was, until Harper sent her mom in to insist that her daughter was more qualified for the role. She'd raised enough stink that Hale sat me down to explain that the role had been reassigned to Harper and that hopefully, we could work together the following year instead. Hale ended up leaving that year unexpectedly, so I never got that chance.

An uneasy rivalry had already been festering between Harper and me. When she usurped my ambassador position, a line was drawn in the sand. She became increasingly catty that year, and I refused to have anything to do with her. Even after Hale was gone, the divide between us grew. Any friends we'd had in common had been unofficially forced to choose between us. Most of the girls who followed Harper mirrored her shallow behavior, making that group absolutely intolerable in my eyes.

They knew not to mess with me overtly, but that didn't stop them from the occasional petty jab. When the two girls came toward us, I steadied myself for snide comments, but they were seemingly absorbed in conversation. I'd almost let my guard down when Addison swung her bag from one shoulder to the other, slamming it into Reyna in the process.

Reyna stumbled forward, nearly dropping her phone.

Addison drew to a stop, mouth gaping in exaggerated shock and contrition. "Oh my gosh. I'm *so* sorry. I totally didn't see you there. My bad."

Penelope snickered, drawing a satisfied smirk from Addison as they started to turn away.

"Puking your guts up every day after lunch must be affecting your vision," I shot back dryly. "Might want to get that checked."

Addison's head shot around so fast it nearly came unscrewed, but she didn't say a word. With eyes narrowed to slits and lips puckered so tight her mouth resembled an asshole, she just glared before storming away.

It took precisely thirty-five seconds for Reyna and I to burst into a fit of laughter.

"They haven't tried something like that in a while," she said when our giggles subsided.

"Just testing the waters after break, I'm sure. Hopefully, that put them back in line." I glanced down the sidewalk in the direction they'd gone, only to find Kane watching us intently. He was too far away to hear our exchange, but I had no doubt he'd witnessed the entire scene. All signs of the suave Casanova had melted away, and what remained startled me. Brutal intensity. Savage ferocity. A predator.

What the hell was his deal?

Every ounce of that concentrated scrutiny was aimed at me, and I held his stare with my own unwavering strength. He absolutely would not intimidate me.

After what felt like an eternity, he finally severed our connection. My eyes stayed glued to him. I watched as he threw his leg over a sleek black motorcycle, strapped on a helmet, then gracefully glided away from the school.

"What kind of parents let their kid have a motorcycle in high school?" Reyna mused. She'd been watching him too.

I peered at her with raised brows, thinking of the shiner she'd had a month before from her monster of a father.

She caught my drift and shrugged. "I guess it takes all kinds."

My eyes trailed back to the street. While I couldn't see him anymore, I could hear the acceleration of his bike in the distance. "Yeah, but he's definitely unique. I don't know what it is, but I get an odd vibe from him. He makes me anxious."

"It could just be that he's the hottest guy to walk the earth."

I smacked Reyna on the arm. "You said you weren't paying attention to that stuff right now!"

She giggled. "He's kind of hard not to notice."

"It's so annoying." I sighed. "Why do the pretty ones have to be such pains?"

"Oh, that's me." She nodded toward a black Cadillac sedan. "I'll see you tomorrow!"

I waved her off, then walked to my mom's car when she pulled up. She hated to sit in line, so she waited for the crowd to die down before coming. I had a driver's license but no car, which left me subject to her whims.

I was the baby of the family. A surprise baby, no less. My parents had thought they were done with diapers and bottles until I came along. What they say about the youngest in the family is true. There were no set nap times for me. No homemade baby food or cloth diapers. Not that my mom was the type anyway, but once she'd already had two girls to contend with, her parenting style was more of a lesson in survival than anything else.

It worked for me. I was given a good deal of freedom so long as I stayed inside the lines. I made good grades and went to church without complaint—at least, not outwardly—and that was pretty much all they asked. I wasn't overly deviant behind their backs, but I did sneak out on occasion. However, now that I knew my father was in the mafia and our lives were more dangerous than I'd ever suspected, I was more cautious about breaking the rules. My most egregious infraction was Reyna. My parents would be livid if they discovered we were friends, but I refused to turn my back on her. I just had to hope I didn't come to regret that decision later.

"How was the first day back?" my mom asked after I was in the car.

"Just a normal day. Nothing to report."

"Well, only a few months left. This is the beginning of the end. You really need to commit to where you're going after graduation."

I watched sightlessly out the window as we passed scenery I'd seen most every day of my life. "I know, Ma. I'm getting there."

I'd been accepted to all five schools to which I'd applied. The problem was, I couldn't seem to decide on one. College, in general, held little interest to me. I couldn't care less about a degree in finance or architecture or any academic pursuit for that matter. Nothing compared to the way I felt when I played the piano. That was my one true love, yet no matter how confident I was in life, piano was my one insecurity. I was uncomfortable playing for others, and there would be too many other talented musicians for me to get into a music school like Juilliard or NYU.

My eldest sister, Giada, never went to college and relied on yoga to keep her busy. Something like that was an option because we each had ample trust funds, but that life sounded boring as hell. I needed a focus. A purpose in life. I'd assumed I'd go to college because I was a high achiever, but none of it truly interested me. How could I decide on a life path when nothing fit?

The only time I felt perfectly at ease was sitting at my piano. When my fingers danced across the keys, the world around me melted away until all that was left was the comforting embrace of a haunting melody. Some people wrote in a journal or talked to a therapist. My coping mechanism was the piano. Every emotion under the sun was there to be drawn forth with the right combination of ebony and ivory. A lively Chopin mazurka for bright sunny Saturdays. Beethoven or Rachmaninoff when my emotions were dragging me under. Music was everything to me. But if I didn't want to play for others, how could I ever take my music further? Being a music teacher was one thing, but being at a university would require performances. Just the thought terrified me.

My father called me his songbird. Without the freedom to play my music regardless of the audience, I was a bird in a cage of my own making. Fear was holding me back, but I wasn't sure how to overcome it, and going to a music school felt like an enormous leap from the safety of my bubble. It was so scary that I hadn't even explored the options.

Oblivious to my existential crisis, my mom continued. "I'm hoping we can all get together this weekend. Maybe you can give Camilla a call and help convince her to come. I'd like to have all my girls together for a change." Something in her voice drew my attention.

"Everything okay?"

"Yeah, yeah. Just being a mom, that's all." Her forced smile wasn't at all reassuring.

Was there something bothering her, or was I just being overly sensitive? I had no clue, and between the pressure of helping Reyna and the irritation of dealing with Kane, I didn't have the capacity to worry about my mom too. Instead of pressing her for an explanation, I debated what song I would practice when I got home.

Something dark and intense.

Something suited to amber eyes glowing like a wolf's deep in the forest. If I could work through the complicated emotions Kane evoked, maybe I could relax around him. Maybe we could even become friends.

I recalled the penetrating intensity of his gaze, the masculine cut of his powerful physique, and his natural abundance of confidence that was present in only the most capable apex predator. The combination was intoxicating. Breathtaking. I couldn't imagine being around him and not being affected by his presence. Just the thought of him shot a zing of electricity from my belly out to the very tips of my fingers.

Kane Easton wasn't friend material.

He was the type of man who elicited only the most extreme emotions from the people around him. Love or hate, there was no between. If I learned to see past my dislike for him, I shuddered to think where that might take me.

CHAPTER 4
Kane

"Hey, man. I didn't think to ask you yesterday at lunch, but do you play lacrosse? We could always use new talent on the team." Bryson caught me just as I walked inside the school, his face open with eager anticipation. Too bad I had to squash his hopes.

"I can't, man. Busted knee ended my sports career."

"Ah, man. That sucks. What'd you play?"

"Football, receiver."

"That's right—Texas. They love their football down there." He smirked. "Too bad about your knee. That's a tough break."

"Yeah, no more contact sports for me." I grimaced,

thinking about everything I'd had to give up as a result of my injury. I'd gotten over a majority of my anger, but the bitter aftertaste of resentment still lingered.

"Not sure if anyone mentioned yesterday but Blake Masterson is having a back-to-school party on Friday. His parents will be at their place in the Hamptons, so his house is all ours. You should definitely come. His parties are always sick."

"I've got nothing better to do. Count me in."

I could only imagine what a high school party would be like for people who ran through money like water. It would probably just piss me off, but it was my first big social opportunity, and I needed to take advantage. I got Bryson's number and the address for the party, then went to my locker before class.

Xavier utilized traditional scheduling rather than block scheduling, so each school day followed the same routine. That meant I got to start each day with Val and Reyna. I was reconsidering my first impression of Val after witnessing her jump to Reyna's defense yesterday after school. I couldn't hear what she'd said to the bitchy blonde, but whatever it was had sent the girl away fuming. Valentina had jumped to Reyna's defense like a mother bear protecting her cub. The exchange made me realize that Valentina's cool demeanor around me may have been more complicated than an aloof rejection. If she saw me as a threat to her friend, she'd do anything she could to push me away.

The realization raised a couple of key questions. Why was she so protective of Reyna, and why did she deem me a threat when she hardly knew me? I erased the mental image I'd first created of Valentina—the spoiled rich girl who considered herself above everyone around her—and decided to let her show me herself who she was. I suspected that beneath the callous exterior she exhibited at school lay a ruthless loyalty—the true heart of her character that she only revealed to those she deemed worthy.

My view of her had morphed from beautiful and bitchy to beautiful and fierce—a key distinction that only magnified her intrigue.

I shook my head before walking into English. No matter the reason, interest in anyone at Xavier was a terrible idea. I needed to stay focused and get the hell out of there before I fucked my life off course more than it had already been derailed.

I slipped into the desk I'd occupied the day before and scrolled through my phone as the other students filtered in. Like Siamese twins, Reyna and Val entered together. The girls were clearly inseparable whenever possible.

Val's eyes darted straight to me when she entered. I gave both girls a broad smile—one that was guaranteed to melt hearts, even the ice-coated heart of a merciless prom queen.

"Careful flashing that thing around here this early in the morning. You might be accused of being a morning person," Val deadpanned as she sat at her desk.

"Would that be such a bad thing?"

She swiveled to look at me, eyes narrowed as she studied me. "Your looks would counteract a lot, but it'd be a serious black mark on your name."

A wry grin tugged at my lips. "I take it you're not a fan of mornings?"

"I couldn't care less. But the others?" She tilted her head toward the rest of the students behind us, each one hunched in their seats, worshiping a cup from one local coffee shop or another. "They get pretty testy in the mornings."

"I'll keep that in mind," I mused playfully. "Bryson told me about the party on Friday. You two going?"

She stilled in the process of turning back to the front. Her eyes cut to Reyna. "No, we won't make it."

"Yes," Reyna shot back. "Yes, we'll be there."

Val's brows furrowed, but she didn't argue. Interesting. A good sign that their friendship wasn't entirely dictatorial.

"Great. I'd love to see y'all there." I smiled at Reyna, whose warm, coppery skin turned a deep shade of rose.

"All right, everyone. Let's get started." Mrs. Adams turned on her laptop projection system displaying a poem on the whiteboard. "Hopefully, you all read the assignment last night. It was an easy one to start the semester."

Robert Frost's "Nothing Gold Can Stay" flickered onto the screen. I hadn't done the homework, but it was easy enough to scan the simple eight-lined poem to familiarize myself. Not only was it short but the poet also spoke of a concept I was all too familiar with.

"It may seem straightforward at first glance, but the poem can be interpreted in a number of ways. What are your initial impressions of the poem?" the teacher asked.

I didn't raise my hand. "Nothing good ever lasts." It was a Nihilistic perspective but had proven true in my experience.

"Well, that's certainly one way—" Mrs. Adams began to respond but was cut off by a sharp female voice.

"I disagree," Valentina blurted. "Frost doesn't imply that change is good or bad. He's simply saying that life is always in a state of change. To project a negative connotation to the passing of time is a product of the reader's own state of mind." She couldn't see me from behind her, but I was certain she was aware of my eyes on her.

"*So Eden sank to grief.* You don't think that implies a degree of sadness?" I asked.

Val turned to face me. "I believe he's assuring us that even sadness doesn't last, the same way a flower can only bloom for so long. Regardless of what passes at any particular moment in time, that moment won't last. Whether that encourages us to relish the best parts of today or assures us that the hardest parts won't last forever, I'd say the poem is about encouragement and endurance rather than loss and helplessness."

Our eyes remained locked even after Mrs. Adams began to impart her own interpretation. After Val finally turned around, I took out a piece of notebook paper and scribbled a short note.

Careful with the optimism. People might think you care. I tapped her arm, discreetly passing her the folded paper.

I don't care what people think of me, but you, on the other hand, are in grave danger of smearing the carefree image you work so hard on. She wasn't wrong. I'd spoken honestly about the poem, and my true beliefs were far more cynical than what I portrayed.

I suppose both of us may be more complex than we seem.

Too bad we'll never be close enough to know. Her parting quip made me smirk.

I had to resist the urge to reach out and run my fingers through Valentina's chestnut waves to verify that she was real and not some figment of my imagination. Some heaven-sent enigma meant to test me. Tempt me. Everything about her was meticulously designed to appeal to me in a way that could only be divine retribution.

What the hell had I done in a past life to deserve such a gauntlet of obstacles to overcome?

It didn't matter. Just like Robert Frost had said, as Valentina so eloquently pointed out, my time at Xavier was limited. No matter how tempted I was or how captivating the distraction, I would not allow myself to be swayed from my goals.

I forced my gaze back to the board, severing my connection to the girl who was so much more than she seemed.

CHAPTER 5
Valentina

KANE WAS ALREADY SEATED AT OUR LUNCH TABLE WHEN I arrived. His eyes sliced through the air and collided with mine the second I entered the cafeteria as though some internal radar had alerted him to my presence. His stare was rope snagged around my middle, coaxing me forward. Seeing him at our table reminded me of the day before when his arm had casually rubbed against mine. The warmth of his skin radiating against me and the shock of electricity that jolted through me with each accidental connection of our bodies.

Just as he had in English class, his eyes held mine longer than appropriate. Longer than societal norms dictated for a chance occurrence of eye contact. His gold and mine silver, like the sun and moon, forever at odds with one another.

I'd challenged him from the moment we met. Why did I get the feeling my resistance had only sparked his interest? Most men shied away from potential rejection. Kane was totally impervious.

As long as he left Reyna alone, I could handle him. Despite her claims that she was tougher than she seemed, I was much more confident in my ability to manage a playboy like Kane. No matter how coaxing his playful manner and mesmerizing good looks, I wouldn't lose my head where he was concerned.

Do you hear me, Valentina? You will not *fall for Kane Easton.*

With one last mental pep talk, I made my way to the table and took a seat on the opposite side as Kane. I wasn't going to sit next to him and risk becoming addicted to the feel of his body touching mine. Just to be sure I set a clear boundary, I didn't even acknowledge his presence.

"Where's Reyna?" he asked, ignoring my cool demeanor and bridging the gap between us.

My temper flared. I was annoyed that he wouldn't take a hint and leave me alone, but if I didn't know better, I would have said some of that anger was also rooted in jealousy, which was absurd because I wasn't interested in dating someone who charmed his way through life. He was only faithful to his own self-interest. His eyes tracked my movements, but he was the consummate flirt and harbored an unquenchable interest in Reyna. Was he hedging his bets and going after the both of us? Probably. Definitely not someone who should stir feelings of jealousy inside me.

I had to stop dwelling on this Kane Easton. I had

something infinitely more important to contend with in my life.

I clamped down on my wayward emotions and smiled. "She wasn't feeling great, so she went home for the day." She'd gotten cramps, but that was none of his business.

He lifted his chin, letting the subject go but continued to watch me as I laid out my lunch. "Those girls picking on her after school yesterday?"

I flicked my eyes up to where he toyed with his sushi before returning my feigned concentration to the engrossing nature of my food. "They tried to when she started at the beginning of the year, but I put an end to it."

"That was very charitable of you, considering you must have hardly known her at first."

I shrugged. "Not exactly. She was incredibly quiet and made an easy target for jerks who take advantage of people weaker than themselves. Stopping them was just human decency." At first, I'd stepped in partially as a way to keep Harper and her cronies in check. Does a person truly have power over others if they don't exercise it on occasion? I found it prudent to throw my weight around when the opportunity arose just to make sure they knew I could. Otherwise, Harper would have gotten a big head and thought she ruled the school. What started as a power play became a friendship. As I got to know Reyna, I found that I wanted to keep the bullies away for her sake rather than my own self-interest. Looking back, I was embarrassed at how self-centered my motivations had initially been.

"That how you two became friends?"

"Yup." I took a bite, hoping to end the conversation. When he didn't say anything more, I glanced up to find him smirking at me like a hungry cartoon shark. "What?"

"I don't suppose you'd give me her number so I could tell her I hope she feels better?"

What the hell was up with this guy? Did he realize how odd it was that he stared at me then asked for my friend's number? Maybe that's the reason he moved across the country and changed schools. He'd probably gotten his ass kicked by an angry mob of women.

"I don't suppose I would." I took a big bite of my sandwich with a hostile glare.

Kane only laughed.

Impervious? Clueless? What was his deal? He bulldozed his way through life with a smile on his face and a trail of bodies in his wake. Did he see the consequences of his actions, or did he wear a set of blinders, purely focused on his goals? I couldn't figure him out, and it both irritated me and fascinated me. For the moment, irritation won out. I kept my nose down and thanked the heavens when Bryson snagged Kane's attention for the rest of lunch.

I was free of my tormentor for the next few hours until poli-sci. He entered the room just before the bell, teasing me that perhaps he was skipping class and had left for the day. His appearance destroyed the sliver of hope I'd clung to that I might escape the day without any further encounters with him.

Our teacher instructed us to pull up a page from the e-book on our iPads, then directed us to pair up to go over the study questions from the prior night's homework. Before I could look around to pick a partner, Kane took hold of my desk and pulled it next to his. I gasped and gaped up at him, now only inches away from me. His eyes were hooded, and a sultry curve hooked each corner of his lips.

"That wasn't necessary," I whispered, eyes darting around the room. No one else had bothered moving their desks.

"I don't have my iPad. This way, I can see yours." He was smug. Satisfied. But his admission was just another black mark against him for being irresponsible and not caring about school. Students at Xavier were academically competitive, often motivated by overachieving parents with oppressive expectations. There was nothing attractive about coming to class unprepared, so why did my heart begin to thrum in my chest at his proximity? Why did the air in the classroom suddenly feel suffocatingly thin?

I took in a deep breath, hoping to compose myself, and moved my iPad between us where we both could see. I wasn't going to make a scene by pushing my desk back to its original location. Kane leaned forward, placing his elbows on his desk and clasping his hands together before him. He wore a long-sleeve Henley like he had the day before, but for the first time, I noticed a set of three colored friendship bracelets on his left wrist. At least, I thought that's what they were. They were crudely made—essentially a collection of threads knotted in random intervals.

"You have a little brother or sister?" I asked quietly, completely forgetting about our assignment.

He followed my gaze to the exposed bracelets and fingered the strings. "I've got a brother." His words were surprisingly tender.

I had no response I was so taken aback by the sudden change in his demeanor and the emotion in his voice. The sincerity. He'd struck me as phony with all his schmoozing and cocky showmanship, but this brother of his elicited something more genuine from him than I expected.

"What about you? Have any siblings?" he asked.

My eyes sought out his again for some unknown reason, and when I peered into those warm molasses depths, I saw a tiny glimpse of the man beneath the surface. Someone with passions and fears. His truth hid beneath the harsh line of his brow and straight, humorless lips. Genuine curiosity unearthed in his gravelly murmur. All signs of the cavalier playboy had disappeared. It made me wonder if that person even existed or if every bit of it was a mask.

Had he meant to pull back the veil, or had it slipped without his permission?

"Um, yeah. Two sisters, both older," I finally answered.

He cleared his throat and directed our attention back to the device on the desk. "We should probably glance at these questions. Did you read the assignment last night?"

I nodded.

"Good. At least one of us did." He smirked, slipping back into the skin of his school persona.

I sighed. "Okay, first question. According to the essay, why is it important to protect speech, even if that speech is unpopular?" I crooked an eyebrow at him, putting the onus of answering on him despite knowing he hadn't read the assignment.

"If the government was allowed to censor speech, our fundamental democratic rights would be at risk. The sharing of ideas would be stilted and thus inhibit progress. Freedom of communication, just like education, is essential to the prosperity of the people who make up a nation."

I stared at him speechless. Kane may not have deemed homework worthy of his time, but he was unquestionably intelligent. Maybe even smarter than I cared to admit.

"You sure you didn't read the assignment?"

"Just a fan of the constitution."

"Seriously? Who even says that?"

He grinned, his teeth tugging on his bottom lip playfully. "I think I just did."

I shook my head, unsuccessful at stifling my own smile. "Whatever. Next question. According to the essay, what kinds of actions are included in the term 'speech' as it is found in the first amendment? And I guess it's my turn to answer." I paused to collect my thoughts. "According to the essay and not just some wealth of knowledge I acquired through an unnatural fascination with government," I glared at him coyly, "speech includes any expression of opinion—verbal or written words, non-violent actions, or any other form of expression that doesn't infringe on anyone else's rights."

Kane slowly nodded his head as if processing my statement. "So, if I jumped up on this desk and began to yell about the benefits of an increased minimum wage, and the school forced me to stop, would that be an infringement of my rights?"

"No, the First Amendment protections apply to censorship by the government. Xavier is a private institution."

"What about if we were in a public school?"

I had to think about his question for a moment. "Well, I would think that my actions would constitute a disruption of the other students' rights to an education. The school must have some kind of right to regulate student speech—at least to some degree." I peered at Kane, my brows raised theatrically. "Is that correct, oh great master of the constitution?"

A salacious smile spread wide across his face as he slid down languidly in his seat. For the briefest of seconds, a swarm of butterflies fluttered up from deep inside me at the approving gleam in Kane's eye. Then everything changed when his knee relaxed against mine. I gasped at the tingling desire that emanated from the warmth of his touch. We both dropped our gazes to the point of contact—my naked knee resting against his khaki-clad thigh.

When I peered back up, the playful young man sitting next to me had turned to stone. His body rigid and smile turning rancid, Kane was suddenly a stranger.

He sat upright, stiff and mechanical, severing our connection. "I'll read the next one." He slid the iPad from my grasp, a grimace in place of his smile.

I had no idea what had happened. He was clearly upset, but why? Because we touched? His response made me feel like I had the plague. I wanted to lash out defensively—shame him for being so egregiously rude—and simultaneously hide under a rock.

He was the one who'd pulled my desk over. He was the one who touched me, not the other way around. Why had the contact seemed to disgust him? He'd appeared happily engrossed in our exchange seconds earlier, so what had changed?

The longer I thought about it, the angrier I got that I cared at all. What did it matter to me if he was upset? Why did I care if he was the most mercurial man I'd ever met?

I considered a million scathing admonishments throughout the rest of class but didn't voice a single one. In the end, I decided that ignoring him entirely was the best recourse. An emotional response to his actions would only concede that he held a small degree of power over me, and that was an admission I wasn't willing to make.

When the bell rang, I packed up my things and left without giving him a second glance.

I AVOIDED Kane as best as I could for the rest of the week. It was actually easier than I expected because he seemed to be employing the same strategy. My need to understand what had changed between us ate away at my conviction to stay away from him. I managed to hold firm, but it cost me every ounce of self-control I possessed. I was short-tempered and overall irritable for two solid days. By the time school let out on Friday, I wasn't fit company for anyone, but Reyna had insisted we go to Blake Masterson's party.

I was especially conflicted about going because I was bound to run into a certain amber-eyed nuisance who was slowly creeping his way under my skin. I rationalized that it was probably best to go to the party if only to ensure that the mere presence of a man couldn't keep me cowering at home —especially a man who tied my emotions in a knot. He reminded me of those theater masks where half the face was smiling, and half was crying. I couldn't predict what he might say or how he might act. He hadn't slipped into a neatly defined role among our student body like most new students. Kane laughed in the face of conformity, blew it a kiss, then did whatever the hell he wanted. I couldn't even begin to predict what he might do at a house party where everyone was swimming in hormones and alcohol.

I had to prepare myself in every way I could. And in my world, the proper attire could make all the difference. I had to pick an outfit that made me feel confident ... but also sexy because I wanted to make sure Kane knew what he was missing. I mean, I didn't *want* him, but I wouldn't have minded him wanting me. The problem was, my outfit couldn't be too sexy because that would look like I was trying too hard. This was one of the few times he would see me in something other than my school uniform. Whatever I wore had to be perfect.

After an hour of floundering between patterns and solids, cotton and flannel, I finally settled on ripped jeans and a silky button-down with a delicate black camisole underneath. I left the buttons undone but tied the bottom of the two front panels at my waist. I slipped on brown leather booties with a short heel, set my hair in loose waves down my back, and made sure my makeup was on point. I felt cute but casual. Sexy but not slutty. Confident and committed to not letting Kane get the better of me.

I'd told my parents I was going to bed about an hour earlier and turned on the security system after setting the alarm panel to silent. That way, I could quietly turn it on and off as I came and went. I'd turn the sound back on in the morning so that my parents wouldn't know the settings had been changed. Once the lights in the house went dark, I crept downstairs and disarmed the alarm, then set it to away and slipped out the back door.

Reyna and I lived about a mile from one another. Halfway between our houses, a large oak tree had become our meeting place on the few occasions when we'd snuck out in the past. Rey was first to arrive, waiting for me bundled in a heavy coat.

"I should have worn something heavier," I said as I approached her, hands shoved in my tiny pockets. The evening was cold, but we didn't have a long walk. Had Blake lived much farther, we would have had to arrange for a ride, but as luck would have it, his house wasn't but a couple of blocks away from ours.

"Then you would have covered up that killer outfit!"

"True, but that won't do me any good if I freeze on the way there." I started us in the direction of Blake's house with quick strides to keep me warm. "Remind me again why we're going to this party?" I was trying not to be cranky, but it was harder with every step I took.

"Because my dad could send me back to Mexico at any moment, and this would be the last time I'd ever get to experience a high school party. I want to take advantage of every opportunity while I'm here." Her voice was unaffected, but the truth of her words was a vise around my heart. She'd been taught at home by a tutor all her life, and now her entire existence was uncertain. I needed to get my head out of my ass and stop worrying about Kane so that I could focus on helping her.

"I'm sorry, honey. You're right. I want you to get to have some fun. And I promise I'm working on figuring out a solution to keep you here." I bumped her shoulder gently as we walked. "Hopefully you didn't have any trouble getting out of the house?"

"Nope. My mom was passed out, and the guards Dad left to watch us aren't all that diligent. I think they're more worried about someone raiding the house than they are about me sneaking out."

"Hey, we'll take that as a win."

"Absolutely."

When we turned the corner onto Blake's street, a dozen or so cars were parked along the sidewalk. It would have been more, but a lot of us didn't have our own vehicles.

There wasn't any point if we were just going to move to the city after graduation.

Aside from the cluster of cars, the bass undercurrents of music hung in the night air as evidence of a gathering. The houses weren't particularly close, so chances were slim that neighbors would report the party. The mansions on his street not only had large lots but backed up to a forested preserve, providing plenty of privacy. Blake's house was an impressive Tudor monstrosity nestled among full-grown oaks and maples that would be gorgeous once their leaves returned. The house was primarily constructed of red brick but had two front-facing panels in the traditional cream-colored stucco with dark wood trim. It was stately yet quaint and alive with activity.

We were arriving well after the party had begun since we'd both had to wait to sneak out of our houses. Laughter could be heard from around the side of the house where the party had spilled out into the backyard. I debated walking around to slip in from the back but decided against it. Instead, we let ourselves in the front door and took in the scene.

The home had been renovated inside, so despite the traditional façade, the inside was open and well-lit with a sweeping great room and high ceilings. People were gathered in small groups throughout the space, drinks in hand and talking while Billie Eilish's "Bad Guy" pulsed from the home's speaker system. A wealth of drink options were scattered across the kitchen's granite island that bordered the two spaces. Outside the large picture windows lining the back wall, more people were clustered around a flaming stone firepit.

My eyes flitted from person to person as we submerged

ourselves into the fray. Several people waved and shouted greetings, but I didn't pause to talk. I was too distracted scanning the room for a single individual. I shouldn't have been looking, but I was. My eyes flitted from one face to the next in search of sandy brown hair that always looked sun-dried after a swim in the ocean. I sought out the imposing stance of a broad body that commanded attention even though its owner projected an air of nonchalance. My breath caught for a set of kissable lips that challenged me in ways I'd never encountered.

When I finally spotted the object of my growing obsession, my hands curled into tight fists, my nails burrowing painfully into my palms. I was still upset about the way he'd acted at school, but seeing him cozied up to Harper on one of the two long sofas stole the air from my lungs.

The wretched truth of my reaction was exactly why I'd been wanting to avoid him. I was furious at myself for feeling such a nauseating sense of betrayal over a man who was as easy to read as ancient Sanskrit. Why did I expect any sense of loyalty from someone who couldn't be bothered to follow a single rule?

I knew better, but why did it have to be Harper of all people? She was so much more than my nemesis. She was the stereotype each of us as women was working to overcome. Shallow. Inept. Catty. If Kane couldn't see the vast differences between someone like her and myself, then he wasn't worth my time anyway.

"Think you could grab us some drinks?" I asked Reyna. "I'd like to head out back and get some air."

Her eyes shot briefly to where Kane was seated before she

gave me a tight smile. "No problem. You head out, and I'll find you in a few."

I gave her hand a squeeze and moved toward the sliding glass doors. I should have stayed with Rey to make sure she was okay, but I couldn't stand to be in the same room as *him*. Once I was outside, I discovered a second cluster of people around several propane heaters and a keg. The wafting heat from the fire and heaters banded together to create a bubble of warmth that made the patio more tolerable than I'd expected.

"Hey, Val," Bryson called over from the fire. "Want a drink?" He left his seat and grabbed a red Solo cup from beside the keg.

"Sure, thanks." I wasn't a fan of beer, but I preferred to have something in my hand. It acted as a talisman—or maybe camouflage—however you explained it, the simple red cup could transform any outcast into a member of the crowd. I needed its magical properties to help me disappear.

"Lookin' lovely as always." He grinned at me with glassy, hooded eyes.

I took the cup from him and chuckled. "Nice try, stud. It's not happening." And certainly not when he was too drunk to see straight.

He lifted his hands in a wide shrug. "Can't blame a guy for trying."

"Hey, Bry," someone called from behind us. "Tell them about the little guy you panced at the last match!"

"Gotta go!" Summoned by his rabid fanbase, Bryson was eager to regain his role in the spotlight and hurried back to the group.

Given the opportunity to be alone, I stepped to the edge of the patio, looking deep into the shadowed tree line. It was cooler away from the heaters, but I wasn't in the mood for people, no matter how hard I tried.

"It's awfully cold out here for someone without a coat." Kane's rumbling voice resonated through me from behind just as I was enveloped in warmth. He draped his jacket over my shoulders, immersing me in his uniquely masculine scent —spiced cedar, stargazing at midnight, and a winding ride in an open-top convertible. The intoxicating pull on my emotions was disorienting. I wanted to breathe deeply until my lungs threatened to explode.

Damn Solo cup had failed me. That or Kane's sorcery was no match for its piddly magic. Either way, I'd been found. I slowly turned around and craned my neck to look in the face of the man who was quickly chipping away at my sanity. The darkness cooled his eyes to a deep maple, sticky and sweet and irresistible.

"It was a little crowded in there for me," I said with a dryness that should have clued him in to read between the lines. But that wasn't Kane's style. If he did catch my jab, he ignored it.

His eyes strayed to my lips before his tongue wetted his own. "Did Reyna come with you tonight?"

What other guy would have the gall to ogle me but ask for my best friend? None. Not one. Only Kane could send such mixed signals with reckless abandon. His callous disregard for anyone around him made me furious.

I set my drink on the ground and slid his jacket from my shoulders, shoving it against his chest. "*Here.* I'd rather be cold than take anything from *you.*" I started to turn and flee, but a large hand clamped down around my arm.

"What the hell did I do?" he snapped, bringing his face down close to mine where I could smell the harsh bite of spiced whiskey on his breath. I figured he'd been drinking, but how long had he been at it? Maybe he was drunk enough to be real for once. I wanted to know what was going on in that complicated head of his, but I was too angry to listen.

"You didn't do *anything*. Not one goddamned thing." I tugged against his grip to no avail.

Kane yanked me several feet farther into the shadows. His entire body bristled with furious frustration. "You're not going anywhere until you tell me what crawled up your ass."

If looks could kill, I would have become a wanted woman.

"You want to know what's wrong? *You're* what's wrong. You and your fucking charm and your … those god damn eyes that see everything and *nothing*." I shoved at his chest, my words jumbled from aggravation. "For someone so smart, you are so fucking clueless."

His jaw flexed and nostrils flared. "You don't know what you're talking about."

"*I* don't know? *Ha*! That's fucking hysterical." I was acting like a psycho, but I couldn't help myself. Hurt and anger spewed from deep inside me where it had been festering all week.

"It's not that simple, okay? I'm not trying to hurt you or anyone else." Kane's brows furrowed over pleading eyes set deep in shadow.

I shook my head, not about to take his bait. "Stay away from me and stay away from Reyna. Okay? Just pretend she doesn't even exist."

"What does Reyna have to do with this?"

"She's got a lot going on and doesn't need someone in her life who's going to screw her over." I yanked away, and he finally released me.

"What makes you so adamant that I'm going to hurt either of you? What if all I've been trying to do was be friends?"

I scoffed, my hands settling on my hips. "You don't lead on your friends, string them along like love-sick puppies, only to move onto the next *friend* like it meant nothing."

His eyes narrowed to furious slivers. "Did I do something to lead on Reyna? Because I don't recall doing a damn thing."

"If you can do it to one girl, you can do it to another. Her skin isn't thick like Harper's or … or mine. You go grinding on every girl you see, flirting and charming whenever the mood suits you, that will devastate her. I can take it—the way you look at me then act like I don't exist. I won't let myself fall for that bullshit, but she's different. You can screw with anyone else at Xavier, but leave Reyna the *fuck* alone." I stormed away from him, furious at myself for revealing my own hurt. I should have kept my argument solely about Reyna or Harper. By showing him my hand, I'd given him even more power to toy with me.

What a cluster fuck.

I charged inside and found Reyna with two drinks in hand, leaving the kitchen.

"Hey, I was just heading outside to find you." Her smile faltered. "Is something wrong?"

"Nope. Just ready to get this party started." I took one cup from her and downed its contents. If I couldn't escape Kane's presence, I was going to need a good deal of alcohol to numb my emotions.

Reyna's eyes rounded. "That's like solid vodka, honey. You might want to take it easy."

The drink scorched my throat the whole way down, making me grin, head back and eyes shut. "That was *exactly* what I needed." I brought my gaze back to her and took a deep breath. "Let's dance."

A Post Malone song filled the air around us with his unique mellow rap style. With a surge of alcohol quickly flooding my veins, I gave myself over to impulse. Reyna's eyes widened, but she didn't stop me from raising my hands in the air and slinking over to a group of girls gyrating to the music. I was easily absorbed into their swarm, becoming one with the rhythmic beat around us.

I buried all my emotions and allowed myself to become the music. To feel its ebb and flow in each cell of my body. When I was one with music, there were no problems or pain, only melody and harmony and the pulse beating in each of us. When I gave myself over to music, I was free.

I danced until my throat ached with the need for a drink. When I went back toward the kitchen, Reyna was nowhere to be found. I wasn't sure how much time had passed. A half hour. Maybe an hour. My hairline was matted with sweat, and the room was spinning a little, but I felt alive. Unconquerable.

"Looking for something?" Giovanni Capelli asked from across the counter. He grinned, a deep dimple slicing through his cheek.

My face widened in a grin. "Yes, I am. I need something to drink." And a distraction. It was a bad idea, but alcohol-laced choices were rarely prudent.

I'd gone to school with Gio forever. I'd only ever dated one guy in high school, and Gio was his best friend. So even though Gio was sufficiently hot to get almost any girl he wanted, I'd stayed away from him. Talon and I were no longer a couple, but he was a good guy, and I had no desire to hurt him by dating his best friend. Besides, I'd realized I wasn't all that interested in dating the guys at Xavier. Guys I'd known since kindergarten. I still wasn't interested in dating Gio, but he was guaranteed to make sure I didn't think about other more frustrating individuals.

"I think that can be arranged." He winked and began to throw together a mixed drink.

I took the cup when he was finished and sipped the pink liquid. "Tastes like lemonade!" I walked around the counter to stand by him, leaning gently into his side. "Thanks, G," I purred.

"You bet." He eyed me curiously from beneath a plethora of dark lashes. "Care to dance?" He wrapped his hands around my middle and pulled me against him, rocking us to the music.

I held my drink out to the side, not wanting to spill, and brought my other hand up to his shoulder. I tried to enjoy the feel of his hard body against mine and the way we swayed in half-time to the beat, but a dueling set of voices inside my head wouldn't be silenced. They bickered back and forth like angry children.

I hope Kane sees us dancing.

And did you even consider how shallow it is to use Giovanni like this?

People dance at parties. It's not like he's in love with me.

Still, it's not necessary. We'll probably just look pathetic to Kane.

If he even sees us.

What does it matter if he sees us when he doesn't even care?

The voices were a serious buzzkill. I began to debate leaving the party altogether when Giovanni stopped moving, his eyes trained warily over my shoulder.

"What's up, man?" Gio asked.

I turned to find a wall of vibrating fury staring down my dance partner before Kane's eyes cut to me.

"I need to talk to you, *now*." He grabbed my wrist and tugged me off toward a dark hallway.

My stomach lurched and roiled, but not with fear. No matter how angry Kane appeared, I didn't think he'd hurt me. It was a melee of other emotions that stirred my insides and lit my veins on fire with liquid adrenaline.

Once we were down at the far end of the hallway away from prying eyes, Kane released my hand but kept me rooted in place with his vicious stare.

"I act like you don't exist because everything would be so much simpler if you didn't," he hissed.

The words barreled into me, bruising me from the inside. I opened my mouth, but no sound came out.

"The problem is, you *do* exist," he continued, backing me against the wall. "Not just at school; you're everywhere. In my thoughts—my fucking *dreams*—I can't escape you."

I searched between the specks of molten gold in his simmering stare for understanding. I'd thought at first that he was spewing his hatred for me, but when I strung the words together, I realized there was more. He hated that he couldn't stop thinking of me. But if I was the one on his mind, why was it Reyna and Harper he sought out? He'd hardly said two words to me at school for days. Granted, I hadn't exactly ingratiated myself, but if he liked me, wouldn't he have made an effort to talk to me?

"Well, you're doing a damn fine job of trying to escape me. Between ignoring me at school and cozying up with Harper, you were blissfully free of me."

Kane sneered. "If you'd been here instead of hiding from

me, you would have seen that I removed Harper from beside me as soon as she sat down."

"Oh, yeah. And I just happened to come in during that thirty seconds when her hand was on your thigh. Look, you don't have to explain anything to me. There is absolutely nothing between us that warrants an explanation." I shook my head and tried to push forward, but Kane was rooted to the ground, blocking my way.

Seconds passed, my ears ringing from the thunder of my own pulse, yet time stood completely still within the tomb of the hallway—a world away from the party raging under the same roof.

Finally, Kane broke the tension with a murmured confession rife with turmoil. "Maybe it's best if you hate me." The words were barely loud enough for me to hear, but their impact rocketed through me, crumbling the resolute foundation I'd stood upon.

"Best for who?" I breathed. My emotions were so tangled that I wasn't sure how I'd feel even if I could understand what Kane was trying to tell me.

Something dark—a ravenous hunger—flashed behind his eyes just before his lips collided with mine. I breathed him in, instantly clutching his shirt to keep him close as my tongue tangled with his. He kept his hands anchored to the wall on either side of me but pressed his chorded body against me so that I could feel just how affected he was. The taste of his whiskey mouth and the press of his marbleized hardness molded to my soft curves made my head spin beyond the effects of alcohol, but it was the knowledge that I caused him to lose all self-control that liquified my insides.

Kane, the unflappable man who shrugged his way through

life, was off balance because of me. I did this. Something about me drove him absolutely wild. While his lips were devouring mine, I ignored the part about how he hated that loss of control.

When he pulled away, chest heaving with ragged breaths, his eyes widened with shock and horror. The disgust on his face doused my veins in buckets of ice. At that point, the truth couldn't be ignored.

He hated what he felt for me.

His reaction made me feel dirty and wrong, and I hated him for that.

He took a single step back, spun, and put his fist through the sheetrock with a string of cursed expletives. White dust and particulate scattered across the wood floor opposite me. My hand flew to my mouth, but Kane paid me no mind. He shook out his hand then stormed down the hall without a backward glance.

CHAPTER 6
Reyna

WHY ON EARTH DID I INSIST ON GOING TO THIS DAMN PARTY? I hadn't expected Val to up and disappear on me, for starters. She hadn't gone totally MIA. She was somewhere in the crowd dancing her troubles away, but that wasn't my scene. I was self-conscious enough on my own—grinding on a makeshift dance floor would only make matters worse.

Without Val to act as my anchor, I felt adrift. I didn't blame her for having fun. If anything, I regretted that she assumed such a heavy responsibility just by being my friend. She was incredibly thoughtful, always worried about how people or situations would affect me. I appreciated that she was taking an opportunity to let loose. I wanted to be able to slip in and out of groups, chatting with people and having fun, but just the thought of jumping into a conversation was painful. I found myself peeling away from the crowd and becoming one with the wall. I desperately wished I could be like everyone else at the party. Uninhibited and carefree.

I glanced down at the drink in my hand, knowing it could give me the freedom I wanted, but I refused to lift the cup to my lips. Not after watching my mom lose her battle with alcohol day after day for years. I didn't judge anyone for choosing to drink; it just wasn't for me. Aside from the increased chance that I'd have a propensity to be an addict, I also couldn't stand the idea of losing control over myself. I liked to have all my senses sharp in case I needed them. The only reason I had mixed myself a drink was so that I would fit in, or at the very least, not stand out.

As the music transitioned from one high-energy beat to another and the people around me shed their inhibitions like an unwanted skin, I became more removed from the scene until I was no more than a ghost, able to see the living but unable to interact.

My heart ached as it thudded heavily against my ribs.

When a loud crash cut through the music, I startled so badly that half of my drink sloshed onto the floor. A glass lamp had been knocked off an end table and had shattered on the stone floor. A few people near the incident gasped or giggled, but the rest of the room never even noticed. The revelry continued around me while my pulse mimicked the rapid-fire release of an automatic weapon.

I couldn't do this. Coming to the party had been a mistake.

I didn't want to leave without Val or have to cut her dancing short, so I decided to wait outside where it was quieter, and I could hide in the solace of the shadows. I set down my untouched drink and hurried to the patio doors. Being invisible could be lonely, but it also enabled me to slip away without a chorus of questions, which was a blessing when all I wanted was to be alone.

I took in a lungful of the cool night air to soothe my frayed nerves and moved past the crowd of people around the firepit without drawing any notice. A vacant heater sat near the edge of the patio, too far from the party for anyone to bother with. I would have stood in the cold if needed but preferred not to shiver to death if possible. I breathed a sigh of relief once I was alone under its radiant warmth.

Glancing at the ocean of darkness beyond the trees, I realized that someone leaned against a nearby trunk. The man wore jeans and a black wool coat, hands stuffed in the pockets, and he was staring at me. Just enough ambient light from the patio illuminated the yard for me to see his features and feel a sense of recognition, but I wasn't sure from where. He had the look of the Hispanic men back home, and his relentless gaze was unwaveringly trained on me. There could have been any number of explanations, but my fears hissed adamantly that the man worked for my father.

My spine stiffened, and my breathing quickened as if to prepare for a fight. I glanced at the other people nearby for reassurance when the man slowly ambled forward. It might have been a false sense of security, but having people I knew close by, no matter how superficial our acquaintance, gave me the courage I needed to hold my ground. Once the man was fully within view, I could see that he was definitely a few years older than me. Handsome in a stoic manner with dark, deep-set eyes over high, angular cheekbones. His black hair was nearly shaved on the sides but longer and swept back on top. A shadow of facial hair drew his face in stark repose and highlighted the perfect shape of his lips.

I didn't detect an immediate threat emanating from him, but I couldn't imagine his appearance was a good thing.

"Who are you?" I asked, cutting to the point, pleased my words were steady.

"My name is Santino Cardenas." His masculine voice was softened by the caress of a faint Spanish accent.

I was right. This wasn't a chance encounter. Did he work for my father or, worse, one of his enemies? Fear sank its icy talons deep into my skin, rooting me to the spot.

"What do you want?" It was hardly more than a wheezed breath, my lungs suddenly too frozen to cooperate.

Santino lifted his chin as his vigilant gaze swept the patio and its occupants. "I'm just keeping an eye on things."

"*Things* or me?" I bit out, finding a touch of courage.

He only smiled. The look wasn't remotely reassuring.

"Well, feel free to stay and keep an eye on *things*. I'm leaving." I started to step past him to walk around the outside of the house toward home, only thinking about getting away. From him. From the party. From my life.

"I can take you home," he offered coolly.

I pulled up short, snapping out of my panic-induced escape. There was no way in hell I was getting in a car with this guy, nor was it a good idea to go off alone.

Come on, Rey. You're smarter than that.

"Actually, I came with someone." I stepped back toward him and the sliding glass doors.

He smirked. "I'm happy to give you both a ride."

Was he toying with me? Because I didn't find any of this remotely funny. I faced him fully, staring deep into his eyes. "Do you work for my father?"

He slowly shook his head. "No. I work for a man named Javier. You might have known him as Primo."

My lips parted with recognition. "That's the man who killed my uncle." He was dating Val's sister and had saved her from my uncle. If this man worked for Javier, he could be an ally—the enemy of my enemy was my friend. But if these men considered me an extension of my father, not knowing how much I hated the man, they would see me as a threat. That, or a pawn to get at my father. Hell, this guy could be lying to me and not even work for Javier. Any way I looked at it, I couldn't trust him. He was following me for a reason, and I doubted that reason was good.

"Your uncle was a bad man," Santino deadpanned.

The statement was a test, and my reaction would feed him information, but I wasn't sure what he was looking for. If he did, in fact, work for my father, anything but a staunch rejection would seem like a betrayal. If he worked for Javier, any support of my uncle made me look loyal to my father. Nothing I could say was safe, so I chose to skirt the comment. "My head is starting to hurt, so I better get going." I gave him one last look before heading to the patio door, relieved when he didn't move to follow.

What a difference a few minutes could make. The loud music and throng of people enveloped me in comfort. I now felt safer inside and wasn't looking forward to walking home, but it was best if we left. I scanned the dancing bodies for Val, unable to spot her until my eyes landed on a girl leaning forlornly against the wall just as I had been doing minutes before.

I wove my way over to her and slipped her hand in mine. "You ready to go?"

When her eyes collided with mine, I was stunned by the

sharp pain clouding her stormy gaze. We fell into each other's arms without a word. She was my rock, always there to steady me, so I was pleased to comfort her for a change. I was desperately curious about what had happened, but I didn't want to push her for answers.

"Let's go home," she murmured when she finally pulled away.

I nodded and led the way to the front door, pausing once we were alone on the front porch. "Are you familiar with a man named Santino?"

She cocked her head, brows furrowed. "Yeah, sort of. He works for Javier, so my sister Giada would know him better."

I breathed deeply at her confirmation that the man had been who he said he was. "Okay, that's good to hear. I saw him outside and talked to him briefly. I wasn't sure if he was a danger to us walking home."

"He was here? What was he doing?"

"He said he was keeping an eye on things, whatever that means."

Val's protective mask slipped back into place, burying whatever hurt she'd been feeling. She scanned the front yard for anyone lurking in the shadows. "Okay, neither of us is walking home alone, but I don't want him to see us together. I'll be right back." She yanked the front door open and disappeared for a minute, reemerging with a New England Patriots baseball cap on and an enormous gray hoodie hanging off her body. "Ta-da. It's not fool-proof, but it's something. Hopefully, if he sees us leaving, he won't see me well enough to know who you're with."

I couldn't help but giggle. "Did you just steal that off some guy in there?"

"Yeah, he was too drunk to care."

"And what about you? Think you're okay to walk home? You were having a pretty good time not too long ago."

"Psh, I'm fine. Nothing like a fight to sober a girl up." She tugged me forward, but I refused to budge.

"What? You're going to have to explain."

"Yeah, yeah. It's cold out. I'll tell you all about it while we walk. Now, come on!"

CHAPTER 7
Santino

MY QUIET NIGHT IN HAD UNEXPECTEDLY FOUND ME OUT IN the cold. I wasn't thrilled with the change of plans, but a house full of drunk teenagers had its entertaining moments. While I wasn't that much older than them, my days of reckless drinking had started much earlier and curtailed itself years ago. When someone grows up on the streets, alcohol is just a way of life. However, I quickly learned that if I wanted to work with Javier and earn my place in the cartel, I had to show I was responsible. We might have been as close as brothers, but our relationship alone wouldn't have ensured my future.

Now, I wasn't at all enticed by the sight of young rich

kids binging on their parents' alcohol. My place was in the shadows, which suited me perfectly. A wealth of information was available for anyone who was patient enough to slow down and observe the people around them. I enjoyed watching people, but on this particular Friday night, I was following orders.

I'd only just settled behind the thick trunk of an oak tree when Valentina Genovese appeared in the backyard. Her lips were drawn down in a scowl, and I guessed the young man who followed her outside was likely the cause. I couldn't hear what was said, but the emotions between them were palpable, even from my hidden location in the darkness. Her features initially softened when he joined her, then something he said made her furious. Teenage hormones could be brutal.

Once they returned inside, I continued to survey the scene. The large windows were unobscured by drapes or blinds and allowed for easy viewing of the brightly lit interior. However, the sheer number of people inside made it hard to track any one individual. I took note of what I could, surprised when I was treated to yet another close encounter.

Reyna Vargas emerged from the house alone close to an hour after Valentina had come out. She slunk to the far end of the porch to an empty heater, positioning herself as if she were hiding behind it. Unlike most girls at the party, she wore a bulky coat like a barrier between her and the outside world. I watched her release a long exhale into the night air and wondered at her thoughts. If she was so clearly uncomfortable at the gathering, why had she gone? Or had something happened inside? Whatever the cause, her distress was apparent. She was more fragile than I'd expected. Considering who her father was, I had expected her to be hardened. Callous and self-centered. That didn't seem to be the case at all. If I hadn't known better, I would have said she was on the verge of tears.

When she turned those water-logged eyes in my direction, I found myself advancing forward. Like a moth drawn to the flame, I couldn't resist.

The courage she exhibited was breathtaking. I could almost taste her fear, but she kept it caged as best she could and held perfectly still beneath her battle armor. It was a sight to behold. Angelic beauty, dauntless bravery.

I was surprisingly compelled to ease her worries, assure her that I wouldn't harm her, but that would have been misleading. She was smart to fear me. That truth sat like a rotting stump deep in my belly long after she'd fled inside.

I called Javi once I was alone again.

"There a problem?" he asked in greeting.

"No, although I was spotted," I admitted. "I should have known that anyone who grew up in Juan Carlos' house would be vigilant."

"Reyna?"

"Yes."

Javi was quiet for a moment. "I find it surprising that anyone saw you." A subtle accusation. He thought I'd intentionally let myself be seen. Looking back on the encounter, I realized he might have been right. I easily could have slipped behind the tree trunk when Valentina was outside, but I'd remained visible, nonchalantly leaning back against the frozen bark after I first spotted Reyna leave the house.

"I'm not sure what to say, except that I'm sorry." I should have told him that I'd talked to her, but I couldn't get the sticky words to rise to the surface. The brief conversation I'd shared with Reyna felt private. If I'd learned anything of importance, I would have handed over the information. Our words had been harmless. Innocent. And I preferred to keep them for myself.

"They know we're watching them; that's no secret. I don't like putting women and children at the center of our wars, but we may need to use her, so continue to monitor the situation. That's all we can do for now."

"You know I'll do whatever is needed." My words to Javi were tainted with the bitterness of a lie—a rare occurrence. I had always respected him enough to honor him with the truth, but if our strategy would result in harming Reyna, I wasn't sure I could follow through. For the first time in our friendship, I might have to defy the man who'd saved my life on more than one occasion. I would have to pray it never came to that.

CHAPTER 8
Valentina

I RELAYED A SIMPLIFIED VERSION OF WHAT HAD HAPPENED between Kane and me to Reyna as we hurried home from the party. The only thing I left out was the kiss. I had no good explanation for the secrecy other than it felt private. I walked through all the ways he'd given me mental whiplash—his subtle flirtation then his baffling rejection. Inside, though, I was consumed with thoughts of the kiss. A kiss so passionate it had been transformative. Nothing else in life had been more important at that moment than the touch of his lips. It was as though my brain had been rewired with Kane Easton as its sole programming.

It was in the retelling of his flight that I had a revelation. I realized the one way his actions made sense—he loved someone back in Texas and believed his attraction to me was a betrayal. That was why he hated himself for wanting me. When I examined his behavior from that new perspective, it all made sense. Horrible, heartbreaking sense.

Once I had soundlessly crept back inside my house, I sank deep into the covers on my bed and allowed a swell of negative emotions to drag me down beneath the surface. Aside from despair over Kane's relationship status, I was overwhelmed with anger at myself for developing feelings when I'd known he was nothing but trouble. I started to wonder if my initial wariness of him had ever been about Reyna or if I'd known subconsciously that I was the one in danger.

I hadn't fallen in love or anything so tragic. I'd fallen into hope. Excitement. Longing. I'd seen how Kane was different than the guys I'd gone to school with and fostered hope that maybe he was precisely what I was looking for. When hopes were crushed, it might not be as devastating as the loss of a loved one, but the pain was still real.

My heart hurt, and I was the only one to blame.

I was so distracted by my own troubles that I didn't contemplate Reyna's run-in with Santino until the next morning. My first instinct was to confront Javier about his spying activities and assure him Reyna wasn't a threat, but that would have clued him into our friendship. He would then tell Giada, at the very least, and, in all likelihood, my father. Not an option.

I could do nothing but worry about why they were watching her. I didn't like to think my family was capable of hurting an innocent girl, but until this year, I never would have imagined we were a part of organized crime. Would they use her to get her father to comply with their demands? Knowing what a bastard he was, I doubted such an attempt would work. If he did try to protect her, it was only for his own selfish reasons rather than any real concern for her safety.

I started to wonder if I should tell my father about my friendship with Reyna in the hopes that he wouldn't harm her, but then images of Giada unconscious in a hospital bed surfaced. No degree of pleading would stop my father. If he was convinced Reyna was the best way to accomplish his goals, nothing I said would matter.

Pins and needles of urgency pricked at my muscles, coaxing me out of bed. I had to get Reyna to safety, and the sooner, the better.

"I grabbed fresh bagels this morning," Mom said when I trudged downstairs and began to rummage through the fridge.

"Mmm ... perfect, thanks." I grabbed the cream cheese and turned to the pantry. "You working at the church today?"

Mom volunteered so frequently it could have been a full-time job. I enjoyed the feeling of community I experienced when I went to Mass, but I wasn't devoted to the church like my mother.

"Only until about three, then I'm going to come home to get ready. We're having dinner tonight with Aunt Lottie and Uncle Enzo at that new Greek place that your aunt keeps raving about over by Fort Wadsworth." I was surprised to hear they would be out for the evening. My dad was a bona fide homebody.

"We?" I asked warily.

Mom shot me a look. "You're welcome to join us, but it's not mandatory."

Ordinarily, I wouldn't mind going to dinner with them—it was a chance for yummy food in the city, and Aunt Lottie was always fun—but an idea struck me the minute Mom told me about their plans.

"I think I'll pass. I have some reading to do for English, but you guys have a great time."

"Okay, hun. I'm headed out. See you after lunch." She placed a kiss on my cheek and breezed out of the house.

That evening, I waited until my parents had been gone for thirty minutes before I went to my father's office. From the day we'd learned to walk, my sisters and I had been taught that Dad's office was off-limits. I had never once snooped through his things. I'd never had a reason to. What did I care about a bunch of boring work files? However, considering the mafia's potential interest in Reyna, I had to see what information I could gather.

The solid wood door that separated a standard suburban home from the inner workings of the criminal underworld creaked loudly. The sound pierced the silence, causing my shoulders to surge up to my ears. I'd never been so paranoid before, but I'd also never felt like a traitor in my own home. I was doing the right thing; I just hoped my father would understand if he ever discovered what I'd done.

His office was large, containing an executive desk floating in the middle of the space and a sitting area overlooking a window to the backyard. One wall was lined with bookshelves filled with decorative memorabilia. The opposite wall contained a credenza with his desktop computer and a two-drawer filing cabinet with an old printer on top. His computer was the ideal place to search, but it had been turned off and was password protected. The filing cabinet might also be of interest, but I decided to start with his desk drawers. Surely, he would have kept documents relevant to the current cartel situation within easy reach.

The top center drawer was filled with office supplies, while the drawer to the left contained a number of household bills, several charging cables, and a slew of business cards. The two drawers below it were equally unhelpful. Moving on to the other side, the top drawer on the right contained a padded ledger book, each page filled with numbers that meant absolutely nothing to me. There was also a small notepad, the top page blank.

I started to close the drawer when I took a second look at the notepad. I'd seen in mystery movies where people left inadvertent clues from the indentation of their writing. It sounded silly, but I grabbed a pencil and lightly scribbled back and forth over the top piece of paper on the pad. I was stunned speechless when words emerged.

Viper 10k weekly

I gaped at the message, unable to tell if it was even relevant. What or who was Viper? I'd have to google the name once I was done. It could have been a new car payment plan for all I knew. Dad wasn't the Dodge Viper sort, but I hadn't expected him to be in the mafia either.

I tore off the top page and shoved it in my pocket. The two drawers below were both locked, and the filing cabinet contained folder after folder of documents pertaining to my uncle's construction business. If anything in there would help me, it would take an eon to figure out.

Making sure everything was returned just as I'd found it, I stepped back and scanned the room one more time with a demoralized sigh. I wasn't sure what I'd hoped to find. Maybe Dad's little black book of contacts with *Document*

Forger highlighted in yellow? Or perhaps a detailed plan for the mafia's takedown of the cartel? Regardless of the grandeur of my delusions, the odds hadn't been in my favor.

I was taking tiny steps forward, but my progress was too marginal to see with the naked eye. I could only hope that in time, each little surge forward would get me where I needed to be.

CHAPTER 9
Kane

I WAS SO PISSED AT MYSELF FOR WHAT HAPPENED AT THE PARTY that I hardly spoke to anyone the whole next week. I wasted my entire weekend in a video game, which helped me temporarily forget my Friday night, but there was no avoiding Val once I was back at school. The best I could do was keep to myself while I tried to sort out my shit. Between being the new guy and acting like a surly motherfucker, it wasn't hard to isolate myself. I needed the time to think and get my head in order.

I never imagined I'd meet a girl at Xavier who would erode my control the way Valentina had. It wasn't unusual for girls to bat their eyelashes in my direction and smother me with attention, but not Val. Her concern for her friend came before any attraction she might have felt for me. That made her more than a pretty face. She was multifaceted when everyone around her was two-dimensional. I wanted to peel back those layers and see what was beneath, so much so that I couldn't get her out of my damn head.

Kissing her had only made the compulsion worse. Now, her sultry taste and the feel of her hands clutching me close haunted me day and night. My lack of control grated on me worse than nails on a chalkboard. I couldn't just beat the shit out of the person annoying me because that person was me. No matter how hard I tried to repress my urges, my eyes were drawn to the curvy brunette each day at school. My lungs ached to breathe in her floral scent. My ears strained to hear the commanding way she ruled those around her. I was practically obsessed with the girl, and I hated myself for it.

I'd never been so fucking conflicted in my life.

By Friday, I was so on edge that I snapped when some douche with braces checked my shoulder in the hallway. Looking back, I realized the contact had probably been accidental, but at the moment, it was the perfect outlet for my frustrations. Before I'd even thought about what I was doing, I had the kid up against the lockers pissing himself.

"All right, big guy. Better let the little shit go, or you'll end up in Principal Ruiz's office." Bryson clapped his hand on my back good-naturedly as if I hadn't just acted like a lunatic.

I glanced around at the circle of students surrounding us, then stepped back. My traumatized victim scurried off, disbursing the onlookers.

"Thanks, man. I guess I lost my cool," I murmured to Bryson.

"No sweat. It happens to all of us. You just gotta survive one more class till the weekend." He gave me a conciliatory chin lift, then merged into the stream of students flowing down the hall.

One more class. If only it were that easy.

It would be yet another hour of torture sitting next to the source of my torment. When I entered class, she was already seated, eyes directed straight ahead as though she were alone in the room. I slumped down in my chair, expecting her to continue ignoring me as she had most of the week in response to the icy blast of air I'd interjected between us.

To my extreme annoyance, Barnard instructed us to get with a partner. The class immediately began to pair off with their usual partners. Val and I surveyed the nonexistent options before looking back at one another.

Her lips thinned. "Let's hope you're feeling more civilized after throwing your tantrum in the hallway. At least I know I'm not the only one being subjected to your temperamental mood swings." Her voice carried over to me like the scent of Eve's apple tempting Adam. There was hurt buried in the bitterness, and I yearned to soothe the pain I'd caused. I hated that I couldn't even give her an explanation.

"It's complicated," I murmured sullenly.

She snorted on a choked laugh, drawing my narrowed gaze. "That's what they all say. You don't have to explain anything. I got the picture loud and clear."

It was that spark in her—the innate fight that stiffened her spine—that drove me wild. She stood up for herself and those around her, calling a spade a spade without apology. Her ferocity called to an elemental part of me that wanted to coerce the lioness to show me her soft underside. To convince her to walk beside me rather than battle against me.

It was madness. A sickness in my bloodstream that I was powerless against.

I clamped my hand on the corner of her desk and started to pull her in close to me, but she slammed her feet down on the floor and glowered at me, keeping herself rooted to the spot. My lips peeled back to reveal a wicked grin before I slid my own desk next to hers. Her eyes widened a fraction as she craned her neck to maintain eye contact.

I slowly leaned in, my lips settling close to her ear. "No matter what you think you know, I can promise that you *don't*." A whispered confession, or the closest I could get to one.

When I pulled away, confusion lined her pretty face. I slid over her iPad and began to read the class exercise, determined to ignore just how reckless I was near Val. It wasn't the first time in my life I'd struggled with impulse control, but I'd thought I'd remedied that little problem. Where Val was concerned, I was just as self-destructive as I'd been as a kid.

CHAPTER 10
Valentina

KANE BEGAN TO READ ALOUD FROM OUR ASSIGNMENT, BUT I hardly heard a word he said. Between the ravenous intensity of his glare and the fervor of his snarled defense, I had to wonder if I'd been wrong. Had I misinterpreted his behavior toward me? What else could possibly explain the bipolar nature of his actions—flirty and alluring one minute, then cold and withdrawn the next?

Something kept him from opening up and getting close to me. What secret was bad enough to justify pushing people away in order to keep that secret safe? What all did I even know about Kane? He'd come from Texas and had a little brother. He was intelligent and had a strange fondness for political history yet no real interest in excelling at school. He had a knee injury that kept him from playing sports, and he rode a sleek black motorcycle to and from school. It wasn't the most comprehensive breakdown, but it wasn't entirely devoid of detail. There was still plenty missing. I wanted to fill in every crack and crevice. More than ever before, I wanted to know what made Kane Easton who he was.

My shift in attitude transformed my anger into curiosity.

I forced myself to focus on what Kane was reading, listening intently to the gravelly hum of his voice. Although he had pulled our desks together, our bodies never made contact—accidental or otherwise. We discussed each question from the reading like any two students without a mountain of awkward baggage between them.

Near the end of the exercise, Kane pulled out his phone when he received a text. Phones weren't allowed out during class, but something silly like rules didn't seem to hinder Kane Easton. He texted a quick response, then set his phone on the desk, concealing it from Mr. Barnard by stretching his arm outward. Kane was reading our next discussion topic aloud when a follow-up text came through, the notification appearing on the screen. My eyes shot to the phone from instinct, enabling me to catch the short message before Kane turned the phone facedown and continued to read from the iPad. I, however, had lost all capacity to concentrate on political science as the short series of words danced in my head.

Encontraste a la chica todavía?

My stomach steadily rose higher and higher in my throat as my mind raced, and I tried to make sense of the message. Chica was Spanish for girl. Why would Kane be receiving a message in Spanish? The language was used relatively frequently in the city, somewhat less so in our area, but it wouldn't be unusual enough to raise a red flag ... if we hadn't been in the middle of a war with a Mexican cartel.

Holy shit!

Was I totally paranoid to worry that Kane had ties to the cartel? Could they have planted him to get at me? I wasn't sure that made sense. Why not just take me if they wanted me? Although, my eldest sister had been tricked into running off to Mexico by one of the cartel men. Was Kane part of an elaborate scheme to get to me? If that was the case, he was shit at his job.

No, that didn't make sense. I was missing something, but I had no clue what.

I needed to know what those other words meant so that I could understand the whole message. He was from Texas, so maybe it was a text from an old classmate. Maybe Kane had learned Spanish at school and had told a friend about our kiss. There were plenty of explanations for him to receive a message in Spanish, right? I was overreacting. Surely, I was just overreacting.

"Earth to Val. It's your turn."

I blinked at Kane and debated asking him about the message, but something held me back. "I'm sorry, I totally spaced." On the off chance the text was cartel-related, the last thing I wanted to do was let him know that I was on to him.

"You okay?" He studied me with increased scrutiny.

"Yeah, just got lost thinking about plans for tonight." I hadn't intended to invite him to the movie night I'd thrown together earlier in the day, but so much had changed in the span of a half hour. I needed to know more about Kane and fast. "We're going to see the new Chris Hemsworth action movie—hotties for the girls and guns for the boys. You're welcome to join us if you want." I tried to sound indifferent. I figured that was the proper tone, considering the awkwardness between us, but inside, I silently urged him to agree.

"We?" he asked smoothly.

"The crew—me and Reyna, Bryson, Chloe, Presley, and I think Elliot is coming."

"That sounds cool. What time?"

"I'm not sure exactly when we're meeting up. I can text you if that works." I could have told him the plan, but it was a great excuse to get his number. I wasn't sure how knowing his number would help me, but I wanted any information I could get.

He listed off his digits just before Barnard called for our attention and led the class as a whole through each exercise until the bell. Once I slipped from class, I went to the nearest bathroom and entered the text I'd seen into Google translate.

Did you find the girl yet?

Find the girl? What did that mean? I wasn't exactly hidden. Could he have been after Reyna? Maybe he worked for an enemy cartel. She wasn't any more hidden than I was, though maybe from another cartel's perspective, she would seem hidden.

Hell, I was more confused than ever.

Was I being absurd to even entertain that he was working for a cartel? Maybe. Maybe not. I definitely needed more information before I jumped to conclusions and went running to my dad. A night out with Kane would be the perfect opportunity to start my investigation.

I had expected Chris Hemsworth would be enough eye candy to keep me entertained, but the military movie about US troops in Afghanistan was *not* my thing. I'd already debated a dozen times whether I could pull out my phone without getting fussed at.

My friends and I had met at the theater. Kane had shown up just minutes before the movie started, so there hadn't been time to talk to him, and Chloe had weaseled her way into the seat next to him. I was sandwiched on one end between Reyna and Bryson, counting down the minutes until the damn movie was over.

Unable to take any more, I slipped from my seat and fled the theater toward the lobby where I could sit and kill some time people watching. The place was buzzing with the Friday night crowd. I propped myself against the wall, leaning my head back wearily and taking in the various moviegoers as they bought popcorn and talked with friends. As my eyes flitted from one group to another, they eventually collided with an amber stare locked on me.

Kane stood just like myself, leaned against the opposite wall some fifty feet away. He wrapped his full lips around the straw in his drink and took a long pull, eyes never leaving mine, then slowly pushed off the wall. My skin heated and buzzed with awareness as I watched him stroll casually closer. Once he reached me, he relaxed back against the wall next to me, both of us facing the busy room.

"You're missing the movie," he murmured.

"I could say the same to you." I couldn't help a glance up at his chiseled profile beside me. He was sexy as hell in ripped jeans and a long-sleeved shirt scrunched up above his forearms. He towered over me by about eight inches. I was only five-three, so it wasn't unusual for guys to be taller than me. But with Kane, it wasn't just his height. He was broad and solid. His sheer mass made me feel tiny.

"Not my thing, I guess."

"I'm surprised. I thought all guys loved movies with fighting and explosions." I sensed his gaze fall toward me and lifted my own.

"Guess I'm not like most guys." He tore his eyes from mine, sipping from his drink to settle the sudden increase in electric tension between us. "What about you? I thought all girls drooled over Chris Hemsworth." Was that a tiny smirk I detected?

"Totally. An hour of Chris and my panties were soaked. I was going to run to the restroom and change them, but I forgot to bring another pair." My turn to smirk.

Kane bit his lip to keep from grinning.

"So," I continued. "If war movies aren't your thing, what is?" I turned to lean my shoulder against the wall to face him.

"I like movies that make me think. Movies like *Inception* or *Interstellar*." Complex movies that involved a deep level of deception. A clue about the man himself?

Take it easy, Val. You like murder mysteries, but that doesn't mean you want to kill someone.

"Those were a little heavy for me. I like to keep my entertainment a bit lighter, thus my waning interest in tonight's chosen flick."

His head rolled to face me. "Please tell me you aren't a rom-com girl."

I lifted my chin haughtily. "I can be if the mood strikes. But not always. I'd say my favorite movie lately has been *Knives Out*—a little mystery, humor, and action all rolled into one. Perfect."

"At least it's not *The Notebook*."

"Oh, God, no. That movie was depressing as hell."

Kane rolled to his side, mirroring my pose with his shoulder leaned against the wall. His piercing stare held me captive for long seconds before he finally spoke. "Why did you have to be so different from all the girls around you?" His rumbled words, barely audible above the overhead music and chatter of excited voices, were plenty loud to coax my pulse to a frantic thrum.

Even when I suspected him of deception, he still had the power to make my body respond to him.

"You say that like it's a bad thing." I ran my tongue along my suddenly parched lips.

His eyes tracked the movement. "You're just very … unexpected." His eyes fell again, this time down toward my chest. My lips parted on a shuddered breath when his hand slowly lifted, then gingerly swept a lock of hair out from where it had become trapped beneath my jacket. His warm fingers had brushed my skin to first collect the hair, and the brief contact was a tattoo permanently inked on my body.

"There you are." Reyna's voice sliced through my lust-filled haze.

I shot upright away from the wall and ran my fingers through my hair. I couldn't have looked more guilty if I'd tried. "Hey, Rey. Movie's not over, is it?"

"No. I just got worried when you didn't come back." Her eyes flicked back and forth between us before giving me a questioning look.

"Sorry, we got talking, and I guess I lost track of time."

"No problem. If you're not into the movie, we can wait out here until the others get out."

"No," I barked out more forcefully than I'd wanted. "Let's go back. I'd hate to miss the end at this point." I took her hand in mine and led her around the corner toward the theater. My interest level in Kane might have changed, but I still didn't want him around Reyna. He was a possible threat more now than ever with so many unanswered questions surrounding him.

I glanced back to see if Kane was with us. He'd rounded the corner so that he was still in view but had found a new resting place against the hallway wall. He was silhouetted by the brightly lit lobby behind him, but I knew those eyes tracked our every move.

CHAPTER 11
Valentina

I walked up to Reyna's front door on Monday morning, trying to convince myself I wasn't being incredibly idiotic. It was a school holiday, and we'd wanted to see each other. My place was definitely off-limits, and the brisk winter snap that had blown in the night before made it impractical to spend much time outdoors. I had agreed to come by her house but was questioning the sanity of my decision. Her father and his men knew who I was, but it wasn't the brightest idea to deliver myself up on a silver platter.

Oh, well. Guess I was doing it anyway.

Dad had insisted on having one of his men drive me. Ever

since Giada's ordeal, I'd noticed an increased presence of scary-looking men in and out of the house. In order to keep my destination a secret, I used Chloe as my alibi. We weren't the best of friends but had come to a mutually beneficial arrangement years ago that had become the foundation for an alliance. If either of us needed an excuse or an alibi, we were there for each other, no questions asked. The relationship had evolved to a sort of actual friendship, but nothing like the easy closeness I'd quickly established with Reyna.

I let Chloe know I was stopping by, had my escort drop me off, then made the trek to Reyna's house. It wasn't an ideal setup, but it gave us the freedom to hang out for a few hours. No school. No boys. Just two friends catching up. It was way overdue. Hopefully, our visit didn't end with me being kidnapped and shipped off to Mexico.

Fingers crossed.

I had to pretend to be oblivious about Reyna's family dealings, so when a strange man opened the door, I smiled broadly and announced I was there to see Reyna as if I had no clue the man had a gun tucked beneath his jacket.

"I'm here!" Rey called out from somewhere behind him. She wedged herself in front of the guard. "Hey, Val. Come on in."

I was whisked away up a set of winding stairs and down a hallway to a huge room perfectly decorated from the plush mint duvet on a tufted gray bed to the shiny gold chandelier with matching wall sconces.

"Your room is gorgeous!" I gaped at the magazine-worthy setup, complete with a shaggy fur throw draped over the corner of a loveseat by her picture window. "How come you've never invited me over before?"

Shame weighed on her features. "I was trying to keep you safe," she said softly.

I pulled her into a hug, enveloping her in gratitude and reassurance. My chest ached for the horrible position Reyna was in. "We'll get you out," I whispered fervently.

Reyna only nodded before pulling back, her eyes screaming at me to be careful with my words. There was no telling who all might be listening. I nodded discreetly to signal my understanding.

"So, is your mom here?" I asked, wondering about the other half of Reyna's parenting cesspool. I imagined her life had been pretty rough, but that didn't stop me from being a little judgmental. Her sole job as mother had been to protect her baby, and she'd done a shit job so far.

"Yeah, but she's still passed out. She doesn't usually get up until lunch when she has a bloody Mary and starts all over."

No siblings. No real parents. My poor friend was utterly alone in the world.

I squeezed her hand, not wanting to be overheard reassuring her that things would get better.

"Okay, I don't get to have my friend over often, so I want to make the best of this. Come over here to my living area and tell me exactly what was going on with you and Kane on Friday."

"You have your own *living* room?" I screeched.

"You are not changing the subject. You. Kane. Spill." She led me across the hall to a large room that was a cross between a family room and a game room with a classy sectional sofa and entertainment center. Contemporary framed cityscapes dotted the walls, and a game table sat in the back corner—all decorated in the same style and color scheme as her bedroom.

"Okay, okay. But this setup is crazy awesome, just so you know." It didn't make up for her shit situation, but it was a tiny perk. I plopped down on the sofa next to her. "As for Kane, there's not much to say. I happened to see him in the lobby. He told me he wasn't into the movie, so I asked him about that. Usually guys love war stuff." I shrugged. "That's about it." I debated whether to tell her about my cartel suspicions, but I was still not convinced I wasn't just being paranoid. She already had so much crap to deal with. The last thing I wanted was to give her one more thing to worry about.

"You sure? Because you two looked seriously into each other when I showed up."

"You know how he's rubbed me the wrong way since the day he arrived. I just started to realize on Friday that I hadn't given him a fair break, so I was trying to be civil and get to know him a little better."

Her eyes softened. "I'm so glad to hear that. I think he's a decent guy." She raised a hand to stop me before I could say anything. "Don't get me wrong. I'm not interested, but I also don't think you should be so hard on him. That's all."

"Fair enough. I'm willing to give him a chance. You and I have more important things to think about anyway." I peered around the room, wondering about cameras and listening devices, then leaned in close to her ear. "I don't want to forget to ask you if the word *viper* means anything to you."

"Like the snake or the car?" she whispered.

"Well, I figure it means something more than that, but I have no idea what. I was hoping you could tell me." I dropped my voice back to a whisper, pretending to rub my nose to cover my lips. "I saw it on a note in my dad's office."

"Sorry, but it doesn't ring any bells."

I frowned. "Nothing else to share at the moment, but I'll keep at it."

"There's time," she whispered. "Come on, let's watch a movie." Her face split into an enormous grin that clamped down on my heart. She'd been so neglected in life that she was genuinely thrilled just to watch a movie with a friend—something I would have taken for granted before I met Rey.

We spent three hours together watching a chick flick, talking about celebrities as we leafed through a gossip magazine, then painting each other's toes the same pale blue for spring. They were mundane activities that I wouldn't have given a second thought before. Seeing the world from Reyna's perspective, the time together became a precious gift. I just hoped it wasn't the last time we were able to hang out like two normal teenage girls.

I left Reyna's house buried in an avalanche of emotions so deep I almost didn't notice the man walking on the opposite side of the street. He was bundled against the cold, but I would have recognized that tousled hair anywhere.

"Are you stalking me?" I called out wryly, hoping he didn't detect the genuine concern in my voice.

Kane stopped and met my gaze, those maple eyes of his pinning me to the spot. "Maybe I should ask if you're stalking me."

"Just walking home from a friend's house." I didn't want to say I'd been at Reyna's and give him her home address if he didn't already know it. "What's your excuse?"

"Just out for a walk." He mimicked my tone, stepping forward and slowly entering the street.

"If that isn't suspicious, I don't know what is. It's freezing out. Who voluntarily goes for a walk in this weather?"

"It's refreshing." His lip quirked up in one corner.

I shook my head and continued walking with him beside me. "Definitely a crazy stalker."

"Hey, you chose to walk home in the cold. You're telling me no one could give you a ride?"

I shot him a side glance and fed him the same explanation he'd given me about his temperamental moods. "It's complicated."

He huffed out a laugh. "Touché. You live nearby?"

"So, you're not a very good stalker?"

"Maybe I'm so good at what I do, I've gotten you to drop your defenses."

I studied him from the corner of my eye, wondering if he could be right. "Whatever, it's cold as balls out here. Give me a better answer than it's refreshing."

He blew out a foggy cloud of air. "Mom died when I was younger, and Dad is working overseas at the moment. Sometimes I just like to get away from my house." His tone was matter-of-fact, but the reality behind his words reeked of loneliness.

"That really sucks." There wasn't much more to be said. I couldn't fix his situation, and no positive spin would change the truth. He was alone, stuck raising his younger brother. His situation was mildly better than Reyna's, but not by much. Together, they made my mafia household look like the Huxtables.

Assuming what he said was true.

"It's not as bad as it sounds. I just needed a breather."

"What is it your dad does that keeps him away from home?"

"He practices international law for a big firm with offices in other countries. Depending on what case he's working on, he has to bounce between offices. He used to work at the

Houston office but transferred up here to be closer to the European team. What about you? What does your dad do?" He peered at me curiously.

"He works for my uncle's construction company, and it's mostly out of his home office, so he's always around." That was the story I grew up believing. It wasn't totally untrue, just not the whole picture.

"Mom?"

"She volunteers at the church mostly."

A low humming sound resonated from his chest. "So, parents are around, yet you had to walk from your friend's house. In the cold. You say it's complicated, but I'd say it sounds awfully intriguing."

I slowed to a stop, Kane doing the same. We eyed one another—my gray gaze warring with his golden stare.

"You explain your complicated, and I'll explain mine," I dared him breathlessly.

Kane sobered, his face growing harsh. He took a small step forward. "*You* are my complicated, Valentina Genovese."

The words hung in the air, accented by the pounding of my racing heart.

"I want to know *why*. If there's not someone else, then what's so complicated?" I stepped closer, his magnetic pull drawing me in.

He reached his hand around to cup the back of my neck, then paused, his face twisting in torment before he brought our lips together. Cold to warm. Firm to yielding. Opposite yet perfectly matched.

My soul levitated at his touch. There was no other way to describe it.

I could live a lifetime in his arms, yet our kiss was brought to an end just as quickly as it had begun. Yanking away as though I'd burned him, Kane severed our connection. His eyes blazed with the intensity of emotions I couldn't grasp. Mine were surely riddled with confusion.

"When I'm around you, I have no control," he said between shallow breaths. "Once I start, I won't be able to stop, no matter how wrong it is." His jaw snapped shut as though he'd said too much. The light in his eyes dimmed, and a veil of indifference cloaked his features. "I better head back home. See you at school tomorrow." His retreating form stalked down the sidewalk, leaving me dumbfounded in the cold.

CHAPTER 12
Reyna

The second after Val left my house, I raced back up to my bedroom to watch her from the window. I wanted to make sure she left our property safely. It had been selfish to have her over, but I cherished every minute. If my father's men nabbed her while she was here, I never would have forgiven myself.

Once she walked the length of our driveway and disappeared around the corner, I took a long, deep breath. I continued staring out the window at nothing in particular—just the world carrying on despite the chaos of my life. It was soothing to see the leaves sway in a gentle breeze and birds leap from one bald branch to another. In a few months, the landscape would be repainted in vivid colors marking the arrival of spring and new beginnings. No matter how dire my situation appeared, new opportunities would arise and life would go on.

I stood watch at my window for fifteen minutes when I noticed motion from the edge of my view. A figure stepped out from beside a tree in the neighbor's yard, and his gaze was trained up at me.

Santino. He'd been watching my house.

Had he seen Valentina? He had to have been there the whole time I was at the window, which meant he saw her leave.

Anxiety wrapped its greedy arms around my chest and squeezed. If he told her family that she'd been at my house, would they keep her under lock and key? Maybe they would demand my father withdraw me from school to ensure I never saw Val again.

If Santino could see the worry on my face, he didn't show it. He simply turned and disappeared as if he'd never been there in the first place.

I sighed and finally stepped away from thoughts of freedom to face the walls of my prison. It was time to check on Mamá. I went back downstairs to the master suite, where I found my mother still in bed, snoring softly. It was later than she usually slept but not totally abnormal. In the past two years, her issues with alcohol had worsened, and she'd added prescription pills to the mix. She'd started using alcohol to escape the reality of her marriage early on, so she never had a chance against addiction. Sometimes, I wondered if she just didn't know a better way to cope or if she truly wanted to die. Either way, she was working herself toward an early grave.

I'd spent years of my childhood trying to protect her and worrying about her, but as each year had gone by, I learned to separate myself from her disordered life. Even at a distance, watching her self-destruct was a challenge, and being emotionally invested in her struggle was more than I could bear. I'd had to pull away for my own sanity. It helped that I harbored a certain degree of resentment. She was the mom. She was supposed to be the strong one—the person who protected me against the world.

In the past, when she'd be passed out in the middle of the day, I used to sit next to her for ages, wishing she'd wake up and realize she wanted to change. That she wanted to be my mom again. I'd daydream about living in a small house with just the two of us. We'd cook dinner together and play cards in the evenings like we used to do when I was little and she was still a functioning alcoholic. Now, I hardly gave her unconscious form a second glance before locating her discarded purse on the armchair and pulling out her wallet.

The weekly allowance my father gave her was enough to support a small family. Considering how out of it my mom was half the time, she never had any idea how much she spent. I'd been pocketing money from her for a year—from the minute I learned I'd be going to America—hoping to build up enough of a reserve to help me escape. These months in New York were my best opportunity to get away, but that window was closing, ratcheting up my level of desperation.

I pulled three hundred-dollar bills from her red leather Gucci wallet and slipped them into my bra. Once I was safely back in my bedroom, I grabbed the large teddy bear that decorated a shelf over my desk and pulled back the duvet on my bed. I curled up beneath the crisp linens, hugging the bear to my chest until I was hidden beneath the covers. I had no idea if my father had cameras in my room and didn't want to chance him finding my stash, so I pretended to nap anytime I needed to make a deposit.

I'd opened a small hole in the bear's neck seam that I kept secured with a safety pin. Only once I was hidden beneath my covers did I slip off the pin and add the new bills to my collection. For a moment, I allowed myself the luxury of imagining a life away from my parents—something I tried not to do too often because it made the return to reality that much harder to take.

CHAPTER 13
Valentina

KANE'S CRYPTIC WORDS HAUNTED ME ALL NIGHT. WHAT COULD be so wrong with us being together? It wasn't like we were brother and sister, for God's sake. And if by some insane chance he *was* working for a cartel, I couldn't imagine he'd have such a crushing sense of morality that kissing me would bring on a barrage of self-loathing. I was at a loss for what could possibly explain his warring emotions.

Nothing made sense. No matter how I twisted his words or scrutinized his actions, I couldn't see the full picture. I needed more information, and the only way to get it was from Kane. If he wouldn't tell me directly, then I'd gather every breadcrumb I could find until they led me to the answer. And once I understood his hang-up, I'd decide for myself if the obstacle was truly insurmountable.

I went back to school Tuesday with renewed purpose. For the first time since Kane started at Xavier Catholic School, we began to settle into a new normal. I allowed him to insert himself into our friend group, and he didn't intentionally push too many of my buttons. The underlying current that buzzed between us still stirred to life whenever he was around, but I attempted to pretend I didn't notice.

On Thursday, my mom convinced my sisters to come for a family dinner. I loved getting to see them, so instead of playing piano right after school, which was my usual routine, I dove into my homework the second I got home, hoping to have it finished before anyone got to the house.

I was still wrapping up an English assignment when Giada poked her head into my room. She usually called from the bottom of the stairs when she arrived, so I was surprised to see her in my room instead.

"Hey, there. You have a minute to talk?"

I grinned warily, happy to see my sister but concerned about what she wanted to discuss. "Yeah, I was just working on some homework. What's up?"

She sat on the bed across from me, fiddling with the fabric of my duvet. "I know this sounds a little weird, but I saw you on Monday over at a girl's house. I haven't told Mom and Dad, but that family is seriously dangerous. You have to stop going over there."

Those were the words I'd been dreading for weeks.

I was suddenly overcome with desperation, fear scooting me to the edge of my seat and making my pulse thrum in my ears. "Please, G, you can't tell them. Dad will make me break off the friendship, and I can't do that. Her dad is *awful*, her mom is an alcoholic, and now she's having to move. I can't just abandon her." I couldn't tell Giada about Reyna's escape. She'd think it was too dangerous, so I threw out everything else I could to try to sway her.

"He's not just awful, Val. He's a *cartel* boss and Dad's *enemy*," she hissed, now perched on the edge of the bed.

"I know, okay?"

"You *knew*?" Giada's perfectly sculpted eyebrows leapt to her hairline. "Then why the hell were you over there? *How did you get over there?* Doesn't Dad have someone protecting you?"

"Yes, he has some thug shadowing me. I had the muscle head drop me at another friend's house, and I snuck out the back. Look, if I promise not to go to her house again, will you please not tell Dad? She can't help who her father is, and she needs me. *Please*."

She flopped back on the bed, ever the drama queen. "Now I know how Alessia felt," she muttered.

"Huh?" What did our cousin have to do with this?

"Nothing." She waved it off with a flick of her wrist. "Okay, I'll keep my mouth shut, but I expect you to swear on your life that you will not go back over to that house. And she needs to know that she cannot tell her father who you are. That man may have gone to Mexico for now, but that doesn't mean the threat from his cartel is over. We don't know what will happen, so we have to be safe." She had no idea that Reyna and her family knew my mafia connections. It was never a coincidence that the two of us found ourselves at the same school.

I wrapped her in a tight hug. "Thank you, G. You're the best!"

She smiled, but it didn't erase the worry in her eyes.

"Yeah, yeah. This blows up in my face, and I'll make sure they never let you out of the house again, capisce?"

I raised my right hand. "Scout's honor."

"Alright, let's get downstairs. I think Ma has something she wants to tell us."

Thirty minutes later, I was trying to digest the news that I had a brother somewhere in the world. My mother had just brought out the homemade lasagna when she dropped the bomb that she'd had a baby at the age of sixteen and given him up for adoption. She went on to explain why she decided to finally tell us, but my ears were ringing too loudly to hear.

"Breathe, Val. You're going to pass out," Giada called to me from across the table.

I glanced up at her and Javi, who was now settling in as a part of our family, and realized my lungs had frozen. I gulped in a lungful of air.

Holy shit, I had a brother.

I'd thought the mafia secret was life-changing, but this somehow seemed even bigger. This wasn't just my father's job. A secret baby meant I didn't know my mother half as well as I'd thought. The strict Catholic woman who always strove for perfection and was hyper aware of appearances had gotten knocked up as a teen.

Everything suddenly made so much more sense.

I tore off a small piece of bread from the slice on my plate and rolled it around my mouth. My stomach no longer felt hungry, but I needed something to do while I processed this new information.

"Well, Ma," Giada broke the silence. "I think it's incredibly exciting. We've only ever had girls in the Genovese family, so a boy sure would spice things up. Is there any way we could find out who he is?"

What the hell? Giada was acting like we'd added Disney Plus to our Roku channels rather than learned about a secret brother. I couldn't fathom how she'd assimilated the news so quickly... unless she'd already known.

My eyes traveled back and forth between my mom and sister as if I were a spectator in a studio audience, ignorant to the plot unfolding before me. I felt like a stranger in my own house.

"Oh, I don't know. I guess I'd have to look into it if we decided that's what we wanted. For now, I just wanted to tell you girls because you deserve to know. I'm sorry I kept it a secret for so long. It just never seemed like the right time..." My rock-solid mother, who didn't even cry watching *Titanic*, began to tear up.

The table was engulfed in awkwardness. My frantic stare cut to Camilla beside me, who returned my helpless look with wide eyes of her own.

"Hey, um, we've got some news as well." Giada to the rescue. "Javi and his friend Santino have started up a security company. They've already rented a small building and started talking with clients. How exciting is that?"

Mom smiled through glassy eyes. "That's wonderful, Javier. I'm so glad you've been able to settle in here so quickly."

Talk about Javi brought my thoughts back to the other reason I'd been excited about our family dinner. Reyna had told me about seeing Santino in her yard on Monday. He had to have seen me there, which means he knew about our friendship. If Santino knew, then Javier knew. Maybe that was how Giada had learned I'd been there. Either way, Javier knew about my friendship with Reyna, which meant I might be able to ask him for help.

A surge of excitement added a new element to my emotional roller coaster of an evening. I'd been panicking about how to help Rey and had debated begging Sofia for help, but if anyone would know how to escape the cartel, it was someone who had been in the cartel himself. Javier could be our answer to everything. He wasn't sworn to my father, so in theory, he could help me without telling a soul. And if I needed help persuading him, I had a feeling I could count on Giada to make it happen. First, I'd see what Javi said before I brought her into the mix, but she was a strong plan B.

I perked back up, engaging in dinner conversation and forcing down some food. The second dinner finished, and I was able to get Javi away from the others, I made my first move.

"I need to talk to you," I whispered discreetly. "Can you meet me before school tomorrow? I know it's a pain to drive out here, but it's really important."

He lifted his gray eyes, not totally unlike my own, and peered over at where the others were taking dishes to the kitchen. "If you need me, I can be here."

I squashed down the premature wave of relief that tried to mount. "Seven thirty at the Dunkin' on Hylan. That work?" School started at eight fifteen, which would give me just enough time to give him a quick rundown of the situation before getting back to school in time for first period.

Ever the stoic badass, Javier only nodded one single drop of his chin. The stage was set, so now, I just had to reel him in.

THE FOLLOWING MORNING, I told my mom that I needed to go in early for a study session with a teacher. She dropped me off out front of the school, and I rushed down the sidewalk the second her car disappeared from view.

When I stepped through the doorway at Dunkin', Javi was already seated at a table with Santino, and they were both sipping from steaming paper cups. I realized I hadn't explicitly told him to come alone. I pulled out the chair across from them like a felon fessing up my crimes to two hard-nosed detectives.

I could feel my lips thin when my eyes drifted to Santino. "I guess it's good you're here. I'd love to know more about why you're following Reyna."

Santino didn't respond. He didn't even move a muscle.

"Is that why you wanted to meet?" Javi asked. "To discuss Santino?"

I sighed, placing my hands on the table. "No. But before I can tell you that, I need you to promise me that you won't tell my family what I'm about to say."

"Valentina, surely, you know I can't make such a promise. I'm in a precarious position as it is with your family."

"But this doesn't have to have anything to do with them."

Javi lifted his free hand in a kind of shrug. "That's something I could only determine after I've heard what you have to say. It's a gamble you'll have to take if you want my help."

I stared at the man who had left everything he'd known to be with my sister and decided to take that chance. If anyone understood the need for a fresh start, it was Javi.

"As you already guessed, I need your help. I hadn't asked

before because I didn't realize you knew about my friendship with Rey, but after Giada talked to me last night, the cat's out of the bag." I lifted my gaze to his. "Reyna is a good person. She's not like her dad, and she needs our help to get away from him."

Javi sipped from his cup before responding. "We can't steal her away from her father."

"It's not stealing her away. It's helping her escape. She's the one leaving. She just needs papers to give herself a chance to stay hidden," I argued passionately. "You got away from the cartel, so there's no reason she can't as well."

"She'd have to be willing to disappear completely—become someone new and leave behind everyone she cares about permanently—and not many people are willing to go to those lengths."

"We know." The ragged words came from the depths of my soul, where I wept for Reyna. I hated that she'd have to be on her own, but I hated leaving her with her father even more. "She's willing to do whatever it takes."

Javi exchanged a look with Santino. "It's only papers you're after?"

I sat taller in the small metal chair. "Yes, and for you not to tell my father."

"Papers are one thing, but a secret from your father is another. I'll do what I think is best, and that's all I can give you."

"I understand but know that if Dad learns about any of this, he'll keep me from seeing Reyna. Right now, I'm all she has."

My attempt at an emotional plea fell on deaf ears. Javi might as well have been a castle guard outside Buckingham Palace—totally impervious to anything I said. His lack of response stirred up a swarm of emotions that clamored for an explosive release, but I'd only be hurting my chances. Instead, I gritted my teeth together and rose.

"I'd better get back to school. Thanks for meeting with me."

Javi nodded again. "I'll be in touch."

I said my goodbye and left the shop, desperately hoping I'd made the right decision.

CHAPTER 14
Santino

JAVI AND I BOTH REMAINED SEATED AFTER VALENTINA FLED the donut shop. We'd known the two girls were friends, but this was the first we'd learned of Val's efforts to help Reyna escape. We sat quietly for several minutes as we processed the implications.

"What do you think?" Javi asked, breaking our silence.

A frown tugged at my lips. "We're not left with much choice. The girl's father is a bastard. There's no question about that, so I can only imagine what she's been subjected to by living with that man. And if we allow Valentina to involve herself, she could end up in danger. Besides, giving the girl papers would only be a small interference." Each was a valid argument, but the reality was, I would have wanted to help Reyna even if it hadn't made any sense at all. I wasn't entirely sure that if Javier declined our services, I wouldn't defy him and assist the girl myself. I felt compelled in a way I couldn't explain. A compulsion that had me stepping from cover and allowing her to see me from her window.

"True." Javi sipped from his cup. "And your impressions of her?"

I considered his question for a long moment. She was beautiful yet broken—a rose had taken root in the jagged crevasse of a city sidewalk. Her delicate strength should have been crushed out of her years ago, but she persevered. She was enchanting in a haunted way that made me want to protect her. Nurture her. Seeing her trapped in that house, a bird in a cage, made my fists clench with rage. The last time I was there, I'd had to leave her house before I took matters into my own hands and did something I would have regretted. Something that could have gotten me killed.

I could have told Javier about my feelings, but I didn't want him to discount my input as emotionally flawed. Instead, I tried my best to produce an honest, logical response. "She comes across as meek, but she's stronger than she appears. I'd say she's observant. Intuitive. My instincts tell me she'd be successful on her own because she's never had the luxury of relying on anyone before. In that way, she's not unlike we were when we first encountered the Vargas family."

Javier eyed me, surprised at my assessment. "We could make her disappear easily enough, but Juan Carlos would know she had help. He hasn't truly tried to come after us—not to the degree he's capable—but a personal affront such as this might do the trick. I'd rather not take that risk if possible. It isn't only our lives at stake."

"True, but we got a second chance to be free from the cartel. Isn't it our duty to help others do the same?" I tried to keep the frustration from my voice, but Javi was the most perceptive man I'd ever met. Fooling him was not an easy feat.

He grunted in response. "We can have the documents ready should we decide to help, but for the moment, the family hasn't decided if they want to use the girl or not. She may be the best way to draw out Vargas and his men, and we can't deny the Genoveses that possible avenue. For now, we wait."

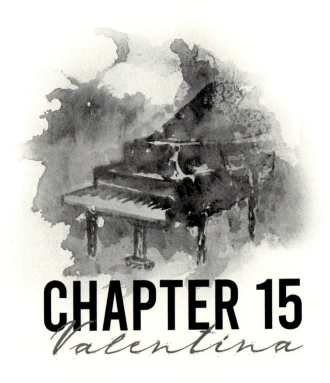

CHAPTER 15
Valentina

It was a good thing I'd always been such a good student because I was using up all the brownie points I'd earned over the years in a matter of hours. I was scolded in all four of my morning classes for failing to pay attention. How the hell was I supposed to concentrate on calculus after my meeting with Javier? I couldn't. It wasn't possible.

Javi insinuated he would get the papers for us but hadn't been totally transparent. I'd have to wait and see if he came through, and in the meantime, my mind was racing with the possibilities. If he did get the papers, would he give them to us before Reyna's father sent her back to Mexico? What if Javi didn't end up helping us? What if he told my father and I never saw Rey again? What if we *did* get the papers and were able to get Reyna away—where would she go?

There were so many uncertainties, and trying to plan for them all was going to make me crazy. I needed to ask Javi for a timeframe. Having an expected date of receipt would at least cut out some of the variables. When I got out my phone in class to text him, I realized that I never asked for his number. As I berated myself for being such an idiot, I received my fifth warning for the day—this time for having my phone out in class.

I slid the device back into my backpack and considered asking Giada for her boyfriend's number, but she'd insist on knowing why I wanted to talk to him. I didn't want her and her big mouth to know anything about our plans. Though I adored my sister, she was a notorious blabbermouth. I'd just have to plan as best as I could and try not to give myself a stress-induced heart attack at the age of seventeen.

Lunch was a welcome distraction. Talking with my friends helped finally stop my mind from looping through the same damn questions. Plus, seeing Kane reminded me that I had more than one problem to obsess over. Lucky me.

"What's the plan for this weekend?" asked Bryson before smashing half a slice of pizza in his mouth.

"Weather's gonna suck. We need someone's house to hang at." Chloe turned her devious gaze to Reyna. "We've never been to your place, Rey. How about hosting a little gathering tomorrow night?"

Before Reyna or I could shoot down the idea, Kane chimed in. "I think that sounds like a great idea. It doesn't have to be anything crazy, just a place to hang out."

I glanced at Reyna, who looked like she was actually considering the possibility, and cut in before she could get herself in trouble. "Isn't your dad super strict?" I said pointedly, eyes boring into her. "I can't imagine he'd be okay with you hosting a party." She wanted to have friends over like any other teenage girl, but she wasn't just anyone. Aside from pissing off her dad, having people over might put them in danger too.

"Come on, Val," Kane pushed. "She could at least ask. You never get anywhere without trying."

What the hell was his problem? My teeth ached from the strain of my clenched jaw. "I don't even know why we're discussing this when *your* dad is out of town, so your house is completely available." I tilted my head and smiled with a challenge.

Take that, you bully.

"Hey, man." Bryson shoved Kane's shoulder. "That's perfect. If your place is available, we can chill over there—order pizza and have a few beers. Nothing crazy."

Kane assaulted me with a glare. "Yeah, that's cool. We can hang out at my place. Maybe Reyna can host next time."

I grinned, not caring how pissed he was because I'd just won an all-access pass to Kane Easton's house. I couldn't imagine a better place to dig up clues about a person than in their own personal space. If Kane was hiding something, I would do my best to find it.

"I wish I could join," said Presley, "but I'm on the decorations committee for the Valentine's dance, and we have a meeting tomorrow evening."

"On a Friday night? That's bullshit," Chloe groused.

"The dance is only two weeks away. We have to paint signs and get some other stuff ready. Several people were going to be in the city this weekend, so they decided to get it done tomorrow after school." Presley was surprisingly sweet, considering she was Chloe's friend. Who knew, maybe that's what everyone said about Reyna and me. I wasn't totally blind to the similarities. While they weren't quite as inseparable, they usually did school stuff together, but it appeared the decorations committee was where Chloe drew the line.

I'd been so wrapped up in other stuff that I'd completely forgotten about the dance. I thought about Kane and how it would feel to dance with him—our bodies pressed together, my arms draped over his broad shoulders, and the smell of his cologne warming me from the inside out.

My cheeks began to radiate heat. When my eyes flew up, I found Kane's eyes glued to my face, his harsh features a storm of condemnation. Did he know what I'd been thinking? There was no way, yet I sensed his intuition deep in my gut.

"Hey, Val," Bryson called. "I saw you dancing with Gio at the back-to-school party. You gonna go to the dance with him and finally give the man a chance?" He smirked, knowing I hadn't gone out with anyone since dating Talon, Gio's best friend. More than one rumor had circulated after our breakup about why I hadn't dated anyone since. I couldn't care less about rumors, but I did enjoy the sour look that crossed Kane's face at the mention of Gio.

"I guess that depends on who asks me." I tried not to look at Kane, but my eyes flicked in his direction for a split second. Just enough time to see his gaze drift to Reyna.

The next two classes dragged on as the emotional strain of my day wore me down. Fortunately, I had seventh period office aide, a privilege granted to seniors if they could fit it in their schedule. It was an hour reprieve from learning and a chance to mentally rally for the last class of the day. I worked on whatever admin tasks were needed and sometimes used the hour as a study period.

"Hey, Mrs. Kennedy. Whatcha got for me today?" I asked, dropping my bag next to the school secretary's desk.

"First, I need you to man the fort. I told Principal Ruiz I'd pick up the cookies she ordered for our staff meeting after school, but Shannon is out sick today, so I haven't been able to leave. I've got some absentees for you to put in the system while I run to the bakery, then you're free to do homework." She pulled a worn leather purse from the desk drawer. "I'll be back quick as a flash."

"No problem. I'll grab the phones and make sure the place is still standing when you get back." I grinned at our sweet secretary and lowered myself into her desk chair.

Seven names were scribbled on a mini legal pad, which I recognized as her absentee list—people who had not shown up or had to leave early for the day. Typically, I used my own student aide log-on when I worked on the computers in the office, but today, Mrs. Kennedy had been in such a rush to leave that she'd forgotten to log out.

I stared at the screen for endless seconds, a restless energy making my palms tingle and sweat. Student files were confidential, but as the school secretary, Mrs. Kennedy had access.

I could take one little peek, and no one would ever know.

My throat tightened as my hand lifted to the mouse, directing the cursor to the shortcut link for the student file database. One simple click and I was in.

With my eyes darting between the screen and the office door, I typed in Kane's name and pulled up his file. Kane David Easton. Parents: Steven and Amelia Easton. Mother: deceased. Father: attorney at DLA Piper. Siblings: none.

CHAPTER 16
Reyna

I UNDERSTOOD WHY VAL WAS SO ADAMANT AGAINST ME inviting our friends over to my house. It was a horrible idea, and I probably wouldn't have done it even if she hadn't cut in and redirected everyone's attention to Kane. But that didn't stop me from being a tad annoyed—at Val, at my father, at my entire situation. I felt like a diver watching my air tank slowly drain to its last puffs of oxygen. I had so little time left, and I desperately wanted to cling to every vestige of life around me.

If I ended up back in Mexico, I would undoubtedly find myself married to one of my father's associates, my life forfeited for his business purposes. What kind of life would that be? Depending on my new jailer, it could be a fate worse than death. The days and weeks I spent at Xavier might be all the life I had left. I wanted to experience everything I possibly could—hoard away every scrap of joy like a squirrel hoping to survive the long winter.

That was why I considered having friends over.

That was why I snuck out to go to the movies and obnoxious high school parties.

That was why I agreed to go to the dance with Kane when he asked me after lunch.

"Me? Um ... are you sure you're asking the right person?" I could hardly understand what I'd just heard. Surely, there'd been a mistake. I liked Kane, but I hadn't gotten the impression he was all that into me. Then again, what did I know? I'd never had a boyfriend in my life.

He grinned down at me, his bottom lipped pulled playfully between his teeth. "Yes, silly. I'm absolutely asking the right person. I know this isn't the most romantic way to ask, but I wanted to make sure I got to you before anyone else."

I glanced around the hall where we stood just outside our next class and wondered if this was a joke. Students were filtering into doorways, their noisy ruckus dwindling to a few hurried footsteps and slammed lockers. There were no snickering kids with phones filming my anticipated humiliation—no signs whatsoever that this was an elaborate scheme to tease the awkward, quiet girl.

He truly was asking me to the dance.

Val had been absolutely adamant nothing was going on between her and Kane. She was the only true friend I'd ever had, so I didn't want to hurt her, but if she swore she wasn't into him, and it was the only chance I had at going to a high school dance, I had to accept. I'd missed the homecoming dance, and this was the only other dance besides prom. I might not even be in the country by the time prom rolled around.

"Okay," I croaked, my voice abandoning me. I brought my eyes back to Kane—a guy who was almost too pretty to be real—and let my emotions override logic and rationale. I wasn't sure I was even interested in dating Kane, but the chance to show up at the dance with such a hottie made my head spin.

He grinned even wider and nodded toward our sociology class. "Excellent, now we better get to our seats. I don't want you to end up in trouble because of me."

"Oh, yeah." I jumped into action, rushing into the classroom and praying I hadn't just destroyed my friendship with Val. If she did harbor secret feelings for Kane, surely she'd understand that this was a once-in-a-lifetime opportunity for me. I wasn't expecting to marry the man. I just wanted one magical night out with friends in a fancy dress with my hair done and my problems forgotten.

I spent the rest of the afternoon debating whether to be up front with my father's men about the dance or if I should sneak out of the house that night. It wasn't like I was just taking a quick walk to meet Val, and getting out in a prom dress would be almost impossible. When one of our guards arrived to pick me up after school, I decided to be up front and use Val as an excuse for the outing.

"I've been invited to the school Valentine's dance in a couple of weeks."

"I'm not sure that would be wise, señorita. With your uncle dead, your father's ... *associates* have been challenging his position as boss. Going to a dance wouldn't be safe." His response somewhat surprised me. I hadn't heard that my father was facing problems other than the mafia here in New York. Had he been even the tiniest bit of a caring father to me, I might have worried about him. Instead, my initial reaction was relief. His problems in Mexico would surely keep him preoccupied, his focus far removed from me.

"That's terrible to hear," I said solemnly, "but Valentina invited me to get ready with her. It would be an excellent opportunity to get close to her and her family. My father was insistent that I use every opportunity possible to get close to the Genoveses." God, I hoped this didn't backfire.

He glanced at me in the rearview mirror, brows drawn tightly together. "I suppose if you're with her, you'd be safe enough." I wasn't sure if the wariness in his voice was uncertainty as to my safety or concerns of upsetting my father, nor did I care. Getting to the dance was my newest mission, and I intended to make it happen.

CHAPTER 17
Kane

I SHOULD NEVER HAVE AGREED TO THIS. HAVING MY NEW friends over was risky, but the challenging glint in Valentina's cool metallic stare had pushed me beyond sanity. With just one defiant look from her, I did crazy things. Insane, reckless, dangerous things. She was the kryptonite I never knew I had.

The group of us had been watching a movie for an hour, but I'd hardly heard a word of it. I was too absorbed in thoughts of the girl who was quickly turning my world inside out. My mood grew darker at the reminder of my precarious situation. I relished control, but with Valentina, I was utterly powerless.

One silver lining cast a hopeful glow on my shitstorm of a life, though. Reyna had agreed to go to the dance with me. It was the precise turn of events that I'd needed. I didn't want to toy with her feelings, but our date would send a clear message to Valentina and move me in the right direction.

I glanced around at the swarm of bodies strewn about my living room—almost twice as many as had originally been invited. I scanned each form in the dim light as they watched the large-screen TV for the source of my temptation. I couldn't help myself. My eyes were drawn to her whenever we were together like a moth to a flame. After pausing to identify each person, I realized that Val was gone.

I'd been so lost in thoughts about her that I hadn't noticed the object of my obsession had slipped from the room. She could have simply gone to the restroom, but my gut said otherwise. Something told me the girl who saw more than she should have let her curiosity get the better of her. She'd been suspicious of me since the day I walked into Xavier. If she suspected I was keeping a secret, she was the type who wouldn't stop looking for answers—the exact reason this whole night had been an epic mistake.

I eased myself up from the sofa and began to wind through my empty house, surveying each room for the mischievous pain in my ass. It didn't come as a surprise when I found her sitting quietly on my bed.

"Can I help you find something?" I asked from the doorway, startling her to her feet. I got immense satisfaction from catching her off guard. Those full pink lips of hers fell apart on a silent gasp, stirring up an urge to kiss her into submission, which only brought on a world of self-loathing. An ocean of irritation simmered just below the surface of my cool exterior.

Valentina's mouth snapped shut as she collected herself. "I'm always up for some answers if you're offering," she quipped, crossing her arms over her chest.

My grin dripped with malice. "Is that so? And what question is it you'd like answered?" There were so many to choose from, I was genuinely curious what she might pick.

Her eyes flicked to my left wrist. "You said your brother made you that bracelet, but when I looked you up in the school computer, your file says no siblings. I wondered at first if maybe he had passed away when your mom died—a car accident or something—but after walking through your house, I'm wondering if it was all a lie. There's not a single picture of any other kids in your house, and the only other bedroom besides yours and your dad's looks like a guest room. I can't fathom why you would lie about something like that, but nothing else makes sense."

So fucking smart.

I couldn't make a single misstep without her catching on. However, the irony was that of all the lies I'd told, the bracelets were the one bit of truth. I'd fallen victim to sentimentality when I opened up and told her who had given me the knotted bits of string. She drew those emotions out of me for some reason—those and so many more. It was a mistake to have told her, but a part of me delighted in knowing she'd focused on the one part of me that was real.

I eased forward, one predatory step at a time until we were toe to toe, my body dwarfing hers. "What do you want me to say?" My words hummed between us, my fingers itching to touch her. "I'd tell you that you caught me, but I *do* have a brother. He doesn't live with me. My family's fucked up, maybe more than most." I leaned forward, unable to stop myself from inhaling an intoxicating blast of her alluring scent, and whispered, "Now, how about you tell me what it is about your life that makes you so damn suspicious of everyone else?"

The palms of her hands flattened against my chest, searing me with their contact. I half expected her to push me away, but her touch softened before gently drifting down the planes of my chest. "Not everyone. Just you," she admitted quietly.

"And why do you think that is?" My lips were now close enough to ghost across her cheek. Playing with fire—a vice I never could totally escape.

I didn't give her time to reply.

"The answer is because you're right. I am a liar. And no matter how tempting this thing is between us, it changes nothing." Pulling back, I glared at her from behind my most intimidating mask but then paused when the next words clogged in my throat. "There's a reason I asked Reyna to the dance and not you. It's better for both of us if this thing dies right now along with your incessant curiosity."

Hurt flashed across her face when I mentioned Reyna. She hadn't known. I was glad to be the one to tell her. That way, she could direct all her anger at me rather than her friend. Better it was hate between us than something far more complicated.

She quickly recovered, face serene as the night sky. "What makes you think there's *anything* between us?" she asked with an impressive degree of apathetic disdain.

My canines made another vicious appearance. "Because, baby girl, your nipples are so hard they're about to shred that pretty shirt of yours. Almost as hard as my aching cock. There may be nothing but chemistry between us, but that shit's real, and there's nothing either of us can do about it except lock it in a box and pretend it doesn't exist." I stepped back, slowly drawing away from her, relieved at the tension in her jaw. I didn't want to be the only one frustrated as hell.

"Fuck you, Kane Easton," she hissed.

I turned and walked away, disappearing down the hall without a reply.

Fuck me, indeed. I was starting to question whether pushing her away was worth the damage I was doing—to her and to me. The anger radiating off her was nothing compared to my own self-hatred. At this point, I was screwed no matter what I did. Let her in or push her away—both came with a price.

Was I honestly considering a relationship with Valentina Genovese?

If that was the case, I was more fucked than I'd ever imagined.

CHAPTER 18
Valentina

I DESPISED THE TEARS THAT BLURRED MY VISION AS I WALKED back to Kane's living room. The only thing worse than being treated like shit was letting your tormentor see your pain. Kane hadn't just toyed with me; he'd been downright mean.

He'd caught me snooping, but I didn't think a little nosiness warranted a full-on assault. Why the hell had he lashed out like that? I'd been difficult that first week of school, but we'd begun to develop a civil rapport. Despite what I'd told myself so many times over, if a part of me hadn't liked the guy, I wouldn't have been curious about him at all. I wanted to know his secrets because I wanted to know *him*.

Regardless of his reasons, he'd made his point clear. Kane Easton wanted nothing to do with me, which was why I went back downstairs and rejoined the party rather than leave. I wasn't about to let him think he'd won by tucking tail and running home. I might have been a little bruised on the inside, but I had still come out triumphant because I'd found more clues before our little confrontation.

A missing brother wasn't the only oddity in Kane's house. The place was suspiciously perfect. It was just him and his father, but there was a difference between a tidy house and a vacant house staged by a realtor. There was an emptiness that haunted the space. It was a gut feeling I had—nothing remotely concrete—but on top of my existing suspicions, it felt important. Further proof that my wariness about Kane was justified.

Even more concerning was the old Spanish Bible I'd found in his nightstand drawer next to a set of worn rosary beads. They were the only things I'd seen in my short search of the house that appeared to have a past. The only things that were real and honest.

Plenty of Catholics lived on Staten Island—that alone wouldn't have been concerning. Why did Kane have a *Spanish* Bible by his bed? The text he'd received could have been a fluke, but the Bible? I couldn't deny that Kane had Spanish ties. That didn't necessarily mean he was connected to the cartel, but it was a possibility I had to take seriously. Especially after learning Reyna had agreed to go to the dance with him.

I couldn't believe she hadn't told me. Confronting her about the omission was the other reason I couldn't leave the party. If I didn't talk to her now, I wouldn't have a chance until I saw her at school on Monday.

I settled back into my spot on the floor next to Rey. Leaned back against the base of the sofa, I waited until the movie was over and Kane had gone into the kitchen to pull her aside.

"Hey, did Kane ask you to the dance?" I asked quietly, eyeing the room to make sure no one was close enough to overhear. When my eyes flicked back to Reyna, her face crumpled.

"I'm so sorry, Val. I've been so worried you'd be upset. I didn't know how to tell you. If you want me to call it off, I will. It's just that this might be my only opportunity to experience something like a high school dance." Her eyes shone with unshed tears. She was visibly upset enough that I worried we might draw attention.

"Shh, I promise it's okay," I assured her. "I was just surprised you didn't tell me." I'd considered trying to talk her out of going, but after hearing her reason, I hated to take that from her. "Wait, why would you be scared to tell me?"

"Well, I know you said there's nothing between you two, but I can't shake the feeling that you like him. I don't know. I just didn't want to hurt you." She peered at me sheepishly. Apparently, the only person I'd fooled with my denials was myself.

I sighed. "There's nothing between us. Even if I did have some ridiculous hang-up over Kane, he's made it perfectly clear that he's not interested. You should go with him. I don't want you to miss out on the dance." A stabbing pain twisted in my belly. I tried to tell myself it was worry for Reyna, but it was time to stop lying to myself. I was jealous, pure and simple.

I wanted to be the one he trusted with his secrets. He

might have been hiding something, but he was also captivating in a way I couldn't deny. I was drawn to him.

Maybe he was right. Maybe I saw his lies for what they were because my life had been full of secrets as well. I recognized myself in him, and that recognition both repelled me and enticed me. The confusing internal conflict left me vulnerable. I'd continued to seek him out even when he'd told me nothing could happen between us.

I wouldn't make that mistake again.

If he could resist the pull between us, so could I.

After giving Reyna a hug, I throttled my internal hopeless romantic, boxed up and buried any feelings I had for Kane, then plopped down on the sofa next to Giovanni.

"Hey, Gio. Enjoy the movie?" I smiled broadly and leaned into him.

In the past, I'd always been careful not to give Gio the wrong impression when I talked to him. He was cute with a sexy boy-next-door look but was a relentless jokester. I liked a good laugh but wasn't interested in dating the class clown —until now. Maybe a little levity was exactly what I needed.

IT HAD TAKEN LESS time than I'd expected for Giovanni to ask me to the dance. With just a couple of texts over the weekend and a coy look in the hallway Monday morning, I'd secured a date. I spent the next two weeks preparing for the dance and showing Kane the depth of my indifference toward him. A crucial part of my emotional warfare would be finding the perfect dress. Acting indifferent toward him wouldn't be nearly as satisfying if he wasn't drowning in desire for me. Everything about that night needed to be just right.

After Reyna explained her need to get ready with me, I set up hair and makeup appointments for us. I was pleased to realize I didn't begrudge her going to the dance with Kane. He was solely responsible for the stilted awkwardness between us. Reyna was just an innocent bystander. I made it clear that I had more important things to worry about than him. A delighted part of me couldn't help but notice he grew more surly and withdrawn with each passing day. I liked to think I was the cause, but with Kane, there was no telling.

On the day of the dance, Giada came to help me with logistics. My mom was a little disappointed when I told her Giada was taking me to the salon, but she was also happy to see her eldest and youngest staying close. I made sure my sister was already at the house when Reyna arrived so we could make a quick exit before my parents noticed. After hair and makeup, she dropped us over at Chloe's house. I'd managed to convince her that we girls should all get dressed at her place where the guys could come collect us so that Rey was technically with me but not at my house where my parents might see her.

The stylist had swept up half of my hair into whimsical braids and left the rest down in long waves. My eyes were heavily shaded with dark eye shadow that made my gray eyes pop, even more so when I slipped on the gown I'd bought. It was perfect for a winter formal—a pale metallic blue satin with shimmering sequins arranged in bursts like fireworks or dandelion puffs from top to bottom. The bodice was fitted with thin spaghetti straps and a plunging neckline all the way to the thin fabric belt ringing the top of the full skirt.

I felt like a queen. The designer dress hadn't been cheap, but it was perfect in every way. Well worth every penny.

While we got ready, we talked about our dates and were

even allowed a small glass of champagne each from Chloe's parents. The day had turned out perfectly, but a kernel of dread stayed lodged in my stomach. No matter how hard I tried, I still hated to think of seeing Reyna, or any other girl, in Kane's arms.

To my relief, Gio was the first to arrive at the house. We took a few pictures, only because I'd promised my mom I would. Chloe's mom urged us to stay and take pictures with the group, but I pretended to forget and ushered Gio from the house. I didn't want to be there when Kane arrived. A part of me considered staying just because I wanted to witness his amber eyes melt to liquid gold when he saw me in my dress. That was almost worth the pain of seeing him in a suit with his arms wrapped protectively around my best friend.

"You look crazy hot, Val." Gio grinned as he held the car door for me.

I smirked. "Thanks, G. You clean up pretty decent yourself." It was hard to be anything but playful with someone who was always cutting up. Someday, he'd meet a sweet girl who adored his antics, but that girl wasn't me. Giovanni served a purpose for me, and I tried my best to keep things between us lighthearted so that he wasn't crushed when I walked away.

"What's the bag for?" He motioned to the duffel I'd set at my feet.

"Just a change of clothes and a swimsuit for the after-party. I heard the suite has a hot tub." The dance was at a nearby hotel where a couple of the guys had rented out the penthouse suite for an after-party. It seemed a bit excessive when this wasn't even prom, but I wasn't going to decline the invitation.

"Nice. I didn't think to grab my suit, but I guess boxers work." He shut the door and hurried to the driver's side.

We talked about our graduation plans on the short drive to the hotel. Conversation with Gio was pleasant. He was easy to talk to and kept the flow going without much effort on my part. His presence was so comfortable that I found my mind wandering. Gio didn't hold my interest like other more enigmatic individuals.

I thought about Kane and how we couldn't seem to have a single discussion without growing emotional. Our turbulent dynamic had seemed problematic, but after spending more time around Gio in the previous weeks, I questioned that assumption. I could never be in a relationship with someone who didn't pique my interest. I needed a man who kept me engaged. Someone who brought excitement to each day and anticipation to my nights.

Someone like ... no, I wouldn't go there.

I forced a smile at my date as he escorted me into the hotel. The elegant ballroom had been decked out in red and white, starting with a balloon tower archway at the entrance. Tables filled one side of the room, each draped in white linen and topped with exquisite bouquets of red roses. The rest of the room was dedicated to a dance floor already packed with gyrating bodies.

"Dance or drink?" Gio motioned to the refreshments table.

"Let's dance!" The music was fast-paced and would stay that way for a while. The slow dances usually didn't kick in until later in the evening, so I was safe for now. Dancing to something slow and sensual would definitely send the wrong message. Besides, letting loose with the music would ease some of the excruciating tension that had been coiling tighter in my muscles with every passing hour.

We inserted ourselves into the crowd, and in no time at all, I was lost to the music. Maybe it was the champagne or perhaps the week's worth of frustration festering inside me, but I shed my inhibitions and danced like no one was watching.

But someone was watching.

When the music suddenly slowed, Gio pulled me in close. Time had gotten away from me. I stiffened at first, wary of the message a slow dance might send to Gio, but then I caught a pair of amber eyes boring into me from across the dance floor. Kane held Reyna loosely, his stare a claiming touch that made my skin feverish.

Didn't he know he was the one who made this happen? Why glower at me when he was the one who pushed me away? He was impossible to understand.

Without a hint of weakness, I held Kane's vicious stare and leaned into Gio. My heart rate stumbled to a gallop. Interpreting my actions as a show of affection, Gio pulled me closer, spinning us until I lost sight of my temperamental nemesis. Once I wasn't putting on a show, a wave of awkward embarrassment crashed over me.

What had I done? I was already abusing my friendship with Gio, but leading him on was unnecessarily cruel. Everything about this night felt like a horrible mistake. Guilt anchored my feet to the floor, halting my dancing.

"I need to head to the restroom." I shot him a forced smile before retreating from the ballroom.

The bathrooms just outside the dance were bustling with students, not helping my need for isolation. I had to have a few minutes alone to regroup, or I was going to fall apart in front of everyone. On a whim, I checked the single-stall family restroom and found it empty. Relief urged me forward. I flipped on the light switch and hurried inside, but before the door clicked shut, a resolute shove forced it back open. The momentum sent me stumbling backward, giving Kane the opportunity he needed to slip inside and lock the door behind him.

"What are you doing?" I gaped at him in utter confusion.

Kane glared, the florescent lights casting his angular face in stark relief. I'd never seen him look so volatile—a hurricane of emotions bearing down on me. "What is your game?"

"What game?" I shook my head, confusion brewing into irritation. "Why were you staring at me instead of your date? If anyone is playing a game here, it's *you*." I stood taller and lifted my chin, unwilling to be intimidated.

He took an aggressive step forward, making me step back so that my butt was pressed against the porcelain sink. He'd gone with a classic black jacket and white button-down with the top button undone. No tie. No frills. The look was pure business—stark and powerful—right down to the fiery sparks in his eyes.

He was teetering on the edge of a very precarious cliff, but why? He pushed me away, and I complied, so why was he so upset?

"I wouldn't send you mixed signals just to fuck with you. I have my reasons." The coarse touch of his voice scraped along my skin as his hands clamped around each of my arms.

"*No!*" I shoved his chest, but he refused to release me. "You can't say shit like that and not give me some kind of explanation. You're making me absolutely crazy, and I can't stand it one more—" My emotional rant was cut short when Kane's lips slammed against mine.

Like our explosive first kiss weeks before, I became instantly drunk on his touch. My blood sang with a desire so consuming it eclipsed all else. I'd had crushes and experimented some with my last boyfriend, but none of those experiences brought on the same mindless desire Kane elicited from deep inside me. The intensity of my feelings scared me but not enough to override the violent thrumming in my veins. A need so elemental it was second nature.

When his hands grasped me possessively and molded our bodies together, I could feel his impossibly hard cock pressing against my belly. The thought of him inside me sparked my nerves but also emboldened me to know he was just as helpless against the web of desire that had us in its clutches.

I hadn't had sex yet because situations in the past had never been quite right. I wasn't ready, or the timing was off, or the guy wasn't the one. None of that was an issue when Kane's lips were on mine. He was all I wanted—the *only* thing I wanted—and judging by his voracious appetite, Kane was suffering from the same consuming hunger. Why was he preventing us from exploring that chemistry? Why reject the desire he so clearly felt?

The push and pull was maddening.

I couldn't allow him to break me, and if we continued the hot and cold any longer, I'd end up in pieces.

Pulling back, I rested my forehead against his, cringing at the ache in my chest. I whispered a single word, knowing he'd understand. "Why?" What was the problem that kept him from getting close to me? Why wouldn't he let me in?

His lips parted then shut before he finally spoke. "Because I'm trying to protect you," he breathed.

I lifted my eyes to his, desperately searching for answers. "From what?"

A ghost of an apology flitted behind his eyes before he pulled away and allowed an iron curtain to fall between us. "From myself." The words were eerily hollow. Cold and lifeless.

He let himself out, leaving me floundering in his wake.

Like a heated glass that cools too quickly, hairline cracks splintered my heart. From the outside looking in, they could hardly be seen, but the fissures were weakening me one tiny fracture at a time. I'd hoped if I could squash my feelings enough, my desire for Kane might weaken, and I could move on to someone else, but it wasn't working. I wanted him more than ever. All our pretending had accomplished was heartbreak and a steady descent into madness. I had to make him see that being with me was worth whatever the risk. How could anything be worse than the torture of rejecting our connection?

I had to take control of the situation—either make him see the detrimental nature of his actions or eradicate him from my system entirely.

The thought alone was gut-wrenching.

I could lock down my desire and ride out the storm safe behind a reinforced wall, but at what expense? How much of my heart would I need to paralyze in order to survive seeing him every day with other girls? I was strong enough to see it through, but I wasn't sure I'd ever be the same. My best hope was to push Kane to the breaking point. Force him to face losing me entirely and hope that he can't face it any better than I could.

CHAPTER 19
Reyna

WHY DID I CONTINUE TRYING TO BE NORMAL WHEN I WAS SO clearly not? Kane had been sweet all evening, but there was an awkward undercurrent that had followed us throughout the evening. When he made his excuses to slip away from the dance floor, I understood. I was different, and he could tell. He probably regretted ever asking me to be his date.

Now he was gone, and I hadn't seen Val since she left Chloe's house with Gio. There was no one else I was comfortable clinging to, so I found an empty table situated in the shadows and sat down to watch the others dance. It was my default setting—observing others rather than living my own life. Passivity had saved me on more than one occasion, but I was tired of barely existing. Living an invisible life. I wanted to be seen. To be wanted. To leave my mark on the people around me. I wanted to live out loud, paint my world in vibrant colors, and experience everything life had to offer.

To be a girl who lived in the spotlight and never hid in the shadows.

I was well on my way to a full-scale pity party when someone slipped into the chair beside me. My lungs seized when I found Santino a foot away, dressed in a perfectly tailored suit as if he were one of the students. He relaxed into the chair, threading his fingers together in his lap with one leg casually crossed over the other. He was breathtaking—a fearless jungle cat, lording over everything in his sight.

"What are you doing here?" I asked, still shocked by his appearance.

He drew his eyes from the crowd, piercing me with their fathomless intensity. "It's a dance. What do you think I'm here for?" Then he did something that left me speechless. Santino held out his hand for mine in an invitation to dance.

My heart pounded frantically until I could feel its punishing rhythm throughout my body. I didn't know what to do, so my arm moved of its own accord. My hand fell easily into his as though it had always belonged there.

Santino rose and led me to our own small section of the dance floor apart from the other dancers. He pulled me flush against him, one hand firm on the base of my back and the other clasping my hand close to our bodies. His hold was warm and secure. We might as well have been in a room entirely alone. The world around me faded from existence as Santino became the sole focus of my attention. From the way he cradled me against him, I felt like the center of his world. No one person had ever made me feel so safe and protected.

It had to be my imagination—the romantic delusions of a girl who'd always been an afterthought. This man was my father's enemy. I should have been on guard, but his touch soothed and warmed me more in thirty seconds than Kane's presence had all night. There was no comparing the two. I reacted to Santino in a way I had never reacted to another person, and I had no idea why. Or more importantly, if I could trust my own responses. Just because I felt safe didn't mean I was.

"How long have you been watching me?" I asked. My cheek was close to his chest, but I knew he could hear me.

"Long enough to know you didn't come alone. What happened to your date?" There was a dangerous edge to his question.

"I'm not sure." Kane hadn't told me where he was going when he slipped away.

"Seems your date *and* your best friend are missing." The warning tone in his voice brought the room into focus.

My eyes darted from person to person, only stopping when I spotted Gio dancing in a group with no sign of his date. It wouldn't have surprised me if Kane and Val had gone off together. I'd known something peculiar was going on between them, and I hadn't lied to Val when I told her I wasn't drawn to Kane, so I wasn't upset at the prospect. Why did I get the odd feeling that Santino was outraged on my behalf? Or did he object to Val going off alone with Kane for some other reason?

I had no idea, and I couldn't seem to make myself care. I worried all the time—planned and strategized every aspect of my life. The brief reprieve I found in Santino's arms left me incapable of pulling away. We danced to our own swaying cadence, nowhere near the upbeat tempo of the song blaring over the speakers. The pace we set was our own, and I relished the bliss I found in that one moment of perfect serenity.

But like any fairy tale, the magic had to come to an end.

Coaches turned back into pumpkins—beautiful gowns back to rags—and this temporary princess was back to an awkward teenager the second my date reappeared.

"That's my date," Kane snapped from over Santino's shoulder.

Santino turned, releasing me just enough to face Kane but keeping me tucked into his side. "Then you shouldn't have left her alone."

Kane's eyes narrowed. "I can't say that I recognize your face from school. Who exactly are you?"

Santino smirked. "No one you know." He lifted my hand to his lips, our eyes catching for a heated second. "I'll see you around." Then he disappeared into the crowd, leaving me cold and alone in a room full of people.

CHAPTER 20
Valentina

I TRIED TO GO BACK TO DANCING WITH GIO, BUT I WAS SO dazed that I could hardly keep a beat. Why would Kane say he wanted to protect me from himself? I'd tossed around the idea that he was tied to a cartel, but deep down, I didn't buy that theory. Was it naïve of me to discount the possibility? What other reason could he possibly have to think he might be bad for me?

Even more confusing was how something that felt so right could possibly be wrong.

When Kane's lips touched mine, pure energy ran through my veins, and my entire existence melted down to the sensation of his body connected to mine. Hands, bodies, mouths. My sole purpose in life filtered down to maintaining that contact as though my life depended upon it. Every molecule in my body was convinced that Kane was made for me, yet he seemed equally convinced that we could never be together.

Dismay weighed on my shoulders while frustration jumbled my rhythm. If I'd been a bad date before, I was positively horrible after my encounter with Kane.

"You okay?" Gio eventually asked.

"Yeah, sorry. My feet are just getting tired."

"No problem. How about we head upstairs to the party?" He was being sweet, and I just wanted the night to end. Could I be any more wretched?

"I think that sounds great." Alcohol was my only chance of sluffing off some of this leaden guilt I was carrying around. "Let me tell Reyna, and I'll meet you by the elevators." I'd been an awful friend tonight, so obsessed with my own drama that I'd completely ignored my best friend. She was dancing with Kane and several other people in a small circle when I found her.

"Hey, Val!" she called warmly when she spotted me. Rey was so generous that I should have known she wouldn't begrudge me an off night. Yet her forgiving soul somehow made me feel even worse.

"We're going to head up to the after-party. It should be pretty cool, so I wanted to make sure you got a chance to go up if you wanted."

"Definitely! Let me tell Kane." She turned to talk to her date, who nodded, his eyes cutting over to me.

He placed his hand at the small of her back, and I cringed inwardly. Once we reached the elevators, I encouraged the couple to head upstairs while I waited for Gio. When my date showed up, he was carrying my duffel that he'd retrieved from his car. I'd completely forgotten about it.

"Thanks so much for getting that." I held out my hand for my bag.

"Nah, I got it." He reached past me and pressed the elevator call button.

"That's sweet of you." The words caught in my throat as they squeezed past a ball of emotion. I might have seemed heartless to some, but I did have an empathetic side. I just tried to keep it in check more than other people might, but sometimes, the pesky emotions got past my barriers. "Hey, G. I've had a great time tonight, but I just ... I feel like I need to tell you. Well, I'm not sure exactly what." I wrung my hands together, my cheeks flaming with embarrassment, and stared at the marble veins webbing across the stone floor.

Gio stepped closer and bumped my shoulder. "S'okay, Val. I've seen the way you and Kane stare at each other. I'm just glad I got a chance, that's all."

Tears burned the back of my eyes. "You deserve someone who'll give you so much more than a chance."

Reaching over, he wrapped his hand behind my neck to pull me in gently and place a kiss on my forehead. "You too, gorgeous."

My breath caught. I had to wipe my eye before a treacherous tear fell.

"Let's go up and finish this night off with some fun. Okay?" He smiled softly, giving me a glimpse of the maturity lurking behind the humor. Had I seen that side of him before Kane showed up, the last few weeks might have played out very differently. But that was not what happened, and there was only one man on my mind.

I nodded, slipping my hand in his. The comfortable

silence between us on the ride up was a welcome relief. I was able to breathe deeply since I first set out on my conquest to distract myself with Gio. Giving him false hope when I wasn't fully invested in a relationship hadn't been worth the hurt I might have caused. I was enormously relieved that the charade was over.

The suite door was open when we reached the top floor. Upbeat party music wafted into the hallway. The guys who had hosted the party hadn't invited all that many people, so I hadn't expected a raging kegger, but there were still fewer people scattered in the main living area than I'd expected. Most were on the extensive patio either at the railing or in the large hot tub with a column of steam wafting up into the night.

Chloe stood with Reyna near the sliding glass door in her swimsuit with a towel wrapped around her.

"Hey, ladies. How's the hot tub, Chloe?"

"Good, you need to get your suit on. I'd stay and chat, but I gotta run to the bathroom before I freeze to death." She scurried back to what I assumed were the bedrooms.

"What happened to Kane?" I asked Reyna as I glanced around again.

"He went back down to get my bag from his car. You must have just missed him at the elevator."

I hadn't thought about how he'd take Rey to the dance, but his motorcycle wouldn't have worked. "What's he driving?"

"Some black car. I didn't really pay attention, but I think it was a Lexus. Why?"

"Just curious. Probably his dad's. I know this may sound creeper-ish, but do you think you could remember the plates when he takes you home?"

Perfect Enemies

Reyna studied me. "Whyyy? What exactly is going on between you two?"

"I'm just curious about something. It's nothing, really." I didn't want to freak her out that I had a paranoid suspicion her date was hiding something, but the plates to his car could prove useful. "How has your night been?"

She was still suspicious, but she let me change the subject. "It's been very ... interesting. You?"

"Same." I didn't want to go into detail about why my night was so unusual, so I didn't press her for details of her own. "Okay, I'm going to change. Get your suit on and come out when he gets back."

A few minutes later, I was lowering myself into the muscle-melting heat of the hot tub. "Oh my God, that feels *amazing*." My head dropped back, and my eyes drifted closed.

"Right?" Chloe chimed in. "And it's huge. We could probably fit ten people in here."

Besides Chloe and I, there were four others in the bubbling water. We all turned to see who was joining us when the sliding door opened. Gio grinned, carrying two cups in his hands.

"Here you go, Val. Got us some drinks." He handed me a cup and set the other one down. "And now, since I forgot my suit, it's *naked* time."

Chloe and I burst out laughing while the other girl shrieked. Gio performed a hilarious striptease, leaving his boxers on before joining us in the water. I wasn't sure if he would have actually gone through with the full monty, but the other guys present insisted he kept his junk to himself. We were all laughing and talking over one another when the door opened again.

"Hey, Rey. Come sit by me," I called over.

Reyna grinned, hesitantly dropping her towel and hurrying into the tub. "Oh, it's *hot*."

"That's the idea, silly. Is Kane coming? There's room for one more." I tried to sound casual, but judging by the side-eye Reyna shot my way, she wasn't fooled.

"He said he didn't want to get in. Bryson showed up and told Kane to just wear his boxers if he forgot a suit, but Kane said he wasn't interested." She shrugged.

Unable to resist, I peered to the side at the living room window. Kane's eyes were already on me. He sipped amber liquid from a clear glass, the colorful liquid bringing out the light in his eyes. Bryson and two girls stood nearby talking animatedly, but Kane hardly paid any attention. I motioned for him to come get in. He refused with a curt shake of his head.

My attention was startled away from Kane when someone flicked water up at my face. "Hey!" I shrieked in protest.

Gio grinned unapologetically. "More than a chance, right, Val?"

I fought the smile spreading across my face. "Oh, you've asked for it now." I flicked my hand, sending a spray of water at him. Unwilling to be outdone, I started to send a second splash when he grabbed my wrist and yanked me against his chest.

"Hey, now. We're even!" he cried. "And if *you* don't stop, I'll be forced to up the ante and tickle you." His arms held me snugly against him, restricting my ability to fight back.

"Tickle me and—" That was as far as I got before his fingers began to squeeze the soft part of my leg just above my knee. I squealed and laughed, writhing from his torturous tickling. "Giovanni Capelli, you *stop* right now, or I'm going to pee in this hot tub."

A riot of voices objected, and Gio let me go. I drifted back to my spot and attempted to glower at my friend, but a treacherous smile forced its way through and gave me away. Gio just winked, knowing I wasn't at all mad.

Conversation resumed, and I relaxed back, taking one small peek at the window. Murderous eyes stared out, but they were no longer trained on me. Kane was shooting a death glare to Gio before his eyes flicked back to me. I turned away to keep from getting sucked back into his dark vortex. Several times over the next half hour, the heat of his searing gaze warmed my skin, but I refused to give him my attention.

Our gathering grew by a dozen or so people, and I wanted to give them a chance at the hot tub, so I eventually got out. My skin was starting to prune, anyway. With my towel wrapped around me, I took my clothes back to the bathroom only to find Kane waiting for me in the dark hallway. I held his gaze and paused within arm's length of the brooding man.

"You have a thing for bathrooms or something?" Between Gio's reminder and the alcohol, I was feeling bold. This time, I wouldn't let him stun me into compliance. This time, he was the one who would feel the pressure.

"Just the only way I can seem to get you alone."

"Why do we need to be alone? For you to *protect* me?"

Kane's jaw muscles twitched and flexed. "Just put some fucking clothes on before you catch a cold, then we can talk."

I don't know what possessed me. Frustration. Defiance. Whatever it was, I tossed aside any care about who could see me. I took a single step back and dropped my towel, all while maintaining steely eye contact with the darkness lurking behind Kane's savage stare. "It's not your job to protect me—from yourself or the cold or any other danger." I reached back and tugged my bikini top loose, allowing the fabric to fall to the floor.

I didn't know what I was doing. Stripping hadn't exactly been a part of my master plan, but it felt like the one thing that might tip the scales of his control. There was a reason he'd waited for me—a reason he hated to see me with Gio, and a reason for the electric current between us—no matter how badly he wanted to deny it.

An unexpected sense of power strengthened my resolve as I stood almost naked before him. My nipples pebbled beneath the touch of his gaze, the featherlight drift of gossamer silk ghosting down my body.

My hands moved down to the bikini bottom strings at my hips.

"*Fucking Christ.*" The words were wrenched from deep inside him as he lunged forward and yanked me inside the bathroom, slamming the door shut behind us. Kane seized me in his arms and placed me down on the counter, but he didn't kiss me. Our bodies were flush together, our foreheads and noses gently touching. "You drive me fucking insane," he said on a shuddered breath.

"Ditto, Kane."

He shook his head, not severing our connection. "You think you know me, but you don't."

"You think I don't *see* you?" I dropped my barriers and showed him my skepticism and suspicion. I displayed all my doubts and insecurities about him. "Just because I *see* doesn't change how I *feel*." It was stupid but true. Kane had secrets, and I knew that. It didn't change how badly I wanted his lips on mine.

His body solidified to sculpted marble when my lips reached forward and hesitantly nipped at his. My touch sent a shiver through his body. Having that kind of effect on him only encouraged me further. I moved forward again, but this time he sucked my bottom lip between his teeth and allowed it to slowly slip back out. With a swipe of my tongue, I licked at his lip. We were two animals meeting in the wild for the first time—scouting one another to determine friend or foe.

"You have no idea how badly I wanted to rip out Giovanni's neck every time he touched you." His lips took mine in a sensual kiss, slow and decadent.

My hands curled in his shirt, pulling him closer. "I made him take me to the dance before everyone else so that I didn't have to see you with Reyna." I breathed in the subtle spice of Kane's cologne, the delicious smell filling my lungs and warming my chest.

He squeezed me tighter, pressing my center firmly against his middle. The pressure was both a relief and a torment because while it felt good, my body craved more.

"I know you see me," he breathed, his lips drifting to my jaw. "That's what makes you so goddamned irresistible. You're going to be the death of me, but maybe that's my fate. Maybe I'm meant to walk right into the flames. I can't see another way around it because this body? It's mine, just like those perceptive eyes and that sharp tongue. It's all mine."

CHAPTER 21
Kane

THERE WAS NO GOING BACK FROM CERTAIN PIVOTAL MOMENTS in life. The loss of a loved one. Starting a new job. Having a baby. Some turns in the road were more poignant than others. Some brought us to our knees, and we welcomed others with open arms. Sometimes, we were helpless bystanders to the whims of fate, while other times, we were the driving force behind these periods of demarcation.

As I stood in that hotel bathroom with a nearly naked Valentina in my arms, I stepped from the cliff of restraint and began to free fall. I couldn't get my footing again if I'd wanted to. The line had been crossed, and there was no going back. I'd put words to the emotions boiling over inside me for weeks.

Valentina was mine—fuck the consequences.

And there would be consequences, but maybe I could mitigate the damages. I pulled back from her and clenched down every muscle in my body to gain control of myself. "But being mine is complicated—more so than you can imagine. You'll have to be patient while I figure things out. For now, I need you to get dressed before I do something both of us will regret. I'll take Reyna home, and you will make sure Gio doesn't lay a fucking *finger* on you when he takes you home, understand?"

She nodded, which was a relief because I could see the questions clouding her eyes. Val could be so headstrong that I never knew when she would put up a fight. I slowly tore myself away from her, then slipped from the bathroom, allowing her time to change and me the chance for my blood to cool.

I waited to take Reyna home until Val and Giovanni were also leaving. I refused to leave her in that suite without me. When the night was finally over, and I lay restless in my bed, I decided that perhaps I'd gone about my time at Xavier the wrong way. Maybe the night hadn't been a total clusterfuck. I could see a new path illuminating. It was likely a one-way ticket to hell, but it was a path, nonetheless. Not fighting my draw to Val would make my time there far more enjoyable. Maybe even more productive.

Yeah, I was definitely going to hell.

I texted Val several times over the weekend. Our conversations were light and easy with only the slightest flirtatious undertone, but I enjoyed having that connection with her. Our relationship had run an emotional gambit, so it was refreshing to simply talk like two normal people getting to know one another.

The first thing I did on Monday morning was locate Giovanni. The fucker had flipped me off behind Valentina's back while he held her in the hot tub, and it was time to put him in his place.

"Hey, G," I said calmly as I leaned up against the lockers next to his. "I know you think you're funny, but you pull a stunt again like you did on Friday, and I'll rearrange your fucking face."

He slammed the locker closed. "Why? So you can keep her dangling on a thread?"

"We've sorted things out. She's no longer available."

To my surprise, the guy smirked. "It's about damn time." He glanced over my shoulder then sobered. "But keep in mind that if you hurt her, I'll rearrange *your* face." Like the cocky son of a bitch that he was, he shoulder checked me as he walked away.

I had to give him credit. Behind the clown mask, the guy had balls.

The rest of my morning unfolded with less confrontation. I could sense the uncertainty in Val's demeanor, so I decided to make things clear to everyone. At lunch, I straddled the bench seat and pulled Val close against my chest. With one leg under the table and the other behind her, I fit perfectly around her.

"Well, hey there," she teased. A flush enveloped her

cheeks. One of the best parts about a strong woman was when she allowed you to see her softer side. Val's ferocity was balanced by a tenderness that I was privileged to witness. She didn't show that side to everyone, and I didn't miss the importance of its appearance every time she opened those doors.

"How was your morning?" I took a bite of my food, keeping my body wrapped around her.

"Um, hello?" Bryson called out. "Did we miss something here?" His eyes bulged as they swept back and forth between Val and me, along with every other set of eyes at the table.

I leaned in close to her ear so that only she could hear me. "Ever heard that old song, 'Something to Talk About'?"

She nodded, turning to give me a curious look when I took her mouth in a kiss that was so explosive it registered on the Richter scale. Guys whooped, and girls sighed all around us. After staking my claim, I took a sip from my bottle of water and glanced at Bryson. "How was *your* weekend?"

He chuckled. "Not half as good as yours."

"Probably right." I grinned and returned to eating, my attention back on Val. "Where's Reyna?" The two were almost always together, but we were ten minutes into lunch with no sign of Val's other half.

The second the words were out, Val stiffened. "Um, she had a tutoring session over lunch." She took a sip from a bottle of tea, then leaned in close to me. "Kane, why do you always seem so interested in Reyna?" She had whispered her question to keep it from the others, but I also sensed her hesitancy to voice her concern, as if saying it out loud gave it validity.

My interest in Reyna had been problematic for Val, and I hoped that providing an explanation might ease her concerns.

"Because I recognize her loneliness. I know what it looks like. How it feels. When you've lived with the feeling, you can see it in others." Reyna was reserved, but unlike most introverts who preferred solitude, I could sense her earnest desire to be with people. I wondered if she was genuinely shy or if her home situation had impaired her true nature.

"Oh," Val breathed.

"Not the answer you expected?"

Val shrugged, then rested her side gently into my chest. "I guess not, but you're right. She is lonely. I hate seeing her like that."

"We should do something together—the three of us," I suggested.

She sat taller and turned to search my face. "Really? You're not just saying that to get in my pants?"

My lids lowered to half-mast. "Baby, if I wanted in your pants, I'd be there already."

A peal of laughter burst from deep in her belly. *Mission accomplished.*

Seeing her tender side was rewarding, but I wasn't sure it topped bringing her such joy that she lost herself in laughter. Valentina Genovese was ambitious, dedicated, calculating, and ruthless when needed. Drawing unguarded laughter from the warrior queen wasn't an easy feat. If I didn't watch out, I'd become addicted to the warm feeling in my chest when her eyes lit with mirth, crave the stirring in my belly when her cheeks flushed, and become mindless for a single touch.

Who was I kidding?

I was already a lost cause for my drug of choice. Valentina fucking Genovese.

CHAPTER 22
Valentina

THINGS CHANGED AFTER VALENTINE'S. KANE NEVER VERBALLY defined where we stood, but everything about his demeanor around me changed. We became a couple. Friends. More. I woke each morning excited to start my day and fell asleep each night smiling at the memory of his touch. The only thing that interrupted my contentment was a sliver of confusion that wedged its way between us. We texted, and Kane made sure everyone at school knew I was his, but we didn't hang out alone, and he never asked me on a date. For each of the past two weekends, he'd had excuses that kept him away—they were valid but still frustrating. The one time we did anything outside of school, we included Reyna, just as he'd promised. I appreciated him thinking of her, but in two weeks, we hadn't spent any time with just the two of us. I tried to remember that he'd asked for my patience, and two weeks was hardly any time at all, but patience wasn't my most abundant virtue.

Each day, I walked through the Xavier entrance with a grin, itching to see Kane since school was the only place we were together. I would round up Reyna from the library, then loiter in the hallway by Kane's locker, waiting for him to come sauntering down the hall. Our eyes would meet at a distance when his towering frame came into view. My heart would leap into my throat. When he finally reached me, he would pull me in close and whisper, "Hey, baby," into my ear. Those two simple words vibrated through me, warming my blood and summoning thoughts no good Catholic schoolgirl should have.

It was a magical way to start a day.

However, on Tuesday, March third, just two weeks after we started in this new direction, I entered a strange new dimension where everything was topsy-turvy. Nothing about that day went as planned.

If it had been possible, I would have bleached the day from my memory entirely.

I waited for Kane by his locker—that was as long as the normalcy lasted. Other classmates came and went. Reyna stood with me briefly before heading to class when the first bell rang. I waited until the tardy bell, but Kane never appeared.

I shot him a quick text before rushing to first period, trying not to worry. By lunch, I still hadn't heard from him. My appetite shriveled up to nothing. Rey tried to reassure me, but I couldn't shake the horrible feeling that something was wrong. Terribly wrong.

Turned out it wasn't Kane I needed to worry about.

I was ten minutes into fifth period when I was called to the office over the intercom system. The secretary had said I was leaving for the day, but I couldn't fathom why. I didn't have any appointments that I could recall.

I dropped my iPad back in my backpack and left class. When the office came into view, my blood went cold at the sight of my mother and Javier. Mom's face was blotchy as though she'd been crying, and Javi was radiating menace.

Daddy. Did something happen to my dad?

I couldn't imagine why Mom would come without him if something was wrong. "What happened? Is Dad okay?" I hurried over and wrapped my arms around my mother, whose body shuddered as she gripped me.

"Your father's fine," she assured me. "Let's get in the car, and I'll tell you everything."

I pushed for answers the second we were outside, away from the office staff. "Please, tell me what's going on before I go crazy worrying."

"It's Camilla," she said without pausing on her way to the car. "She didn't show up for work today. Her boss was killed, and they think it was the cartel. We don't know if they have her or what's happened. Dad is with his men organizing a search."

I slipped into the back seat of the car, numb with shock. I vaguely took note that another man was driving us, leaving Mom to sit in the back with me, which was highly unusual. We were under tight security.

Not again. How could this be happening again so soon?

It hadn't been but a couple of months since Giada was

taken, and now Camilla? I couldn't do it again—the waiting and uncertainty. We'd been so lucky to get Giada back, but what if our luck ran out? I couldn't comprehend losing a sister. Just the notion brought my stomach dangerously high in my throat. I had to force several swallows to keep the pooling saliva from my mouth.

Mom filled me in on what they knew while we drove home. Her voice quivered when she spoke, and each time my chest clenched in response. I couldn't imagine how worried she must have been. On the verge of my own panic attack, I suddenly realized I had to be strong for her. One of her babies was in danger. Looking at it from that perspective helped me rein in my chaotic emotions even though they were threatening to turn me inside out. Being strong for her gave me purpose, and I desperately needed something to think about besides worry for my sister.

I placed my hand in hers and squeezed. "It's going to be alright, Mama. You'll see. She'll be home in no time."

Her childlike nod cracked my heart wide open.

Seeing my mother come undone was more unsettling than I could have imagined. I felt wretched for her, but all I could do was be there to walk the terrifying path alongside her.

Once we were home, I texted Reyna with a cryptic message about what had happened, hoping she could decipher it. Whether her father's men were responsible or not, I didn't want them gaining information from my text. Rey would worry about me if I didn't give her some explanation as to why I disappeared.

The only other person I was interested in telling was Kane. He hadn't been at school, so he wouldn't have any idea something was wrong, but I wanted him to know. I needed to hear his voice.

Me: Where are you? I was worried about you, and now my sister's missing. I'm so fucking scared. Please call me.

My phone rang just a few minutes later.

"Are you okay?" I answered when I saw it was Kane on the line.

"Yeah, I'm sorry I didn't text. I wasn't feeling great today. What's going on with your sister?" His tone was cool, almost as though he were trying not to be overheard, but he was sick, so I tried not to overthink it.

"We don't exactly know. She didn't show up for work today, and that's not like her at all. My family has been trying to find her, but there's no sign of her." I didn't want to freak him out and tell him this was the second kidnapping we'd faced. I hadn't even considered what a boyfriend would think about my family's mafia ties. Was I allowed to tell other people? There'd been no formal rules outlined, so I wasn't sure what was allowed for someone in my situation. But I didn't have the capacity to worry about that now. I shook off the thoughts and decided to keep the grittier details to myself for the time being.

"Is there any way she just forgot to call in sick and is just playing hooky for the day?"

He wouldn't understand, not without knowing our background, and I couldn't explain without giving him possibly secret information. "You may be right," I said wearily. "My parents are just protective." It had been pointless to even tell him if I couldn't fully explain. I wasn't sure what I'd been thinking except that I'd wanted his support. "I better get going so I can keep my mom company while we sort this out."

"Valentina," he said firmly, snagging my attention. "I don't know what's going on, but I'm here if you need me, okay?"

My bottom lip trembled with relief. I hadn't realized how badly I needed him to tell me it was going to be all right, but his words had done the job. I had to keep my shields up for my mom's sake and remain calm. "Okay," I croaked.

"Breathe, baby," he urged softly.

I took a deep breath through my nose, and while I was breathing, I thought I heard male voices in the background on Kane's end of the phone. "Is someone there with you?"

"Just the TV. Let me know when you learn anything about your sister. I can come by if you need me to, but I'm kind of a mess."

"You don't need to go out when you're sick. There's not much to be done anyway. We're just stuck waiting for news. You get some rest."

"Later, baby."

"Later," I whispered, reticent to sever our connection.

I didn't want to force him to be out if he didn't feel well, but having his strength there beside me would have made those interminable hours almost bearable. Instead, I sat with my mother as afternoon bled into evening, and worry devolved to desperation. Giada was there with us, and my aunt Lottie came by, which was an enormous help. For the first time in my life, I didn't even feel like playing the piano.

We sat together, praying for Camilla's safe return and trying to keep one another distracted. We were poking at bowls of soup when my mother's phone rang just after nine that night. For a brief instant, we all froze, eyes wide as we stared at one another. With the second ring, Mom darted into action, picking up her phone with trembling fingers.

"Oh God, please tell me you found her," she answered. There was a brief pause before she burst into tears.

My stomach dropped into my feet, and the blood drained from my face.

Camilla couldn't be gone. She just couldn't.

I looked at Giada, whose face mirrored my own.

"Ma, what happened? You're freaking us out," Giada cried.

Mom lifted her head and smiled through her tears. "She's safe and heading home. It wasn't even the cartel. She's safe."

Giada and I rushed into each other's arms while Ma finished her conversation.

Relieved wasn't the right word for what I felt. A single word was too simple. I was a shredded quilt, tattered and undone, frayed at the seams. I couldn't fathom how people lost loved ones and continued on with life. I'd been lucky not to suffer such a blow in my life. My cousins had lost a brother, but I'd only been a baby at the time and never knew him. The threat of such devastation made me want to seal all my loved ones in protective cages, including the girl who had quickly become my best friend.

Camilla might have been saved, but Reyna was still in grave danger. We were now into March, and I still had no word from Javi and no other ideas. I had to get her away from her father immediately. We couldn't wait. I couldn't stand the pain of knowing I'd been too late to keep her safe.

"Hey, G. Can I get Javi's number from you? Now that he's a part of the family, I feel like I should have his number for emergencies." I purposely insinuated my interest was about safety so she wouldn't ask questions.

Never one to be duped, Giada eyed me. "Yeah. That's probably a good idea." She was suspicious, but she played along and listed his digits. Just as she finished, his face flashed on her phone screen with an incoming call. She answered and wandered into another room.

Mom had finally gotten off her phone, so I turned back to her.

"What did you learn?"

"She was in the city, so they aren't coming here tonight, but hopefully, we'll see her in the next day or so. They think her boss was killed by the cartel—something about money laundering at the bank they worked at—but the guy who took her had nothing to do with that. It was strange. I'm not sure how she knew the guy, but I guess he was stalking her or something. I don't know. Dad didn't have all the details. I'm just glad it's over. I can't keep doing this."

I moved to sit next to her and squeezed her hand. "I know, Ma. It's been a real shit show lately."

"Valentina!" she fussed. Ma didn't like us to cuss.

I shrugged. "Well, it has been."

Then my mom started giggling. Uncontrollable, hysterical, childlike giggles. "You're right. It has been a shit show." She wheezed the words between peals of laughter.

Seeing her so uncharacteristically lighthearted made me fall into a fit of giggles right along with her. We were wiping tears from our eyes when Giada rejoined us.

"What did I miss?" She gaped at us, clearly wondering if we'd lost our minds.

"Nothing." Mom waved a hand at Giada as she composed herself. "Just letting the stress out. It's been a long day."

"No kidding," I chimed in. "I think I've had about all I can take. I'm going to head to bed. Wake me if you need me, Ma." I kissed her cheek.

"Get some sleep, sweetie. I'll be fine."

I gave Giada one more hug, then slipped upstairs to my room. Now that my sisters were grown and moved out, I had the whole floor to myself. I didn't have to worry about anyone overhearing my phone calls. Javi had left us to help with the search once we were safely home. Now that she was safe, he should have a minute to spare. I took out my phone and dialed his number.

"Is everything okay?" he answered. Poor guy had known nothing but chaos since coming into contact with our family. Some of it was his own fault, but still. He was going to need a vacation soon.

"Yes, but I need to know if you have those papers for Reyna. We can't keep waiting."

A long breath hummed over the line. "They're not ready. Things are going on right now, and it's not a good time."

Okay, now I just wanted to punch him. Not a good time? Was he freaking serious?

"It may not be good for you, but Reyna's life is in danger. She could disappear just like Camilla did today, except she'd be in Mexico, and we'd never find her again." I tried to contain my anger, but each word was laced with venom. My only solution to saving Rey didn't want to cooperate, and it made me furious.

"I told you, I'd do my best. That is all I can give." He was as cool and calm as the dark depths of the ocean, completely unfazed by my anger.

I had to refrain from throwing my phone. "I have one other favor to ask. Hopefully, you can at least help me with this one thing. Can you find out information on a person based on a license plate?"

"Yes," he answered warily.

"Do you have a pen and paper?" I listed off the set of

numbers and letters that Reyna had given me the weekend of the Valentine's dance. Things with Kane had vastly improved, but I figured checking the plates couldn't hurt since I had them. "How long will it take?" I wanted to ask all the pertinent questions this time so I wasn't left guessing.

"I'll get the information to you later this week."

"Thank you."

"You going to tell me what this is about?"

"No?" Not if he would accept no as an answer.

Another deep breath. "I'll talk to you soon." The line went dead.

How the hell had my bubbly, talkative sister ended up with someone so dispassionate? It was a mystery I'd probably never understand.

Me: Cam made it home, all is well.

Reyna: Good to hear. You'll have to tell me all about it at school.

Curiosity was probably eating at her, and I was equally as anxious to tell her about Camilla's boss and everything I'd learned. My sister's kidnapping had rekindled my urgency where Reyna's safety was concerned. We would see each other the next day at school, but I hated for anyone to overhear. The cafeteria lunch table wasn't the best place to bring up fake passports and kidnappings. I needed to talk to her, and I didn't want to wait. Despite what I'd told my mom, I wasn't remotely tired. Between the news of Camilla's safety and my own concerns about Reyna, I was too keyed up to sleep.

I wanted to talk to my friend without using code, so that was what I would do.

I bundled up in several layers to ward off the cool night air, then snuck over to Giada's old room situated on the side of the house. I wasn't a fan of climbing down latticework woven with ivy, but it was the only way to sneak out from upstairs. Once I was safely on the ground, I hurried toward Reyna's house. I wasn't particularly worried about being out at night. The cartel hadn't taken Camilla. Besides, they knew who I was and had access to me without tracking me down in the dead of night. If they'd wanted me, they would have taken me already. If Reyna disappeared, I might become an active target, but for now, I was relatively safe.

When I rounded the corner onto her street, I caught sight of a hooded form moving on the sidewalk several houses ahead of me. Close to Reyna's house. I eased behind a tree, not wanting the person to see me. I had assumed it was one of her guards, but the figure peered at the house through the bushes—something a guard would have no need to do. The person watched the house for several minutes before walking away, hands tucked in his pockets. Now fully visible, I could tell it was a man, tall and broad.

I tilted my head as I watched, noting an odd familiarity to his gait. Not just the gait but the shape of the man as well. I'd watched that same form walk down the hallway at school for weeks. I knew how he moved. Why the hell would Kane be spying on Reyna's house?

The cold night air seeped deep beneath my clothes and into my bones.

This was no coincidence. If that truly was Kane, I couldn't write it off like I had the other incidents. Something was going on, and it was time for some answers.

Doing my best ninja impression, I moved from shadow to shadow, following him down the street. With each step the figure took closer to Kane's house, my blood ran colder. I still had trouble believing my eyes when he walked up the front steps to the house. But there was no denying it. The man slid off his hood under the porch light, revealing thick wavy hair I'd know anywhere, and unlocked the door.

It was Kane, and he'd been spying on Reyna. Or her father. What was the difference? Either way, it was a *huge* problem.

I shivered from the hollow cavity that opened up in my chest.

I'd known something was off about Kane, but I figured he had some weird family secret or a girlfriend back in Texas. My initial worry about him working for a cartel had been written off as a moment of lunacy.

Now, it appeared I might have been on to something.

For someone who was so sick he couldn't be with me when my sister had disappeared, he sure was getting around all right now. Kane's secrets were more dangerous than I could have imagined, and I was going to get to the bottom of them, no matter how much I hated what I found.

I snuck closer to his house. Lights blinked on throughout the downstairs. I saw a hint of movement through the front blinds, so I eased closer, traipsing through the neighbor's yard to get at the side windows. My efforts were well rewarded. The drapes were pulled to the side, giving me a view into his living room. I held perfectly still, hardly breathing when Kane walked into the room with a beer in his hand.

He was so freaking beautiful. Why did it have to be a lie? Was he pretty by design? Was that all part of the plan? I didn't hate myself for falling for him, but I had to take responsibility. He'd warned me—my own instincts had warned me—and I hadn't listened to either. Now, I had to learn what I'd fallen into. Who was Kane Easton?

He set down the beer on the coffee table but stayed on his feet, reaching behind him to pull his hoodie up over his head. The T-shirt beneath went with it, leaving him gloriously bare-chested and providing me a perfect view of the large tattoo on his upper arm. He casually pulled the bottom layer out from inside the hoodie and slid the T-shirt back on, but not before I could study the artwork on his muscular shoulder. The piece was probably five inches in diameter and vaguely familiar. It was inked in black—a skull in the center with feathered wings unfurled behind it. Scrolls above and below contained words that I couldn't make out, and the skull had something on its head that flopped to the side.

It was no wonder he refused to get in the hot tub. I didn't know a single classmate with a tattoo—not that it was impossible, but considering the design and the situation, I could tell this was more than a rebellious teen getting ink. At the sight of his muscular torso, along with the tattoo and a beer in hand, he'd never looked so mature.

Kane had a past—more of a past than an ordinary kid would have—and that tattoo had meaning.

How could I have ever confused him for an ordinary high school senior?

My heart thudded so loud in my ears, I half expected him to hear it and know I was outside his window. But he didn't move from where he'd relaxed on the sofa except to sip from his beer. I watched him for several minutes, allowing myself time to feel the loss. To look at the man I thought was my boyfriend and accept that I knew nothing about him.

Some obstacles were insurmountable, and the crevasse opening up between us made the Grand Canyon look like a crack in the sidewalk.

Tears filled my eyes, and my chest cratered with grief.

I slipped away from his house before the howling wail building inside me clawed its way free. The walk home took longer than usual, with each footfall weighted in heartbreak. My mind was such a mess that I completely forgot about Reyna. My only focus now was learning the meaning of the tattoo. It would give me the answers I needed. The tangible proof my heart demanded before it would relinquish all hope.

Once I was safely back inside my room, I booted up my laptop and pulled up Google.

Skull tattoo with wings and hat.

I scoured the images, hoping if I found one similar, it might shed light on his identity. Nothing looked quite right, mostly because the hat was wrong in every image. It wasn't a beanie, but the exact label was escaping me. I searched "types of hats," and the resulting charts gave me my answer. It was a beret. That was what the skull had been wearing.

Putting a word to the object made my fingers begin to shake. I realized why it had been familiar. That was the type of hat soldiers wore—at least, some of them. I didn't know anyone who had served, but I'd seen enough movies to recognize the look.

I tried one more search. *Skull tattoo with beret and wings.*

That was it. Images just like the one on his arm filled the screen. Army tattoos.

Kane was a member of the fucking military.

Holy shit.

My mind couldn't process what I'd discovered. It was so unexpected that my brain kept skipping like one of my dad's records when they got scratched.

Kane was a member of the fucking military.

At least, he had been. But why was he at Xavier

pretending to be a student? He had to be after either my family or Reyna's—or both. I'd wondered about cartel connections, but with a military background, could he be some kind of undercover cop?

My mind couldn't compute the insanity.

Kane looked a little more mature than most guys, but there were a few guys at school who'd developed early. It never occurred to me to question his age. Even when I considered his possible involvement in the cartel, I still assumed he was our age.

Kane hadn't just fed us lies.

Kane Easton *was* a lie.

I fell back in my bed and stared at the ceiling, aglow from the screen of my laptop. Kane hadn't been lying when he said I didn't know him. That might have been the only truth he'd told. That, and maybe he actually did have a brother, but that was inconsequential. Everything he'd said was a lie. Everything he'd done was to further his own objective, whatever it might have been. The specifics of who he was or what he wanted were irrelevant. What mattered was that he'd fucking used me.

Betrayal burned at the back of my throat.

Had anything between us been real? Was winning me over just the easiest means of getting information out of me?

Jesus, I'd been such an idiot.

I should have listened to my gut from the beginning. I'd known something was off but hadn't wanted to believe my own suspicions.

I debated whether I should tell my dad. If I did, there was no telling what would happen to Kane. What would my mafia father do to a man who had used his daughter for information? No matter how angry I was at Kane, I didn't like the possibilities. His offenses against me had been personal, and I wanted to handle it on my own. I wanted to be the one to pull back his mask and expose him.

A simple confrontation would be too easy. I wanted revenge.

Kane planned to slip beneath our skin and trick us into giving him information. He used me like a piece of equipment on the job and toyed with my emotions for his own benefit.

He wanted information? I could give him that.

I'd provide a pretty trail for him to follow, then pull the rug out from beneath him the same as he'd done to me. I'd teach him that you didn't fuck with a Genovese.

In the meantime, the pain of each breath I took was a reminder of how he'd wrenched my heart wide open. Heartbreak fueled my anger, and contempt was the bridle that focused my determination. I was a storm of vindictive wrath, set to annihilate Kane Easton.

CHAPTER 23
Kane

"It's been two months, man. I need you to give me something, and soon," Rizzo barked at me. He was my boss, but we hadn't worked together for long. He didn't know me well enough to realize I didn't half-ass missions, so all he was doing was pissing me off. I'd been in the city all morning dealing with the fallout of the cartel murder—a bank president slaughtered in broad daylight on a Manhattan street.

I was well aware of our need to move faster in our hunt for Juan Carlos Vargas.

And on top of that, I'd been so damn wrapped up in the news of the murder that I'd completely forgotten about school. I hadn't called in sick to the school, nor had I texted Val to let her know I would be gone. My mood had been bleak all day. The last thing I needed was for my boss to point out my inadequacies.

"Don't you think I know that? It's a delicate situation. These are minors I'm dealing with, in case you forgot."

He grunted. "I haven't forgotten, but I know this is your first civilian operation. There's a lot of pressure from above to get some answers here. Cameras from the bank yesterday almost leaked to the media. Can you imagine the shitstorm we'd be dealing with if the public learned that a Mexican cartel had moved in next door? These assholes are getting bolder; we've got to put a stop to this before they get a foothold in our city."

I rubbed the base of my palm against my temple to combat the building pressure. "I know the expectations—that's nothing new to me. I told you I'd get the information, and I will."

"Alright, kid. Check in again in a week unless you get something sooner." He walked away, which was good because I hated the way he called me kid. I was new to the Agency, but I wasn't a kid. I'd done two tours in Afghanistan—that should have counted for something—but the guys I worked with still treated me like I was wet behind the ears. This particular assignment wasn't helping. However, it was the only reason I'd been allowed to go undercover so quickly. No one else in the agency looked young enough to pull it off.

The assignment should have been relatively easy. Win over Reyna Vargas, get in her house, then retrieve everything I could about her father. I never expected her to have a watchdog best friend who would make my job next to impossible. Eventually, I had to accept that my only option was to win over Valentina as well. I'd been hesitant to go that route because it was guaranteed trouble. An invisible link between us had snapped into place the second our eyes met on that first day. I didn't think it was possible to feel such a cosmic pull toward one person without having met them before, but that was what happened. There was no other way of explaining it. I couldn't erase the attraction, and fighting it had proved pointless.

She was seventeen, for Christ's sake.

I berated myself every time thoughts of her surfaced, which was way too fucking often. She'd be eighteen in less than a month, but in the meantime, she was a minor. That was a hard limit for me. I didn't care if the legal age of consent in New York was seventeen. I wasn't going to have sex with a girl until she was at least an adult in the eyes of the law. I could overlook the six-year age difference, but I refused to feel like a fucking pedophile.

As if that wasn't bad enough, Val didn't even know who I was, not really. I was on a job. While the kid I portrayed wasn't totally incongruent with the man I was, it wasn't me. She was falling for someone who wasn't real, yet my desire for her was more real than I cared to admit. The deception was an acid slowly eating away at me until I hated my own reflection.

I'd wanted undercover work, but I hadn't bargained for this situation. I'd never even considered it a possibility.

Initially, I tried to avoid her because I knew deep down how it would play out, but I couldn't make any progress without her. Between the consuming lust and my guilt about lying to her, I'd never loathed myself so much in my life.

As it turned out, I made the perfect emo teen. Fucking incredible.

I spent most of the day in the city, only getting back to my Staten Island home after dark. Normally, I wouldn't have broken my cover, but there was a low risk of being discovered. I was a key part of the cartel task force and wanted to participate in the incident briefings, so I needed the latest news about Vargas and his thugs. When I got home, I decided to take a walk and process the day's events while I checked on the Vargas house. Rizzo's warning had weighed heavily on me, but I was at a loss at how to get the information we needed. Even if I could get closer to Reyna, I wasn't sure she'd be able to give us anything on her father. She wasn't close to either of her parents—that had been obvious. I hadn't lied when I'd told Valentina I could sense Reyna's loneliness. She'd been dealt a shitty hand in life.

I found only darkened windows and silence at the house. The same as every other time I'd passed by. I could only hope that whatever had spurred on the murder at the bank would stir up word on Vargas. All I could do was wait and be ready.

I walked into the school Wednesday morning with a billowing dark cloud over my head, casting a black shadow on everything around me. The stress from the day before had followed me into sleep, trapping me in restless nightmares. The futility of my situation was getting to me, but I should have known seeing Valentina's silver eyes waiting for me at the end of the hall would slice through my gloom. Each step felt lighter the closer I came to having her in my arms.

I'd had to remind myself constantly at first that Val was a minor. It had been hard to grasp. Valentina didn't look anything like a kid, even with the Catholic school uniform disguising her curves.

In the eyes of the law, she was an adult at the end of the

month. At first, I didn't see how one day would change anything—it was just an arbitrary date. But after getting to know her better, I realized that the arbitrariness of the distinction between adult and minor wasn't as critical in her case. Valentina's maturity wasn't an issue. When my hands gripped her supple hips, there was nothing childlike about them. When I peered into those perceptive gray eyes of hers, I could sense a maturity beyond her years.

Come March twenty-eighth, she was legally an adult. That was enough for me.

"Hey, baby," I murmured close to her ear. I'd gotten into the habit of greeting her like that because it gave me the chance to breathe in her heady scent. She smelled like a summer fling in a field of wildflowers, and I couldn't get enough. "How's your sister?" Camilla Genovese worked for the man who had been killed—that wasn't news to me—but if she'd been missing, it was never reported to the police. I was curious about what had gone on.

"She's fine. It sounds crazy, but her boss was killed yesterday. She freaked when she found out and ended up riding a train to Jersey without her phone. It was just a mess, but she's safe now," Val explained while I riffled through my locker.

"That's crazy! Her boss was killed?"

"Yeah, but I don't know much about it. She never liked the guy."

"Still, that had to be traumatic. I hope she's okay." I paused to look at Val, regretting that I hadn't been there with her.

She peered up at me with her bottom lip between her teeth, brows furrowed. "She's fine, really." Her eyes fell to her feet, an uncommon gesture for her.

"You sure?" I brought my fingers to her chin, drawing her gaze back to mine.

"Yeah. I'm just worried about Reyna, actually."

"What's going on with Rey?" I shut my locker door and focused my attention on Valentina.

"I was telling her about my sister last night, and she hinted that something bad was going on at her house. Her father's an asshole, so I'm worried it has to do with him. She wouldn't go into detail. It might be nothing, though. I'm just a worrier."

That was the kind of news I'd been waiting for.

Was Juan Carlos Vargas going to make an appearance back in New York? I hadn't gotten a chance to get in their house, but if I could get word on his arrival so that he could be arrested, that would make the operation a success. I tried not to get my hopes up.

I pulled Val in and kissed her forehead. "You care about her. I'd say it's natural to worry. Anytime it gets to you, I'm happy to listen."

She grinned, a spirited glint reappearing in her eyes. "Thanks, babe."

I felt so fucking two-faced.

I wanted to genuinely reassure her without an ulterior motive, but I had a job to do. I tried to convince myself that I could care for her and do my job at the same time—that passing on any information she'd imparted didn't diminish my feelings for her—but she wouldn't feel the same. She'd see the deception as a foundation of lies, corrupting anything built upon it. If I was honest with myself, I knew she was right.

CHAPTER 24
Valentina

"You need to tell me what the hell is going on." Javi was pissed. It wasn't easy to tell over the phone, considering his reserved nature, but I didn't miss how his words were just the tiniest bit clipped. For Javi, that was one step from yelling.

"I take it you got something on those plates?" I'd been so relieved to finally hear from him after three days of waiting, but now I was a little scared to learn what he'd found.

"The car was a rental, but the ID on file traced back to a George Rizzo."

George? Huh. "Okay?"

"He's fucking DEA, Valentina. How the hell are you

involved with the DEA? No more shrugging off questions. You're going to tell me exactly what's happening, or I'm calling your father."

Javi was definitely pissed.

I didn't suppose he'd see the news as I had and be relieved that Kane wasn't part of the cartel. I couldn't imagine the car he'd driven would be linked to the DEA if Kane was part of a criminal organization. It seemed like good news to me, but Javi was clearly not convinced. I could understand. Law enforcement came with its own concerns. And Kane wasn't just part of some local police sting operation. This was the freaking DEA. My head swam with disbelief.

"Okay, I know this seems crazy, but I don't think we're the target," I urged him.

"How the hell could you possibly know that?"

"I've been watching the man who drove that car. He's been going by Kane and pretending to be a student at my school. He struck me as odd from the beginning, so I've been watching him closely. He's been trying to get at Reyna since the day he walked into the school. I think he's after her father. I was a little worried that he might have been working for a rival cartel. That's why I wanted you to track those plates. He drove the car to take Reyna to the Valentine's dance, and I suspected it wasn't his. He was hiding something, but it seems crazy to think he's DEA. You think his real name is *George*?" It sounded so odd rolling off my tongue. Everything about it was wrong.

"Not unless he's fifty-six. I'd say that's probably someone else in his department. They were sloppy. Figured a teenager would never be suspicious enough to take down tags."

I preened on the inside at the hint of a compliment. I'd been clever, and if it hadn't meant disaster for Kane, I would have loved for my father to have known that I'd seen past the disguise. Maybe one day, but for now, Kane's existence needed to stay secret. "Javi, I know this guy poses a risk even if he isn't after our family, but is there any way we can keep it from my father?"

"Valentina, you can't honestly ask me to do that." Exasperation wore at his words.

"Not forever, just for a few weeks. I want to handle it my way, and you can even be involved so you can keep an eye on the situation. If you're not comfortable with what's happening, you say the word." No matter how angry I was, I didn't want Kane hurt. Bringing my father into the situation wouldn't be good.

"What exactly do you mean by *handle it*?"

I took in a long, steady breath as I mulled over my words. "Kane, or whatever his name is, played me. He lied and used me, and I'm not about to let that slide. I want to give him a taste of his own medicine." My voice had gone eerily cold. Putting my thoughts into words solidified my resolve to come up with the perfect scheme for payback. This girl wanted revenge.

Javi chuckled. "I should have expected nothing less. You are a Genovese, after all."

I smirked. "Does that mean you'll help me?"

"You come up with your plan, and I'll tell you if I agree, but you only have a few days. I'm not letting this get away from us."

"I promise." I grinned. "I'll think about it and get back to you as soon as I can."

The line went quiet for a moment before he responded. "You need to be careful, Valentina." Javi's voice dropped to a grave warning. "From now on, you keep me well informed, yes?"

"Yes, I promise." I was actually relieved to have a confidant, so I had no qualms about keeping him in the loop. Toying with the DEA was no light undertaking.

"Good night and be safe."

"Night, Javi." I hung up and dropped my phone on my bed. I'd already changed into leggings and a hoodie to settle in for a Friday night at home. Some of my friends were going out, but a week of deception had exhausted me. Fortunately, Reyna didn't do anything without me, so I didn't have to worry about her being out with Kane or anyone else. I was free to wallow in an endless stream of questions.

Drug Enforcement Agency. Kane was a freaking DEA agent.

It was almost impossible to comprehend.

Considering he wanted to stop the cartel, he wasn't entirely my enemy since my father had the same goal, but he was law enforcement. I'd been told since I was a child never to trust the police. Even before I knew my family was mafia, we'd been taught never to call 911 unless someone was dying. For any other kind of problem, someone in the family could always help. And here I was, falling for a man who was the epitome of what I'd been warned to avoid.

It was odd. He didn't seem all that different from the men in my family. He lived life on his terms, pushing boundaries and toying with fate. He was charming but calculating. Beautiful but deadly. He had simply chosen to reside on the other side of the fence.

Did he see me as an enemy—a sullied extension of my criminal family? Cops and feds hated criminals. Had he been such a good actor that I'd been totally unable to detect his detest? Or could he see our similarities too? The line between us was faded and gray, chipped away from the tracks of people who had trampled across it before us. When my lips were pressed to his, our bodies flush together, a perfect sense of rightness settled over me. Each time, he'd ended our encounters in a fit of irritation. Had it been my age that bothered him, or a more deeply ingrained dislike? Was he struggling to balance on that line as it grew thinner with each of our encounters? Surely, his struggle would show him that we're all just people doing our best. I had no choice who my parents were—not that I was complaining. I loved my family, but I understood that others might feel differently. It was easy to judge what you didn't understand.

I piled up the pillows on my bed behind me and rested back against their billowing support. I needed to talk to Reyna and tell her what I'd learned. She needed to know the truth, though I didn't think the DEA would be a threat to her. If anything, they might be a help.

I suddenly shot upright, my eyes bulging wide. How had I not considered that Kane could help Reyna? Going to the feds to get help for her had been impossible when I didn't know who to trust, but if Kane was investigating Vargas, he clearly wasn't on his payroll. If I couldn't get papers from Javi, Kane might be able to provide Rey with a new identity.

A whole new realm of possibilities opened up.

With the exchange of a few short texts, we set up a plan to take a walk the following morning. It was going to be a beautiful day, perfect for scheming.

"A FEDERAL AGENT?" Reyna screeched.

"Shh, there's no telling if someone might be following us." She glanced over her shoulder to peek at the empty sidewalk. "Are you serious? There's no one here."

"This whole thing has made me paranoid. I just think it's better to be careful." I'd seen Kane wandering in our neighborhood twice. It was unlikely he was hiding in the bushes, but who knew?

"I just can't believe it. Are you sure? What if he works for my father's competitor? My guards were telling me that my father was facing challengers."

"The car you went to the dance in was rented by a DEA agent."

Her eyes rounded so wide I worried her eyeballs would plunk onto the sidewalk and roll away. "Holy shit! My father would be furious if he learned they'd come so close. In Mexico, the police know not to mess with the cartel."

"This isn't Mexico, and the DEA means business. They might even put your father away for good." I peered over at her. "Then you'd be safe and wouldn't have to run."

She smiled thinly, wary about hoping for such a windfall.

"The other thing we have to consider," I continued, "is that Kane could help you. Maybe he could get you in the witness protection program."

Rey slowed to a stop, her brows pinching together. "I think I have to be able to offer them something, don't I? Like to testify? I don't know anything. My father has always kept me in the dark."

I squeezed her arm gently. "We don't know that for sure, and it never hurts to ask."

She nodded and began to walk again. "I suppose so." The defeated tone of her voice tugged at my heart.

"Try to stay positive. I told you I'd get you out, and it's a promise I intend to keep."

AFTER OUR MORNING WALK, I began Operation Catfish. Kane thought he was duping all of us, but I was about to show him that he was the one getting played.

"Hey, babe. What are you up to today?" I greeted him warmly when he answered my call.

"Not much. Dad told me to get some cleaning done, but that's it." Right. *Dad.*

I rolled my eyes but kept my voice bubbly. "It's such a gorgeous spring day that Reyna and I decided to head out to Wolf's Pond Beach today. Want to join us?"

"Yeah, that sounds great. What time?"

I grinned. "We were thinking three to give it time to warm up." A push of warm air had upped the temperatures, but it was still a long way from summer.

"Sounds good. Let me know when you head over."

"Will do. See you there!"

"See you, babe."

I hung up, hating how much my heart loved to hear him call me babe. No amount of new information about Kane could deter my love-sick heart. She'd jumped in head-first despite the posted warnings and proven herself incapable of leading. I'd had to strip her of all commanding authority. I had business to take care of. It was time for logic and ruthlessness to take the helm.

Mom let me borrow the car to meet Kane. I was sitting on the large boulders overlooking the sandy beach when he arrived, sexy as hell straddling his sleek black bike. A thin smile wavered between triumph and misery as I watched him approach. I wasn't sure I'd ever be able to look at Kane again without being subject to a storm of emotions.

He secured his helmet to the bike, then walked toward the rocks, breathtaking as always—not at all what I would think a self-righteous federal agent should look like. Golden hair glimmered in the sunlight, and his flawless tanned skin was perfectly suited to our beach setting. Everything about him was too good to be true. I should have known.

The wind whipped at his short-sleeve button-down. The top button was undone, giving me a peek at the golden planes of his chest. It was the perfect shirt for a beach day—thin with faded pink flowers over green leaves. The sleeves were long enough to cover his tattoo, but the wind teased as though it might reveal his secret. His choice to wear the shirt and risk detection was yet another example of the way he liked to tempt fate.

"The beachy look suits you," he murmured before bringing his lips to mine.

That treacherous organ in my chest leapt at his touch. I slapped a piece of duct tape over her mouth and shoved her into a closet. "Thanks. It feels amazing to get some vitamin D."

"No kidding." He glanced around after sitting next to me. "What happened to Rey?"

She's home, considering I never asked her to come. I'd known my chances of getting him alone had been slim unless I used Reyna as bait. "She had to back out at the last minute. It's just you and me." My teeth tugged at my bottom lip as I peered over at him coyly.

How had I not noticed the way he tensed when we were alone? Now that I knew the truth, it was impossible to miss.

Pain blossomed in my chest to know his attention was all a show, but I had to play my part. I needed to show him I wasn't a tissue to be used and disposed of.

I could have cut off all contact or even confronted him the minute I figured out his deception, but that wasn't my style. I was more of a get even kind of girl. Eye for an eye and all that. Turning the table and getting revenge took strength. If I'd run to my father, I would have proved myself the child Kane thought me to be.

"That's too bad, but more time for us." His tight smile was unconvincing. "Want to go for a walk along the water?"

"Sure." I eased myself over the boulders toward the sand, waiting for Kane to stand first so he could help me down. I'd crossed that rock barrier myself any number of times through the years, but I was looking for ways to make him squirm. A seductive look. A sultry touch. They were all weapons in my arsenal. "So, your dad had you cleaning this morning? Is he back in town?"

"Yeah, but he heads back out tomorrow."

"Was he in town long? You hadn't mentioned him coming home." We'd gotten closer the past couple of weeks, but I hadn't pushed for information about his family. Partly because I didn't realize I needed to, but also because I'd been too lost in the rush of just being with him. Now, I was going to weasel out everything I could without making him suspicious.

"Uh, he was here for a week. Guess I'm just used to him coming and going."

"He's had the job for a while?"

"Yeah, like ten years." He kicked at the sand as he walked, the wind tugging at our clothes.

"Hey, Kane. I want to ask you something, but I don't want to upset you."

He placed his arm over my shoulders and pulled me snugly against him as we walked. "You can ask me anything, beautiful. Anything at all."

"How did your mom die?" I asked the question softly. Even though his answer would be a lie, the question had still felt invasive.

"It was a car wreck. I was ten, so it was a long time ago." His voice took on an emptiness that sounded eerily close to sorrow. Was there truth buried in his lies?

"I'm so sorry. I can't imagine losing my mom. She's a little crazy, but I love her."

He slowed to a stop, guiding me around to face him before his eyes swept slowly across my face. "I suppose we're all a little crazy sometimes," he whispered into the wind as he lowered his lips to mine. An echo of salt from the sea air greeted my tongue as I sucked on his bottom lip. Kane's hands cupped my face, cradling me like a precious gift. I clung to his forearms as the kiss threatened to cast me adrift. It was tender yet demanding, toying with my heart so viciously the battered organ began to weep.

I pulled back and turned away, bringing my knuckles to my lips.

"Hey, you okay?"

I nodded, blinking away tears. "Yeah, sorry. Just got a little dizzy. Vertigo from the sound of the waves or something."

"You want to go back?"

"No," I said too quickly. "No, I'm fine."

You're going to ruin everything. My head chided my heart,

who had clawed her way out of the closet and fumed churlishly in the shadows.

I forced a smile, trying to turn things around. "So ... my birthday's in a couple of weeks."

"Oh, yeah? I'm glad you told me. Do you have any plans yet?"

"I'm working on it. I wanted to be able to have Reyna over, but her dad has some meeting or something. We're waiting to get more info before we make birthday plans." Adrenaline sparked in my veins as I lay the first crumbs of my trap. I didn't have the particulars laid out, but I'd constructed a basic plan.

"I thought her dad was out of town," Kane noted nonchalantly.

"He is, but I guess he's coming back. Hopefully, we'll know soon."

"Let me know what your plans are. I'd like to celebrate with the birthday girl, too." He bumped my shoulder gently.

"What about you? I've never asked when your birthday is. Have you had your eighteenth yet?"

"Yeah, a while back," he murmured, then glanced at me. "I'm older than ..." He started to speak, then clamped his jaw shut.

I slowed my steps and lifted my brows expectantly, encouraging him to finish.

"I'm just older than you. That's all." He took a deep, weary breath and resumed walking.

"You say that like it's a bad thing," I pried.

He chewed over his words before he replied in a dark tone. "Valentina, you should know that my life was different before I came to Xavier. I was different."

A knowing tingle skittered down my spine. Was Kane

trying to give me a murky window to the truth? My heart wanted to believe it was evidence that his feelings for me were real, but logic slammed the door on that emotionally flawed line of thinking. He was probably just trying to keep me at arm's length out of politeness. He didn't want to deal with drama when the truth came out.

"That's the great thing about a fresh start." I peered at him without a trace of emotion. "We can be anyone we choose to be."

"Yeah, but the past will always be a part of us."

"Well, I'd say that's a good thing because I like you just the way you are. If your past had been different, you wouldn't be the same person you are today." Both statements would have been true had everything about him not been a lie.

A smile teased at the corners of his lips. "You're awfully smart, you know that?"

I was dumb enough to fall for your lies, so not nearly smart enough. I smiled back, but my chest ached with grief.

Revenge wasn't sweet like they said. It was raw and savage and shredded a person's insides like fresh strawberries in a blender. It was messy in every way, but it offered the illusion of control. By tricking Kane, I was taking back control of the situation, and I needed that. I needed to show myself that I wasn't weak. I just hoped I came through on the other side with a pulse. I wasn't sure revenge would be worth it if I lost myself in the process, but that was the tricky part about striking back. Standing up to the person who wronged me was easy; remembering who I was before I got hurt was the real challenge. It would be easier to shut off my emotions and allow bitterness to fortify my defenses. That was what I was doing when I tried to silence the pain— when I didn't allow my heart to feel. True strength was allowing that heartbreak to crash over me without crumpling to the ground. I would rather be shaped by my pain than allow fear to make me unrecognizable. The next couple of weeks interacting with Kane would be difficult but necessary for me to be the woman I wanted to be.

By Thursday of the following week, I'd formalized my plans and been given Javier's approval. Plotting had been energizing, but it wasn't enough to counteract the drain of pretending all day at school. Four days of fake smiles and heartache had taken their toll.

When I walked past an empty music room during my office aide period, I ducked into the silent room shrouded in darkness. I'd always taken private piano lessons and stayed away from school music programs. But I'd gone to Xavier long enough to have seen every inch of the school and knew the music room contained a beautiful grand piano in the back corner—one of the perks of being a well-funded private school.

Enough light filtered in from the hallway to navigate the room and see the sleek black and white keys. Even if it had been pitch black, my fingers would have been at home on the keyboard. The solitude eased the tension from my shoulders, but it was the initial touch of ivory that allowed me to breathe deeply for the first time that week.

My fingers drew out a mournful melody straight from my soul. The haunting strains filled the room, bleeding my heart dry of all its sorrow like a doctor lancing a wound. Up and down the keyboard, my hands wrung out each pent-up emotion until a peaceful hollowness settled in my chest.

My fingers stilled after the last notes of melody hung in the air.

"That was incredible."

The unexpected caress of Kane's baritone voice made my breath catch in my lungs. I turned to find him propped against the wall beside the door. I'd been too engrossed to sense his presence, but he'd been there for a while. Watching. Listening.

"Thanks." I offered a weak smile. The emotional letting had been soothing but drained me in its own way. I didn't have any energy to put into my deception.

"How come I didn't know you played?"

I shrugged. "It never came up, I guess. I mostly play for myself."

His eyes swept the empty room. "So I see. With that kind of talent, it's a shame you don't share it with the world."

"What, like be a concert pianist or something?" The question dripped with skepticism. I couldn't imagine myself worthy of such standards.

Kane lifted away from the wall and closed the distance between us, one achingly slow step at a time. "I just think it's a shame for the world not to hear your music. Not many people play with that kind of passion."

My cheeks warmed at his compliment. I didn't want to be affected by his words, but my heart gave me little choice.

"I should play for people. You should be in class. Looks like we're both falling a little short."

He held out his hand for mine and encouraged me to my feet. We stood chest to chest in the dimly lit classroom, an electric current of anticipation sparking in the air around us. Kane's fingers traced along the edge of my face, drawing my hair back as he studied me. I didn't want to enjoy his attention as much as I did, but I allowed myself this one moment of weakness. In another week, my secret would be out, and our fake romance would be over.

"So much sorrow hidden behind such beauty." The words ghosted across his lips and wrapped themselves around my heart. "How can I make it better?"

You can't. You're the reason I hurt.

A single tear slipped from the corner of my eye. "Kiss me."

Kane reached behind me without breaking eye contact and lowered the lid over the piano keys, then he backed me up until he could lift my bottom onto the covered keyboard. My legs wrapped around his middle, and my fingers clasped his shirt, pulling him closer. When his lips finally pressed against mine, the fervor of his touch sent a shiver down my spine.

"I've never known anyone like you," he whispered between kisses.

I inhaled his breath and words and touch, soaking him into my bloodstream so that I could take a part of him with me. When I lowered my hand to cup his impossibly hard length, Kane hissed. I wanted to push him and see how he'd respond, but I also wanted to feel him. To imagine what it would have been like to have him inside me.

At first, he pressed himself against my palm, rocking once before his entire body shuddered. Then, as expected, he pulled back and met my eyes. "I'll never be able to go back to class with a raging hard-on, and as you pointed out, I *should* be in class." He smirked, but there was no humor in those steely eyes of his.

I set my feet on the ground and wriggled out from behind him, needing space to get my bearings. "Somehow, I don't see you having a problem skipping class," I teased back, hoping to roll with our forced levity.

He adjusted himself and winked, then sobered and snagged my hand to get my attention. "Hey, you going to tell me what was wrong? You can't play that kind of music in the dark and tell me you're okay."

This was it. Time to set the trap.

I took a slow breath in through my nose. "I was just worried about Reyna again. She's upset about her father coming back. From what I can tell, he's a terrible man."

"That's awful. She say when he's coming back? I'd still like to make plans for your birthday."

"The night of the twenty-seventh. Late." Just over a week. The minimum time I needed to get everything in place and the night before my birthday.

"When can I take you out?"

"Rey might need me that night, and my family is having a big dinner for my birthday, so maybe we could go out Sunday. That work?" I didn't want to have to pretend my way through an evening together right before the end. It would be too hard. Once he knew that I knew, we would have no reason to see each other again.

"If it works for you, then it's perfect."

I grinned. "I better get back to the office. You coming?"

"You go ahead. I think I'll give myself a minute to settle." He arched a brow.

I stepped away, allowing our fingers to drift apart. "Oh, I almost forgot. What's your favorite color?"

"Red, why?"

"Nothing, just a little birthday surprise I have for you."

"I think you're confused on how birthdays work. You

receive gifts, not give them." He grinned, and I felt it like a punch to my gut.

Ever the fighter, I refused to show my distress, so I kept my smile bright. "Just sharing the love. And besides, it's nothing big. See you in poli-sci." I waved and slipped into the hallway, my game face crumpling the second I was alone.

CHAPTER 25
Reyna

VAL'S BEEN ACTING ODD FOR WEEKS, BUT SHE WOULDN'T TELL me what was going on. All I knew was that she insisted my mom and I spent the night in a hotel.

That's not true. I knew her odd behavior had something to do with Kane and my dad and some plan she'd concocted, but I didn't know any details. I was just along for the ride, which was often how our friendship worked.

While my mom was coherent early in the week, I told her I wanted to have a girls' night on the twenty-seventh. That was a Thursday, but Mom was too clueless to question why we'd go to a hotel on a Thursday night. She didn't keep track of the days anymore. Mom jumped at the idea to get out and pretend we had an actual relationship. Our guards weren't thrilled, but with her insistence, they reluctantly conceded.

I booked a simple room at the same hotel the dance had been at. It wasn't too far from the house and had an elegant restaurant downstairs, which would be important if I needed to usher Mom to the room earlier than expected. As it turned out, she made it through a surprisingly pleasant dinner but was only back in the room fifteen minutes before passing out on her bed. She'd been mildly annoyed when she discovered I hadn't booked a fancy suite, but extravagance was unnecessary—especially knowing Mamá would be blackout drunk most of the time.

I folded the duvet over her and turned on the television, but before I settled in, I decided to grab some ice from down the hall. Our two guards had the room next door. When I stepped out of our room, ice bucket in hand, I expected one of them to be standing outside the door, but the hall was empty. I should have fussed at them to be more vigilant, but I was too relieved to be alone for once. Constantly having watchdogs at my side wore me down.

I walked back to the elevators where the ice machine was located but pulled up short when I found Santino leaning against the vending room doorframe. He was classically beautiful. Even a jacket couldn't hide the fact that he was built with layers of sinewy muscle. He could overpower me in a flash, but his strength didn't feel like a threat. If anything, the sight of him brought on an unexpected sense of relief.

"What are you doing here?" I blurted.

His steadfast gaze lured me closer. "I told you I'd be keeping an eye on you."

That was an understatement.

His eyes pierced straight into my soul. I'd become an expert at being invisible in life, but I couldn't hide from Santino. I wanted to believe he sensed that inexplicable connection between us. That visceral ability to instantly spot a particular person in a crowded room. Maybe it was foolish of me to believe it worked both ways. I was his enemy, after all.

"I'm valuable leverage, aren't I?" Anyone who wanted to get at my father would have direct access if I was taken. Granted, my father would only want me back to show he couldn't be touched, but I was a useful tool, nonetheless. I understood that it wasn't personal, but it stung to think that was the only reason I continued to find him watching me.

Santino's jaw clenched, his eyes growing impossibly dark. "Do you miss it back in Mexico?"

"I'll do anything to keep from going back there." I might have been more transparent than I'd intended. My father would kill me himself if he learned I'd spoken badly about him. I coaxed my muscles to relax and tried to cover my tracks. "What about you? Do you miss it?"

"There's nothing there for me to miss. Are you going to try to escape your father?" He wasn't going to let me change the subject.

My heart was doing its best to shut me up by lodging itself in my throat. "Maybe. If I was, it wouldn't be in my best interest to tell you, would it?" Valentina had talked to Javier, who was Santino's boss, but I didn't know what all she'd told him.

"Probably not." He slowly reached forward, his fingers snagging the ice bucket. When I handed it over, he took it to the ice machine and quickly loaded it full of ice. "Why are you at a hotel?"

I took the bucket back from him, sliding the lid in place. "We had the house fumigated and decided the smell was too bad to stay there tonight."

He eyed me curiously but didn't challenge me. After years and *years* of practice, I was good at lying.

I glanced around the small elevator landing. "You going to stay here all night?"

"Maybe." A glint of humor shone in his eyes as he returned my vague answer.

"Well, you might want to be careful," I announced haughtily. "We've got guards in the room next to ours. If they discover you're here ... well, just don't let that happen."

Santino strolled closer until only a breath of air was between us. A breath filled with his leather and musk scent that made my head spin. His hands lifted to cup my face, the pads of his thumbs caressing my cheekbones. "How is it that something so gentle and pure could exist amidst such corruption?" His voice was strained with the guttural pull of lust and the weightlessness of wonder.

The one simple question was the most beautiful string of words that had ever been spoken to me. My chest filled with a warmth that made me realize just how desperately cold I'd been inside. Loneliness was an arctic continent that froze over all it touched, but one look from Santino could thaw even the most frostbitten parts of me.

"I'm more than the people who gave me life. I won't let my future be defined by them." I reached up on my toes to give myself the leverage I need to press my lips to his.

A kiss. My very first.

The instant I made contact, a savage moan rumbled from deep in Santino's chest and his lips slanted over mine. Kissing was more natural than I'd expected. My lips and tongue easily followed his lead, taking my body to a place of such intense sensation that I never wanted to leave. I couldn't imagine any drug surpassing the overwhelming euphoria that flooded my veins.

Was it always this way?

Santino slowed, reluctantly drawing our lips apart entirely too soon. I opened my eyes to find his gaze already locked on mine. The intensity swirling in those obsidian depths spoke more than any words. Such desperation and longing. I was certain not every kiss was so heartfelt. Kissing Santino wasn't just kissing. It was everything.

"Go back to your room, princesa," he whispered. "I'll be here watching over you." He stepped back, but it took me several long seconds to convince my legs to walk away.

There'd been little in my life to look forward to through the years. Even the possibility of escape was daunting enough to warrant a small amount of reluctance. But for the first time that I could remember, I was buoyed with hope and anticipation. If Santino was the prize I received at the end of my struggles, it might all have been worth it.

After months of worry and angst, I closed my eyes that night with a smile on my face, knowing exactly where I wanted my dreams to take me.

CHAPTER 26
Kane

"You sure this is the right place? There are half a dozen private airports close to the city," Rizzo grumbled. We'd been sitting in a car along with several other units staked out in front of an airport hangar since before dark. It was now four in the morning, and doubt was creeping in.

"I told you, I got the intel from Reyna herself. I overheard her telling Valentina that her father used this airport. When I checked the logs, this was the only flight that fit the profile of a jet coming in from Mexico."

"Maybe he came in early. He was supposed to be here hours ago. I think it's time we write this one off."

I could feel my heels digging in. I'd been so certain this

was it. My first operation, all tied up with a neat little bow. "If he came in early, then his plane should be in the hangar. Let's at least take a look before we throw in the towel."

Rizzo grunted and flung open his door. We explained the plan to the other team members, then began our approach. Everyone wore Kevlar with earpieces so that we could time our entrance and minimize risk.

"Drug enforcement, put your hands up!" I yelled in warning as we entered the building simultaneously from the two side entrances.

We were met with silence.

Once the lights were on, we made sure to stay covered with our weapons ready, but the hangar was empty except for a single car parked in the middle of the cavernous space.

Rizzo's voice crackled over our earpieces. "Rooney and Hutch, check the office."

There weren't many places to hide, so it didn't take long for us to clear the building. I holstered my gun and let the weight of my failure pull on my sleep-deprived limbs.

Vargas was still in the wind. The nearly three months I'd spent at Xavier had been utterly worthless. Not true. I'd lost my mind to a feisty brunette during that time—I was worse off than I'd started.

I shook my head, running a hand through my matted hair.

"Hey, Kane, this you?" One of the guys called to me from beside the black car, motioning to the windshield.

Everyone moved in on the vehicle to surround the hood. On the dashboard was a photograph of Valentina and me. One she'd taken just a week earlier when we'd walked on the beach.

The room went eerily silent.

"We're all gonna back outta here right fuckin' now," Rizzo ordered softly. "No one touch a goddamn thing." He called up the local bomb squad as soon as we were safely outside the building.

The whole thing had been a setup.

Someone who knew I was after Vargas had arranged for me to find that photo. Someone who wanted to make a show of outing me. I tried to wrap my brain around what exactly had happened, but none of it made sense. We were expecting to find Vargas at the locker, but this appeared to be orchestrated by the Genoveses, considering it was a photo from Val's phone. Could the cartel and mafia organizations have been working together? No way. There was too much bad blood—recent bad blood—for that to happen. All I could come up with was that Edoardo Genovese had figured out who his daughter was dating and was sending us a message.

My fists clenched, and my head throbbed. Not only had the night been a failure, but I'd been made. Our entire operation was over. That was disappointing in itself, but even worse, there was no reason to go back to Xavier, so I might never see Val again.

A frustrated roar clawed at my throat, demanding to be released, but I couldn't let my anger show. Not in front of my fellow agents. I swallowed down the savage desperation that made me want to put my fist through someone's face and sat down to wait out the process of clearing the vehicle.

It took over two hours for the bomb squad to arrive and certify that the undercarriage and trunk were clear of any explosive devices. Two hours of sidelong glances piercing me with curiosity and judgment. Everyone would want to know what had gone wrong. Had the rookie fucked up his first assignment? And I couldn't even clear my name because I had no fucking clue how I'd been made. For all I knew, we had a rat in the department. That one tendril of hope buoyed me through the early hours of the morning while we waited.

Before the bomb squad could turn the car back over to us, they had to open the doors to do a precautionary sweep of the inside. Ready to get our hands back on the car, my team lifted the main hangar door constituting most of the front of the building and watched the technician finish his search. The lead tech, still outfitted in his protective suit, reached for the driver's side door handle. As the door opened, a sharp pop resounded through the hangar, and the man stumbled backward, covered in blood. The guys next to me instinctively crouched to a defensive stance, but I froze in horror. Had my failures as an agent just gotten a man killed?

My ears rang so loud from my thundering heart rate that it was all I could hear.

"Jesus Christ," Rizzo hissed.

Instead of falling to the ground, the man lifted his hands and wiped at his saturated face shield. "It's paint, guys. Just red paint," he called out. "Someone's got a real twisted sense of humor. Help me here; I can't see a goddamn thing."

His teammates rushed over to help him remove the protective helmet, and our guys ambled closer to the car with hands on their hips and questions in their eyes. I didn't move a muscle.

What's your favorite color?

Red, why?

Nothing, just a little birthday surprise I have for you.

I thought back to each snippet of information I'd gathered and the inclination I'd brushed off that Val had been acting weird for weeks.

This wasn't a message from Edoardo Genovese. His

response would have been much more direct. She might have had help, but for the most part, this was all Valentina.

I stared at the car, my head tilting as I took in every detail. I'd have bet good money that was the exact same car I'd used to take Reyna to the dance. Val had never even seen it, so how the fuck had she known?

So goddamn brilliant.

I'd known she was perceptive, but a part of me preened at the astounding acuity of my girl's intuition. My girl... Could Valentina ever be anyone's girl? A man might as well try to own the wind. Val was her own sovereign entity. Good thing I'd been trained to conquer nations.

She'd struck out to punish me. Did she think this orchestration was her way of cutting ties? There was no fucking way. I didn't care if the mission was over. I had to see her again, and I had to explain. This wasn't how things were going to end between us. At the very least, I didn't want her to feel used because she wasn't... not entirely.

Fuck.

I shouldn't even have cared what she thought of me, but I did, and that was the biggest problem of all. It sucked that our mission was blown, but what upset me the most was where that left Val and me. My priorities had shifted somewhere along the course of the past few months.

Where the hell did that leave me?

Standing at Valentina's doorstep, exhausted and furious and ready to lay it all on the line.

CHAPTER 27
Valentina

I SHOULD HAVE KNOWN SETTING UP KANE THE NIGHT BEFORE my birthday was a bad idea. I'd spent every minute of the day stressing over whether everything had gone smoothly, wishing I had set up cameras so I could have watched from a distance. I certainly wasn't able to enjoy my eighteenth birthday like I should have, nor did I have the capacity to deal with whatever my mother was about to share with us. She'd waited until we were all together for my traditional family birthday dinner to make an announcement. Something like that wouldn't have scared me before, but the past year had been insane. Family announcements had become a risky proposition.

"Your half brother was sent my information and given the option to initiate contact." My mother's voice shook as she spoke, which would have ratcheted up my fears if her eyes hadn't been brimming with joy. "It's been a month, so I began to doubt he would respond, but I received an email yesterday. Your brother's name is Connor Reid, and he wants to meet us."

How in the hell had I forgotten I had a brother?

I'd been so consumed with Reyna and Kane that my mother's big reveal from weeks earlier had fallen to the wayside. Now, not only did I have a brother but he also had a name. It made him somehow more concrete in my mind.

Connor Reid.

My big brother.

A breathlessness filled my lungs as though the air around me had thinned. So many emotions swarmed me at once that they canceled each other out, engulfing me in numbness.

What would he be like? Would he be angry that Mom had given him up? She was so incredibly excited that I worried for her. I didn't want this clandestine meeting to break her heart.

"That's wonderful, Ma. I'm so excited for you." Giada hugged Mom while I simply tried to breathe.

"Okay, okay. Let's go eat before the food gets cold. We can all take a guess at what he looks like." She ushered us toward the dining room, sniffling back a barrage of tears.

I had trouble eating but did my best since Mom had cooked my favorite meal. The entire family was present for my birthday dinner. We weren't over-the-top party people, so birthdays tended to be more private affairs. Nothing like my aunt Lottie, who liked to throw black-tie events at every opportunity. Being my eighteenth, Mom had suggested a girls' weekend trip once school was out, and I'd readily agreed. I'd plan where I wanted to go after I could clear my plate of all the other crap I was dealing with.

Tonight, I had to pretend to be in a celebratory mood as I sat around the table with my closest family. Giada had brought Javi, and Camilla's new boyfriend, Filip, had joined us now that the two had recently become an item. Our dining room table sat eight—ten if we were friendly, but those two extra chairs usually flanked Mom's china cabinet. That left a single unoccupied chair at the table. The armed chair opposite my father at the head of the table.

If Connor hadn't been given up, would that have been his chair? How would our lives have been different with a boy in the house? How would things change once we'd met?

Throughout dinner, the empty seat haunted me. I smiled as my family sang "Happy Birthday" and thanked my mom for the delicious cake, but the second dinner was over, I fled to the living room. The pressure over setting up Kane had compounded daily, leaving me ill-equipped to handle the onslaught of emotions that came with the news of my brother.

My nerves were more frayed than the hem of my favorite pair of jeans.

Curled up on the sofa, I opened my phone and scrolled through my social media to help me escape myself. I hadn't noticed that Camilla had followed me until a knock sounded at the door, and she jumped up to answer it. I retreated back to my mindless scrolling until Camilla shot around the corner from the entry and hissed at me.

"Hey, get over here. There's some guy at the door for you.

If Dad figures it out, you know he'll grill the guy, so make it quick."

Anxiety took hold of my stomach and sent it careening into my feet. There was only one guy who would come looking for me, though I never expected him to confront me at my house. He had to know who my family was and the danger associated with showing his face.

Hell, I had to get him out of here before my father spotted him.

I jumped from the couch and hurried to the front entry, hoping I didn't vomit on the way. When I yanked open the door, I was greeted with the sight of an avenging angel—a golden-skinned beauty wrapped in leather and malice.

"Kane, what are you doing here?" My voice stretched thin.

"I think you know." He peered over my shoulder to where Camilla still lurked behind me. "I need to talk to Val alone."

My older sister wasn't about to cut him any slack.

"It's okay, Camilla. I promise. We'll just talk for a minute, and then I'll come back inside. Okay?" I gave her a dose of my most tragic puppy-dog eyes until she finally caved and disappeared back inside the house, but not before cutting Kane with a warning glare.

The second the door was closed, Kane yanked me around the corner with a hand clamped over my mouth. I pulled free of him once we were out of view on the side of the house, but he kept me hostage with my back against the stone wall. His anger was a palpable thing—hissing and snarling just beneath the surface. Leading him on a fake trail hadn't seemed particularly dangerous because I figured he couldn't hurt me. He was law enforcement, and they had rules. Now that I had to face the consequences, I wondered if I'd misjudged him. Maybe messing with a federal agent had been a bad idea.

But he'd messed with me first.

He didn't get to toy with people the way he'd led me on, then act like it never happened. I might have tricked him, but I was only getting even. His deception was the seed that sprouted this entire infestation of lies.

"What the hell do you think you're doing here?" I spat.

"You think I'd just walk away after you pulled a stunt like that? That's not how this works. You showed me how you feel. Now, it's my turn to tell you my side of the story."

"Your side?" I stepped forward and shoved him with all my strength. "You played me like a fucking violin, pulling each of my strings until I gave you what you wanted. You led me on, used me, and toyed with my emotions like I meant *nothing.*" I shoved him again, my vision beginning to blur with unshed tears.

"I knew you'd think that, which is exactly why I'm here. I haven't slept in two days, but the only thing I could think of was getting back here to talk to you."

I shook my head. "You just want to cover your ass and make sure the naïve little girl doesn't get you in trouble. That's why you cringed after every kiss and pushed me away when I got too close. I'm just a loose end that needs to be tied up before you can move on to the next job." Verbalizing the harsh truth sent a stabbing pain deep into my chest.

Kane stepped forward, crowding me back toward the wall. "I may have cringed, but that's only because what I was doing was *wrong.*" He held up a hand. "And before you twist my words, I mean my feelings for you. Needing you—

wanting you—was wrong on so many levels. Besides the fact that I had to lie about who I was, you weren't even *of age*. If I did the things I want to do, I'd have been almost as bad as the pedophiles we put behind bars. Do you think I would have put myself in that position voluntarily? That I would have risked my life just to screw with you? I prayed every day for this desire to disappear, but each time I fell into your silver stare, I became more lost than ever."

I'd gathered that a part of his odd reaction to touching me was centered around my age. It was easy to make that connection once I'd learned the truth, but I hadn't examined his behavior beyond that point. If he didn't want to touch me or get close, keeping me at a distance wouldn't have been a problem. There would have been no cringing or punched walls. No emotion necessary at all. He could have befriended me without any romantic innuendo and still achieved his goals. But he *had* been attracted to me. It had torn him up inside every time we were together. Even now, his bloodshot eyes and the blistering heat of his stare told me his appearance at my house had never been about taking the easy road. Technically, there wasn't even a crime to cover up —we'd only ever kissed. He could have packed up his sparsely furnished house and disappeared without ever seeing me again.

I pulled back enough to search his glassy eyes. "You swear it wasn't all a lie?" My words were rife with a vulnerability I fought to conceal.

He slowly shook his head from side to side. "It would be so much easier if it had been."

We were both so entranced in one another, neither of us noticed footsteps approaching in the dry winter grass.

"You need to get the fuck away from her," growled Javi

the second he stepped around the corner. He took my arm and pulled me away while pressing a commanding hand flat against Kane's chest to stop him from protesting.

"Wait, Javi—" I cried.

It was no use. His grip was absolute.

"Quiet," he barked, his glare still locked on Kane. "I've let this go on long enough. Too long, considering you have the balls to step foot on this property."

Kane lifted his hands in surrender, but his already bloodshot eyes darkened. "I just needed to talk to her."

"You've talked enough. Valentina, get inside, now."

"You don't understand," I started to explain, but Javi wouldn't hear it.

"I said *now!*" he yelled at me, shocking me into silence.

Kane had the opposite reaction. He launched himself at Javier, clutching his shirt and bringing their faces inches apart. "Don't you fucking threaten her again." The animalistic growl of his voice bordered on feral.

How had the situation devolved so quickly? My heart thundered in my chest as though preparing for battle. I lunged between the two men, doing my best to pry them apart.

"*Stop!* Both of you stop right now. I'll go back inside, Javi, but only if you come with me." My voice was laden with panic. If this skirmish lasted any longer, my father would come looking for us, and that might lead to disaster.

Kane released Javier's shirt, and both took a reluctant step back. Neither backed down from the murderous stare passing between them. Only after I tugged at Javier's arm did Kane turn his attention to me. He took two lightning-fast steps toward me, then pulled me into a kiss so devastating it turned my world upside down.

In the handful of seconds we had before Javier wrenched us apart, Kane's lips lavished me with his devotion and desire. His tongue raked over mine with a promise of absolute sincerity. It was practically suicidal to kiss me right outside of my father's house, but Kane was telling me I was worth it. Such a risk would have been pointless if he didn't care about me.

He wanted me to feel the depths of his emotion for me.

Did that mean he still wanted to pursue our relationship? How could that ever work? He arrested criminals, and my family was in the mafia. Those two simply didn't coexist. I couldn't fathom how we could ever be together, and in that case, our desire for one another would be more punishment than reward.

A growing sense of loss shredded me.

I should have shaken off my feelings for him the minute I learned his intent, but instead, they'd grown stronger. He'd never been mine to claim, yet my heart had done exactly that. No guy I'd met in the past had ever enticed me the way Kane had. Maybe my heart had always been his, even before we ever met. I wasn't sure I believed in fate, but nothing else explained our connection to one another. If it had been fate, she must have been a blind old bat because she failed to notice that Kane and I existed in two different worlds.

"That's enough," Javier said through clenched teeth while tugging me with him.

The loss of our connection sent a stab of yearning through my chest.

"This isn't over." Kane's voice called out resolutely behind us.

Javier continued walking at a determined pace, unfazed by Kane's declaration. When he had me back inside, he cornered me in the entry and took two long, steady breaths before speaking. "You have to realize that will never work." His voice was like an eerie fog rising off a lake in the early morning—a serene veil disguising the dangers beneath.

"You think he's just a fed, but it's more complicated than that—like you and Giada," I explained in a whisper.

"No, Valentina. Your sister and I were from different organizations of the same nature. That man works for a government that wants to put all of us behind bars. There is no way the two can peacefully coexist."

I was suddenly winded by the overwhelming desperation of my situation. I'd been so focused in the last weeks on getting back at Kane, I hadn't considered what would happen if I'd been wrong. What if Kane did have feelings for me? How could I ever keep him in my life when we were perfect enemies?

I nodded weakly, my voice abandoning me to heartbreak.

"It's your birthday," he offered in a softer tone. "Let's just pretend this never happened and rejoin the others."

I lifted my watery eyes in surprise. "You aren't going to tell my father?"

"There's nothing to tell, correct?" He peered at me pointedly.

I fought the tears that burned at the back of my eyes. "No, there's nothing to tell."

"Good. Then I believe your father has a gift for you." He placed a warm hand against my lower back to usher me back toward the living room where my family had gathered, drinks in hand and conversation flowing, oblivious to the wreckage of my life.

"More birthday wishes?" my mom asked as I squeezed between her and Giada on the couch.

"Oh, yeah. Just a friend from school stopping by to say happy birthday." My eyes drifted to Camilla, whose unrelenting stare silently interrogated me.

"Now that you're back," my father cut in, "here's a little something to celebrate the beautiful young woman you've become." He extended a small box in pink wrapping toward me.

It was disorienting to dive back into a birthday party after such emotional turmoil. I'd been teased with a taste of pure happiness, only to have it viciously ripped away. My heart was tattered and bruised, a pile of limp flesh on the ground. A birthday present felt inconsequential in light of my heartbreak, but I couldn't let them know. My family would never understand.

"Thank you, Daddy." I forced a smile and peeled back the paper, then hinged open the box to reveal an incredible platinum watch within. "Daddy, it's absolutely stunning," I breathed, true shock catching me off guard.

The thin band was more like a delicate bracelet than a watchband, and the face was a small rectangle no larger than a dime. The piece was artfully crafted with three diamonds at the top and bottom of the face as the sole adornment. I flipped it over to discover a tiny engraving. A bird in flight over a single word.

Genovese.

To my father, family meant everything. The concept was all I'd ever known, and while it had always given me an enormous sense of belonging, the reminder of who we were and how different I was from Kane battered my already raw emotions.

My eyes teared, and I could only hope my family believed they were tears of joy.

"Here, let me put it on." Dad set down his wineglass, then locked the watch clasp in place with surprising dexterity. "I'm so proud of you, songbird." He kissed my forehead, simultaneously warming my heart while shattering it into a million tiny pieces.

CHAPTER 28
Kane

It had taken all of my self-control not to beat the shit out of Javier and steal Valentina away so that we could continue our talk. I managed to keep my emotions on a leash —a much-needed lesson I'd learned in the Army. Lashing out would only hurt my cause. There was plenty of time to wage my campaign to win back Valentina. However, I didn't want to give her too much time alone and risk the small amount of progress I'd made. If Javier or her family got to her while we were apart, they might convince her that I'd only used her for information.

I parked my bike the next morning along the curb two houses down from hers and pulled out my phone. Now that

I'd slept and she didn't have a house full of visitors, I wanted to continue our conversation. Charging up to her front door the night before had been evidence of my sleep-deprived state. I was lucky it hadn't ended in bloodshed. This time, we'd try again somewhere we wouldn't be interrupted.

Me: You up? I'm outside waiting for you.
Val: You're here?! At my house?
Me: I'm down the street. I want to talk again.
Val: This isn't a good idea, Kane.
Me: Come talk to me, or I'll find a way to come to you.

The conversation dots appeared and disappeared three times before her reply finally came through.

Val: You're really bossy, you know that?
Me: I do. Are you coming?
Val: Fine, be there in a sec.

Less than five minutes later, she appeared on the sidewalk wearing leggings and an enormous hoodie with her arms crossed over her chest. "You shouldn't be here."

"There's a lot I shouldn't do, but that's never stopped me before. We still need to talk. I don't give a shit what your family thinks, but if you'd prefer they didn't see us, then we'll just take our discussion somewhere else." I unclasped the spare helmet I'd brought from the back and held it out.

"Why would I talk to you? I don't even know your name."

"My name is Kane, and you know me better than you realize."

"Kane Easton?"

"McKenna."

Her eyes drifted down to my bike. She didn't take the helmet, but her arms uncrossed, and her fingers toyed with the edge of her sleeve. "Where were you thinking?"

"There's a great little beach nearby called Wolf's Pond.

Last time I went, the scenery was stunning." The corner of my lip quirked up, hoping a little teasing would coax her compliance.

Valentina remained guarded but took the helmet. I helped her get it situated, then tried not to moan at the fucking perfection of having Val snug against me on the back of my bike—her thighs gripping my hips, and her chest pressed firmly against my back. She felt like a dream. A dream that left me achingly hard and more convinced than ever that I couldn't let her go.

The morning was cool but warming quickly with the rising sun. I drove carefully, relishing how she squeezed my middle with each turn. A few runners and walkers dotted the beach when we arrived. The sun was about forty-five degrees above the watery horizon, blasting the beach with its reflective rays. I helped Val from my bike, then took her hand and led her to the pathway onto the beach.

"No climbing over the rocks?" Her voice hinted at humor. It helped me to relax, knowing her defenses weren't on high alert.

I smiled. "Next time."

Her smirk tugged downward into a frown, her eyes cast out at the waves. If she doubted the plausibility of a next time, she would find herself proven wrong, but there was no point in arguing. The only way to make her truly believe was to show her, and that was exactly what I planned to do.

"How did you figure it out?" I was insanely curious and had spent hours the prior day thinking over what could have tipped her off.

"I suspected something was off, but it was your tattoo that made me understand."

My steps stalled. "My tattoo? How did you even know

about that?" I'd been well aware the artwork would be a dead giveaway that I wasn't a student, so I'd been exceedingly vigilant about keeping it hidden. I racked my brain, trying to think of when she might have seen it.

She shrugged unapologetically. "I caught you spying on Reyna's house one night, so I followed you home and watched you through your living room window."

I huffed out a laugh. "Sounds like you should have my job." Was it any wonder I was so drawn to her? Beautiful and fucking brilliant—she was an incredible woman. "I wasn't supposed to be undercover. At least, not yet. I'd just started the job when they needed someone who could pass for a high school kid. It wasn't my ideal assignment, but it was better than desk work."

"So ... how old *are* you?"

"Twenty-four." I glanced at her but could detect no outward reaction to my age. I tried to be patient, reminding myself that she had every right to be wary.

"I gathered the tattoo was military. Is that right?"

"It is. I dropped out of high school and enlisted in the Army at seventeen, going straight to Army Ranger training at the first opportunity. After that, I did two tours in Afghanistan before being honorably discharged when an IED shredded my knee."

She nodded, greedily absorbing every tidbit I gave her. "Why didn't you just wait until you graduated to enlist?"

"I didn't exactly have a choice." I inhaled a lungful of the salty sea air. "I fucked up at school and was moved to an alternative learning center. My dad wasn't the patient type and had put up with my bullshit long enough, so he told me to enlist or find somewhere else to live. I may have been reckless, but I wasn't dumb enough to try living on the streets. Two years later, I'd worked my ass off through MOS—Military Occupational Specialty training—and signed my Ranger contract."

"And your mom? Did she have any opinion in all of that, or is she really dead?"

"She is, but she didn't pass until a couple of years ago." My gaze followed the gulls coasting on the ocean breeze. I'd moved past the trauma of my childhood, but I didn't talk about it often, so the words were stiff and rusty. "I told you she died when I was ten because she might as well have. That's when Dad kicked her out because she'd become a drug addict. I never saw her again after she left. After I was discharged, I searched for her. Didn't take long to find her death certificate. The chances hadn't been good that she'd rehabbed and regained her life, but I had to check. So, Dad was a hard-ass, and Mom was a mess—not exactly the American dream."

"Did your mom's drug problem influence your choice to go into the DEA? To help keep drugs off the streets?"

I shrugged. "The only training I had was in special ops, so I had to find something that required that type of specialization. The options are limited. I didn't exactly apply for the job with my mom in mind, but her struggle definitely fostered a revulsion of drugs. Never been high in my life and don't plan to be."

She cocked her head to the side. "What did you do in school that got you in so much trouble if you weren't into drugs?"

"Mostly just stupid stuff, but the thing that tipped the scales was taping a guy to the school flagpole ... naked." I relished the memory of his whimpers, even years later.

"*Naked*? Why would you do that?"

That was the real question. The part the school didn't seem to care about. "He'd been copping feels of the girls any chance he could get but never messed with any one girl long enough for them to rat him out. I was observant and happened to see him do it once, so I kept an eye out. When I verified it wasn't an isolated incident, I taught him a lesson." The administration had given him a slap on the wrist since none of the girls had come forward, but I'd been suspended. It was no wonder the system was fucked.

She stopped and lifted our clasped hands to study the bracelets on my wrist. "And this brother of yours—what's his story?"

Finally, a part of myself I was happy to share. "That's Caleb." I grinned at her and pulled out my phone. "How about I introduce you?" I dialed his number on FaceTime, my smile widening at Valentina's bulging eyes.

The phone rang three times before he answered. "Kane! Tomaste demasiado tiempo."

I laughed, used to his playful chiding, and turned to Val. "He's fussing at me for not calling sooner."

Her face scrunched in confusion as I pulled her in closer to make sure he could see her on the screen. Caleb was visually impaired and wore thick glasses, which only gave him a basic degree of sight. He pressed his face close to the phone to see us in more detail.

"Yeah, but look who I have with me."

Caleb grinned and cried out, "La encontraste!"

I laughed. "I did find her, but she doesn't speak Spanish, so you need to talk English, man." I gave Val a gentle squeeze. "Caleb, this is Valentina. Val, this is my big brother, Caleb."

She waved, a tender smile forming on her lips. "Hey,

Caleb. It's so good to meet you. You look so much like your brother."

"Ella es bonita. Me gusta."

Val looked at me for an explanation, and I stifled another chuckle.

"Yeah, man. She's definitely pretty, and I'm glad you like her. I just wanted to introduce you, but we have to get going. You taking your vitamins in the mornings?"

Caleb rocked back and forth several times. He did that when he was uncomfortable and didn't feel like answering a question. When he did, the framed poster behind him came into view, reminding me of my first day at Xavier. *Tell me and I forget, teach me and I remember, involve me and I learn.*

So much had changed since that day.

"Cuando vendras a verme?" Caleb asked, skirting my question.

"Soon, buddy. I'll come as soon as I can for a visit. I love you, Caleb."

His rocking intensified, and he waved before hanging up. He never said I love you back, but I could feel his attachment to me in the way his agitation always increased at the end of our calls. I was all the family he had, but that was okay because he was it for me as well. We'd only ever had each other—until Val. I was willing to open my small circle enough to include her if … if she wanted me in return.

"That explains so much," she mused, her hands falling on her hips.

My brows furrowed. "Explains what?"

"A part of the reason I was suspicious of you was a text I saw on your phone one day at school. It said, 'did you find her' in Spanish. Then I found a Spanish Bible in your room, and I started to worry that you were working for a cartel."

"My mom was originally from Ecuador, so she taught us Spanish as our first language. Caleb can speak English but not as well, so he mostly refuses to try. When I left town, I had to try to explain to him why I might be gone for a while. I told him there was a girl I needed to go find and would see him again once I talked to her." I wasn't supposed to have given him the number to my work phone—going undercover meant a complete break from normal life—but I'd been unable to sever all connection for that long. Caleb never would have understood. "As for the Bible, it was my mother's. It's the only piece of her I kept."

"I could sense you were interested in Reyna but wasn't sure why. When the Spanish stuff kept popping up, I worried about the cartel, but only briefly. Everything made a lot more sense when you mentioned how you sensed her loneliness. Until then, your unusual interest in her was the thing that made me the most suspicious."

"There was nothing *unusual* about my interest in her," I balked playfully. I'd been reasonably casual about my inquiries, or so I'd thought.

Valentina cocked her head to the side. "You asked about her constantly. That would have been understandable if you were seriously into her, but you couldn't keep your eyes off me. There was no denying the draw between us. The whole thing was so confusing."

I snagged the front of her hoodie and tugged her closer. "Confusing is right," I murmured before bringing our lips together. I could lose myself in her touch and die a happy man. I wanted to taste every inch of her—bury myself inside her and grow roots deep in her soul so I'd always be with her.

Val pulled her lips away from mine but allowed me to

keep her body wrapped in my arms. "Your brother seems sweet," she said softly.

"He's the best part of my world. I hate that he's in a facility, but he's done well there. He's just not able to live on his own with his developmental challenges and near blindness. Dad put him in a state home after Mom couldn't take care of him. I'd always planned to get him out, but after I was discharged, I visited more and came to realize that he was thriving in the structured environment. Taking him out would have been more about my guilt than what was best for him." I placed a hand against Valentina's cheek, my thumb tracing across her soft bottom lip. "I'm selfish by nature, and my feelings for you are no different. There's every reason for me to break this off and end it—for your sake and mine. But I don't care about any of that. I want you, Valentina Genovese. Regardless of our backgrounds or our ages. Regardless of the lies surrounding our relationship. What I feel for you is real, and I'm not about to abandon that." I searched her eyes, desperately hoping she felt the same. To see some spark of understanding that would show I wasn't in this alone.

Her response floored me. Five little words swept the earth right out from underneath me.

"Take me to your place."

It was a whispered command on the surface but encompassed a world of meaning. The precious gift of forgiveness and the chance to earn her trust. It was a bountiful opportunity I wouldn't dare squander. If I could prove to Valentina that we belonged together, the resulting challenges we'd face would be meaningless. She was everything to me.

CHAPTER 29
Valentina

THE ANTICIPATION OF WHAT WE WERE ABOUT TO DO, THE FEEL of my hands flat against Kane's washboard abs, and the vibrations of his motorcycle beneath me combined to liquify my insides. My blood simmered warm despite the cool morning air whipping past me, and the molten need pooling in my belly made my breathing catch with every bump in the road.

The tension between us had been mounting for so damn long that I was ready to detonate before he'd even laid a hand on me. Everything he'd said the night before and that morning had been exactly what I'd hoped to hear, though I wasn't sure to what end. I still didn't see a path for us, but that didn't matter for the moment. Being with Kane was right in every way that counted. I wanted to explore that connection as much as our situations would allow. I'd deal with the heartbreak later.

When we pulled up at his house, a touch of anxiety crept into the back of my mind. I'd fooled around a little with my prior boyfriend, but I'd never been comfortable going all the way. I'd only been sixteen when we'd broken up. Kane would be my first. No matter how safe I felt in his arms, there was still a hint of unease associated with such an intimate act. Having sex with Kane would change me in more ways than one. I wanted him to touch my soul in a way that connected us forever. Even if a relationship wasn't a possibility, I'd always have the memory of our time together.

Kane helped me with my helmet, then took my hand and led me inside his house. He never said a word. The urgency shining bright in his eyes was matched by my own. The second the front door closed, he had me backed against its smooth wood grain. The shock of his quick movement winded me. I took in a shaky breath through my parted lips and shivered at the thin layer of air that separated our bodies. Kane had his hands pressed to the door on either side of me, our bodies in perfect alignment, but a gentle brush of our foreheads was the only place where we touched.

"Have you done this before?" His voice was a coarse, uneven rumble like the distant purr of his motorcycle.

I shook my head.

His breathing shuddered, and his eyes drifted shut while he fought for composure. When his thick lashes lifted again, whatever weakness he'd suffered had been locked away deep behind the copper streaks in his eyes. Kane was now in perfect control.

"Come here." He took my hand in his and led us upstairs to his bedroom, releasing me to turn on the small bedside lamp.

I scanned the room slowly, seeing it again from a new perspective. It seemed small for an adult man. Now that I knew Kane was alone in the house, I was surprised he didn't stay in the master. "This whole time, you've slept in here and not downstairs?"

He stepped behind me and began to gently pull the rubber band from my hair, then loosened the braid I'd used to keep my hair from tangling on the motorcycle. His fingers gliding down my back with each swipe of braid sent a bolt of pleasure down my spine.

"Compared to the shitholes I slept in while overseas, this might as well be a luxury resort. I didn't need the king bed in the master to feel comfortable." Once my hair was free, he stayed behind me, his hands drifting to my bare skin beneath my hoodie. "I want this more than you can imagine, but I have no problem stopping if you change your mind, okay? You get uncomfortable, you tell me." His hands coaxed me to turn and face him so that he could meet my eyes with an expectant look.

"Okay." I gave him what he wanted to hear, but I wanted this too much to ever stop him.

He grunted, then slowly glided his hands up and over my ribs. I followed his lead and raised my arms. Once my hoodie was discarded on the floor, his hungry gaze devoured the curve of my breasts high in the demibra I'd thrown on after he first texted. My skin pressed against the purple lace with each of my labored breaths. Just the sight of his desire for me had me breathing like I'd been dragged along on one of Camilla's ridiculous runs. Exercise wasn't my forte. I was happy with that because I loved my supple curves.

"If I wasn't so desperate to see you naked beneath me, I'd leave that on. Fucking phenomenal." The last was an exhaled benediction that had my nipples pressing urgently against their lace confines.

Kane slipped his fingers beneath the waistband of my leggings and tugged them down to the floor, helping me balance as he removed my shoes and freed my feet from the narrow openings. He took a long time returning to his full height, claiming each inch of my skin with his possessive gaze.

I'd never felt more physically perfect than I did with Kane's eyes devouring me—a dying man at his last supper. My mismatched underwear didn't even faze me. Kane's reverence made me feel flawless. Seductive and mesmerizing.

I wanted to be treated to a show of my own, so I reached for the hem of his shirt. Understanding my desire, he removed it without hesitation. My eyes were instantly drawn to the black ink on his shoulder. I stepped closer, lifting my hand to trace the lines.

Death before dishonor.

Those were the words inked on the scrolls that I'd been unable to read when I first saw the tattoo. Their meaning was an ideal my father would respect. The two men had so much more in common than they could ever imagine, and that truth made my chest ache with frustration.

"Enough," he huffed, sensing the downward turn of my thoughts. He backed me up until my thighs bumped against the side of the bed, then motioned with his chin. "Take off your bra and lie down."

I did as he commanded.

While I scooted backward, Kane removed his pants, taking his underwear with them until he was gloriously naked. The tattoo hadn't been the only reason he'd refused to get in the hot tub after the dance. Seeing him up close, I recognized the difference between the body of a seventeen-year-old and a man of twenty-four. His muscles were more mature—solid mass honed for strength rather than newly developed sinewy tissue.

And his cock. My eyes were entranced with the way his thick member bobbed and hung heavy with each of his movements.

Sweet Mother Mary, how was that going to fit inside me?

"Valentina," he called softly, summoning my gaze back to his as he lowered himself onto the bed. "It'll fit, and you'll love it. I promise."

Good grief. Had I said that last part out loud?

I nodded but was quickly distracted from my worry when Kane brushed his hand up my inner thigh, encouraging me to spread my legs. I watched him raptly, engrossed in the way each featherlight touch brought a surge of sensation rocketing through my nervous system. When he lowered his head and grazed his teeth over my panties directly over my core, I thought my head would explode.

"You smell fucking divine." He slid my panties to the side and licked up my slit.

My back arched off the bed as though I'd been possessed. He tasted me over and over, the velvet caress of his tongue quickly unraveling my mind to the point of primal need. I'd touched myself before and had brought myself to orgasm, but the sensations Kane stirred deep inside me were infinitely more intense.

He lifted his face away just long enough to press my legs together and drag my panties off. His brief absence somehow reset my nerves so that when his touch returned, my pulsing bundle of nerves reignited even more brilliantly than before. My thighs began to shake around his head. Each of my panted breaths was broken and shallow as he pushed me closer to the edge of an impossibly high cliff. My inability to control my own body and the knowledge that Kane was in absolute control somehow added to the intensity. I was his instrument, and he drew a symphonic masterpiece from deep inside me.

"That's it, baby. Come on my tongue."

The vibrations of his words followed by his masterful touches circling my throbbing clit sent me hurdling over the cliff's edge. My mouth widened on a silent gasp as my body dissolved into liquid energy. Pleasure coursed through my veins, wave after wave cresting and crashing through me. I gave myself over to the rolling waters and allowed them to take me to whatever their destination.

When Kane's lips encircled one of my nipples, I was reluctantly dragged from my orgasmic bliss. My body was overly sensitive—unable to handle any more. My eyes flew open, and my lips parted on a shaky breath.

"Shh," Kane urged me. "You'll be fine, I promise." He got up from the bed and rifled through his dresser drawers until he extracted a foil packet. He ripped it open and had a condom in place in a matter of seconds.

The sight had me instantly more alert. I watched breathlessly as Kane lined up our bodies, resting his hip to one side of me and leaning on that elbow. His lips lowered to mine while his free hand teased my breasts. I was stunned to discover a brand-new tendril of lust unfurling deep in my belly. When his hand lowered to the apex of my thighs, I was quickly dragged back to mindlessness. He slid easily through my arousal, dipping a single finger inside me. I moaned his name, writhing in the delicious fullness.

"You're so damn tight, but that's natural. We'll take our time." He slid his finger in and out until my opening welcomed him greedily.

Then he added a second finger.

Again, I gasped at the intrusion, the sensation so foreign. But Kane licked my nipple and placed kisses along my neck, and I was quickly squirming my hips to the rhythm of his hand pumping gently inside me.

How could I feel so full yet ache for more? My body somehow knew what it needed—a primal instinct that had been dormant until this moment.

"I'm ready," I purred. "Please, Kane. I want you inside me." Fear lurked in the shadows of my mind, too remote to penetrate the thick fog of desire.

"Look at me, beautiful."

I hadn't realized my eyes had closed, but I followed his instruction immediately.

Kane's fingers sank deep inside me, his palm pressing down to cup my entire sex. "This is mine. I'll be the first and *only* man to touch you here. Understand?" There was nothing casual or hazy about his declaration. Only perfect clarity and absolute conviction. Kane intended to make me his, but I couldn't fathom how that would work, and this wasn't the time to hash out the details. All I knew was that I wanted to be his, so I let my heart give him what he wanted to hear.

"Yes, Kane. I'm yours."

He raised himself above me, one hand weaving through

my hair to cup the back of my head. I lifted my knees up around his middle to open myself to him. My inner muscles clenched at the scalding touch of his cock when it lined up with my opening.

"Relax, okay?" he urged before angling his hips to nudge inside me.

I gasped, my eyes darting across the ceiling above with a surge of anxiety.

"Val, baby. Keep your eyes on mine."

I did as he said, centering myself in his amber gaze. Kane was here with me. He'd never hurt me. I wanted this more than I'd ever wanted anything before. I coaxed my muscles to ease up, allowing him to press another inch farther. Kane hissed, his eyes briefly fluttering shut.

"Okay, this is going to hurt a bit, but it'll get better. I promise."

I nodded, bracing myself.

Kane lowered his lips, his tongue delving deep into my mouth. Its seductive caress distracted me just enough for his cock to plunge fully inside me. I couldn't help the small cry that escaped me. I wasn't sure what I'd expected, but the pain was real. Kane pressed his forehead to mine, whispering sweet assurances while he let my body adjust.

It didn't take long. When my breathing returned to normal and the pain quieted to a distant murmur, I pressed my lips hesitantly to his.

Kane's eyes flew open, and he seized me in a voracious kiss. He moaned into my mouth—a sound of pure abandon that buried itself deep in my heart. His hips slowly rocked him inside me with heartbreaking tenderness. Only when he sensed me move along with him did he increase the vigor of his movements. Soon, I was clinging to his shoulders, relishing the feel of him lose himself inside me. Kane lowered his hand back down to roll his fingertip around the tip of my clit, sending me into an alternate dimension of pleasure.

"Oh, God," I cried. "I'm going to come again. Kane …" That was all I could get out before my world exploded around me. My muscles clamped down impossibly tight, eliciting a guttural roar from Kane as he found his own release deep inside me.

The moment was utter perfection.

Never in a million years would I regret giving myself to this man, no matter what our future brought us.

Kane pressed three reverent kisses down the column of my neck before easing off me and disappearing to the bathroom. When he returned, he had a navy washcloth in his hand.

"Let me clean you up."

I widened my knees enough to give him access, suppressing a cringe when the use of my abs produced a dull ache down below. "Did I ruin your sheets?"

He gingerly swept the wet cloth along my slit. "One, it'll wash out. But two, the mark of your virginity is evidence of something special. If my sheet was ruined in the process, I would hardly cry about it." Then he winked before taking the cloth back to the bathroom.

A swarm of monarchs took flight in my chest.

I pulled the top sheet up over my rapidly cooling body, making room for him when he rejoined me. I curled up against him, laying my head on his shoulder. He hooked his fingers behind my closest knee and pulled my leg up so that I was more fully draped over him. His solid body felt magical beneath me—warm and secure.

"How do you feel?" he asked. With my ear pressed against his body, his voice resonated through me like the vibrations of a bass drum.

"Probably better than I deserve to feel."

"Why do you say that?"

My hand absently traced the planes of his chest. "I just hope I didn't get you in trouble at work or embarrass you. I kind of meant to before, but now, I feel bad about it."

He gave me a gentle squeeze. "If it had to happen to get us here, it was worth it." His reassurance was incredibly sweet, but it didn't erase the guilt.

"The ironic part about all of it is that Reyna hates her father. If you'd wanted information from her, all you ever had to do was ask."

Kane's body tensed. "Do you think she'd still talk to me?"

"I know she would, although she may not have much to offer you." I lifted onto my elbow. "Kane, is there any way you could help her? Could you get her into witness protection so she can escape him?"

"Is that really what she wants?" His brows furrowed as a myriad of questions passed behind his eyes.

I nodded. "We've been working on getting her to safety ever since her father went back to Mexico. I had a plan, but it's been taking longer than expected."

"I could have her at a safe house in twenty-four hours."

My heart thudded against my ribs as I lay back down. I'd hoped he might be able to help her, but considering our rocky past, I'd been reluctant to set my expectations too high. Now, her freedom was almost assured. The relief was dizzying.

"You don't know how much that would mean to the both of us." My voice cracked with overwhelming emotion.

"I just wish I'd known earlier. I could tell she was lonely, but I didn't realize her situation was worse than that. I'm glad she's had you to help her. How did you two first begin to confide in one another?"

"It only happened in December. Our fathers had a confrontation ending in her father being ordered to leave the country. He took out his anger on her. And unfortunately, I don't think it was the first time." The memory of her bruises brought a lump to my throat. "She came to me upset, coming clean about who her father was and that she'd been instructed to befriend me for information."

"And that didn't upset you?"

"Just for a second, but she was so sincere in her explanation that I believed her when she said she'd never told her father anything. She had no control over who her parents were."

My breath stalled. Would he realize that the same applied to me? Unlike Reyna, though, I didn't want to leave my family behind. I was innocent in my father's dealings, but that didn't change who I was and who I'd always be. Kane was still a federal agent, and I was still a daughter of the mob.

"I should get going," I murmured brokenly. "My parents will be back from church soon and figure out I'm missing." I started to pull away only to be rolled onto my back with Kane towering over me.

"What happened there? I can hear in your voice that something's wrong."

Tears filled my eyes as I gazed up at him. "This has been absolutely perfect, Kane." My fingers feathered over the stubble on his jaw. "But there's nowhere for it to go. How could a DEA agent ever tie himself to a mafia family?"

His gaze caressed my face as he formed his next words. "What if I told you I'd make it work?"

My heartbeat stuttered and stumbled. Make it work? How was it even possible? "What do you mean?" I whispered.

Kane traced the pad of his thumb along my cheekbone. "Just ... just don't give up on me yet, okay? Promise me you'll give me a little time to sort it out."

I couldn't fathom how our situation could be fixed, but I was in no rush. I had all the time in the world.

KANE GOT me back home minutes before my parents returned from church. I'd been given a reprieve from going since it was my birthday weekend. After I showered, I texted Reyna and arranged to meet her between our houses.

"Hey, did everything go as you'd planned on Friday?" she asked as soon as she was close enough not to yell.

"Yes and no. It went as planned, but then Kane came to my house on Saturday."

Her eyes rounded. "Did he talk to your father?"

"No, but Javier had words with him, which was unnecessary. I think he thought Kane was threatening me. But anyway, the point is, Kane wasn't using me like I thought —not exactly. He *does* have feelings for me, but even more importantly, he said he can help you!" I took her hand in mine and grinned. I was thrilled to tell her the exciting news.

Rey gnawed on her lower lip. "Really? He'd be willing to do that?" She was afraid to trust such a windfall.

"Yes, honey. He can get you witness protection and help you disappear. You'd be free." I felt like a fountain since my eyes had produced so many damn tears for one day, but it seemed there were still more to come. Between my joy for Reyna and the resulting sorrow I'd feel when she was gone, the waterworks were at it again.

I wasn't alone. Reyna held back a choked sob. I flung my arms around her and held my best friend tight, knowing these might be our last days together.

"Thank you, Val. For your friendship and for everything you've done for me."

"You need me, and I will *always* be there for you."

CHAPTER 30
Santino

I watched Reyna more than I should have, but I told myself it was a part of the job. If I was being honest, I didn't need to sit outside her house to follow orders. But how could I leave her alone in that house when I knew her father's depraved cruelty all too well? I'd grown up around the Vargas family. For years, I'd felt like I owed them for helping me off the streets, but nothing about their actions was altruistic. The Vargas men were only out for themselves. That became clear over the years, making my departure an easy choice. I was now free of them, but Reyna still had the Vargas gun at her head.

I didn't want to abandon her to that fate.

You sound like a Vargas. Don't gloss over your selfish motives.

My conscience was right. I didn't just want her freedom; I wanted to be the one to free her. I wanted to make her mine.

As if my thoughts had summoned her, Reyna appeared in her window, a vision of divine perseverance. It only took a second for me to realize she was searching the darkness for something. Was it absurd of me to think she was looking for me?

I took a chance and stepped from the shadows. Her face lit when she spotted me, sealing my fate. Never in my life had someone responded to my presence with such pure joy and eagerness. I wanted to bring that look to her face every damn day of my life.

She disappeared momentarily before slipping out the front door and hurrying over. A part of me wanted to scold her for taking such a risk—she didn't truly know me—but I also craved the trust she placed in me. Considering the life she must have known as a Vargas, I couldn't imagine where she could have learned such blind faith. But that was Reyna. She wasn't like the rest of her family.

"I was hoping I'd see you," she greeted me eagerly.

"Is everything alright?"

"Yeah, I just wanted to talk to you. I, uh ... I don't have many people I can talk to, and I know you aren't exactly a friend, but I wanted to tell you something. I know I shouldn't, but ... if I don't ..." She hugged herself to ward off the cool night air.

I slipped my arms from my jacket and wrapped it around her shoulders. "You can always tell me anything."

"Thank you." She gave me a shy smile that made me want to throw her in my car and claim her right then and there.

I managed to control myself, if only out of curiosity for what she had to say.

"I have an opportunity to get away and escape my family."

"You mean the papers Javier is getting for your new identity?"

She shook her head. "No, it's another option to disappear. Something that just came up."

My gut churned with unease. "The undercover fed," I murmured without needing to ask. It was the only obvious explanation, but the two hadn't been in contact since Valentina's big showdown. How had this come about? More importantly, if Reyna became a witness for the state, she would be in grave danger. Assuming she made it out alive, her next step would be WitSec.

She'd be untraceable. I'd never see her again.

I wanted to lash out and demand she refuse to take such a risk. But the truth of the matter was the US government could make her disappear more effectively than if she'd tried on her own. She'd have resources. A future.

What if you were with her? If you disappeared with her, she'd have you.

Was it insanity talking? We hardly knew one another, but I'd do it for her. I'd leave everything if she asked.

"I haven't even talked to Kane yet, and I'm sure I shouldn't be telling you, but I had to. If I do this ... if I entered witness protection ..." Her hands worried at one another, and her eyes searched the darkness for words she didn't know how to say.

"What, princesa? If you do this, what?" I placed my fingers at the back of her neck and ran my thumb along her delicate jaw.

"Then ... I'll never see you again." Her words were a

whispered confession—an admission and a plea—so unexpected they winded me.

Reyna Vargas was drawn to me enough that she was wary to take her best chance at escape for fear she'd lose me. Any man would be a fool to let such beauty and fidelity slip between his fingers.

"Then I'll just have to go with you," I said without reservation. I was spellbound by the woman before me and could think of no better purpose in life than to stand by her side.

"You'd really do that?" She was totally awestruck. I doubted she'd ever been on the receiving end of selfless devotion in her life.

I brought her lips to mine, sealing my promise with a kiss.

"I'd do that and so much more."

She gazed up at me, her delicate fingers clutching my shirt. "You truly are a saint, aren't you?"

I'd always seen the irony in my name, considering the ugly things I'd done in my life, but in Reyna's eyes, I finally lived up to my namesake.

The Saint and the Queen, an unlikely pair in so many ways.

"I need you to give me your number and promise me you won't disappear without me."

Her lips thinned. "My phone is monitored."

"I won't text you anything that will put you in danger. I just need to make sure you can contact me if you need me."

She nodded, then told me her number as I entered it into my phone. I dropped the device back in my pocket, then pulled her in close for a parting hug. The sweet scent of pears filled my lungs before I placed a kiss on her hair, black and glossy as a raven's wing.

"You need to get back inside. Be safe, princesa."

She nodded and slipped off my jacket, handing it back to me. I wanted her to keep it but knew she would be in danger if the guards spotted her with it.

"Good night, Santino." She lifted a hand in a reluctant wave, then hurried back to the house.

I didn't budge from my station until her light extinguished for the night. And even then, it took a mountain of convincing to tear me away. I had to make plans for us, and I needed rest. I was of no use to her exhausted, so I forced myself to trudge back to my car, feeling the pangs of separation worsen with each passing step.

THE NEXT MORNING, I had a meeting set up with Javier to discuss our upcoming week. I debated all night how to tell him about my change in plans. My upbringing had taught me it was disloyal to end my service to a man who had saved my life on more than one occasion. Javi was more family to me than my blood relatives had ever been. He'd understand my need to go, but that didn't make it any easier.

"Reyna's been offered WitSec by the feds," I confessed the moment we sat down. Not how I'd planned to broach the subject, but it did the job.

As always, Javi remained perfectly stoic. "And how do you know this?"

"Because I've been talking to her."

He studied me for long seconds. "Why do I have a feeling there's more?"

This was the hard part. "If she goes, I want to go with her."

"So, you've developed feelings for her?"

"I have. She's unlike any girl I've ever known. If she leaves without me, I'll never see her again."

Javi nodded and sipped from his steaming mug of coffee. "Well, then. We'll need to hurry. I just got word this morning from Mexico that Vargas is in the wind."

CHAPTER 31
Kane

As soon as I dropped Valentina off at home, I raced into the city to talk to Rizzo about getting protection for Reyna. I wasn't familiar with the process and hoped I hadn't made false promises to Val. The rest of the day was spent in meetings and bogged down in paperwork. I didn't get back home until late, but at least I didn't have to get up early for school. My days at Xavier were over.

Where did that leave me?

I lay awake until after midnight, thinking through my situation. I'd gone into law enforcement after the Rangers because it had been a natural progression for someone like me, rather than the product of some unquenchable need to lock criminals away. I liked strategy and teamwork. Maybe I was fucked up, but I enjoyed difficult situations. If I left law enforcement, where would I go from there? I wasn't qualified to do much else, at least in the eyes of potential employers. And I wasn't the type to turn to illegal income streams. I didn't judge Valentina's family for their way of life, but I also wasn't going to adopt it either. What legitimate options were there for someone like me outside of government employment?

There was no fucking way I was flipping burgers, and I'd be damned before I lived off Val's money. Her father would never respect me if I couldn't stand on my own two feet. It was hard to see a solution in such foreign waters, but there had to be one. I was resourceful. I would figure something out, which was why I asked Val for time. I didn't want her giving up on me in the process.

The glowing numbers on my digital clock ticked by for hours before I finally found sleep. Without my alarm set, I slept in until nearly lunch. My system was still off after being awake for two days straight, which didn't help.

I got dressed and put on a pot of coffee to help wake me when a knock sounded at my front door. I wasn't expecting anyone, so I slipped my handgun into the back waistband of my jeans before peeking out the side window. The man on my porch was vaguely familiar. I opened the door, watching carefully for any fast movements.

"Can I help you?" I asked, looking him over with a critical eye. "You were at the dance, weren't you? You were the man dancing with Reyna."

"I need to know how quickly you can get her to safety." There was an urgency to his voice that had me instantly on edge.

"How do you know who I am?" Did he work for her father? Surely not. If her father knew I was a federal agent, they never would have allowed her near me.

"I work for a man named Javier. Have you heard of him?"

"The man who's dating Valentina's sister? Ex-cartel, right?"

He nodded. "Valentina has been keeping him apprised of the situation. We helped orchestrate the small ... production at the airport the other day."

I glared at him, confused. "Why the hell would Val go to him?"

"That's irrelevant right now," he spat with a flare of anger. "We are wasting valuable time. I need to know if you can get Reyna to safety or if I should do it myself."

"I could get her to a safe house right now if needed, but I'm not telling you any more than that. You could be looking to hurt her for all I know." My muscles tensed in response to the escalated energy brewing between us.

The man took a small step forward to bring our faces inches apart. I had to brace myself to keep from taking his ass to the ground.

"Listen," he growled. "We have word that Vargas is on his way back. Reyna is in *immediate* danger, and I need to know if you can keep her safe." His voice was ragged with desperation.

I didn't know the details, but I'd have bet my life he cared deeply for her. His distress was palpable. Simple concern wouldn't have manifested such anguish.

"When does he land?"

"He could be here by now for all we know. Every minute I waste here talking to you is a moment lost unless you can *do* something."

I grabbed my badge and keys from the nearby bureau and joined him outside but stalled when my attention turned to my motorcycle. It wasn't the most secure way to transport an individual wanted by an angry cartel.

"Can you drive us?"

As I jumped in his car, I prayed that my instincts were right and that I hadn't just aided in my own kidnapping… or worse.

CHAPTER 32
Valentina

Kane wasn't at school Monday morning. I'd known that would be the case but hadn't anticipated just how desolate my life would feel without him. His absence was a preview of times to come if we couldn't bridge the gap between us, and I would have done anything to avoid the resulting emptiness. The impending loss was a rancid cancer growing in the pit of my stomach.

I couldn't escape the feeling.

Without Kane in my life, the world around me faded to gray. I couldn't go back to my life before and just pretend he didn't exist. He'd impacted my world in a way I couldn't undo. I'd given him a piece of my heart, and the only way to feel whole was to be with him.

For the first time, I considered breaking from my family.

Bitter tears drained down the back of my throat. I hated all my options, each worse than the last. By fourth period, I was wallowing in a pool of hopelessness so deep I almost missed the office aide come for Reyna.

"What did he say?" I whispered to Rey.

She sat perfectly still, her face as pale as the whiteboard at the front of the class. "He said my dad is waiting for me in the office." Her response was robotic, as though fear had overtaxed her system and caused a total shutdown. My sweet friend was utterly terrified.

I discarded my own petty problems.

"Get your things, let's go," I hissed.

She followed my instructions in a haze. We both stood at the same time, hefting our backpacks over our shoulders.

"Miss Genovese, I don't believe your presence was requested," our teacher warned as we walked toward the door.

"I'm sorry, Mr. Donovan. I have to help Reyna." I shot my parting words over my shoulder, not giving him time to argue.

I shut the classroom door behind us, and we rushed down the hall in the opposite direction of the office.

"Where are you going?" Rey asked breathlessly as we ran.

"We're getting out of here. Your father is *not* getting his hands on you." My instincts took me to the back door that led to the unattached gymnasium building. I paused at the door to give us a chance to catch our breath. "We're going to run."

"We?" Reyna's entire body shook like a leaf.

"Yes, *we*. I'm not leaving you. Now get your phone out of your bag and anything else you want to take with you. Our backpacks will only slow us down."

"He'll just track me with it." She dropped her bag, leaving its entire contents behind.

I clasped my phone in my hand and tossed my bag next to hers. "We're going to do our best to run yet stay hidden. All you have to do is follow me."

"Where are we going to go?" Her voice pitched with panic.

I took her hand in mine and squeezed. "We'll go to Kane's. He can keep you safe." Then I threw open the door and ran.

CHAPTER 33
Kane

"You told me you work for Javier, but I still don't know your name."

"It's Santino," he said just before whipping into a parking spot at the front of Xavier Catholic School.

We both jumped from the car and jogged to the entrance. I was living about a mile from the school, so we were there in under two minutes. I led the charge into the office, finding the school secretary at her desk.

"Mrs. Kennedy, I need you to call Reyna Vargas to the front office."

"Kane? Shouldn't you be in class?" Her eyes darted back and forth between Santino and me uneasily.

I extended my badge toward her. "I know this is a lot to take in, but I was actually undercover here at the school. I'm not actually a student. Reyna is in danger, and we need to get her to safety."

She stood on shaky legs. "Um … in danger? I can't just …" She bent to her phone, hitting the intercom button. "Principal Ruiz, can you come back to the office, please? It's an emergency."

We stood for five excruciating minutes while we waited for the principal to return. Her eyes narrowed on me the second she walked through the door.

"Mr. Easton, what's going on here?" She put a hand on her hip and glared.

I walked through my explanation again, noting her irritation spike at the news that I'd been undercover at her school without her permission. I breezed past that part because it wasn't important. "Reyna is in grave danger from her father. We need to get her to safety immediately."

Principal Ruiz and the secretary exchanged a worried look.

"Mr. Vargas was here just about ten minutes ago to get his daughter, but she didn't come when we called her. I was just in the classroom trying to figure out what had happened. Her teacher said she and Valentina Genovese left class when Reyna was summoned, but neither showed up in the office."

"Both girls?"

"Yes, Valentina seems to be missing as well. I was just going to give her family a call."

"And as far as you know, the girls didn't leave with Vargas?"

"Not that I saw. When they didn't come to the office, I told him I'd go have a look, but he left without waiting."

The terror that knotted my stomach when she said Vargas had already been there eased just a touch. The girls had left the school on foot to run from Vargas. They couldn't be far, but he had a head start looking for them.

"Okay, thank you for your help. You have my cell number in my file. Call me if there are any developments."

Santino and I both pulled out our phones as we walked back outside. I called Val's number only to be sent to voicemail. Why the fuck wasn't she answering? Panic slithered under my skin, threatening to hijack my thoughts. I had to stay calm, or I'd be of no use to the girls.

"I'm at the school with the cop," Santino spoke into his phone. My teeth ground together at his patronizing description of my job—federal agents were nothing like cops—but I swallowed my rebuke and allowed him to continue his conversation. "Vargas was here already, and the girls are on the run … okay." He hung up after only a few words.

"Javier?" I asked.

"Yeah, he's calling Edoardo Genovese and will call me back."

I made a quick call to keep Rizzo informed, hanging up just as Santino's phone rang. He listened briefly, then locked eyes with me. "They're at 5623 Mockingbird?"

My house. The girls had gone looking for me.

"That's his house," he confirmed. "Yeah, okay."

One minute later, we screeched to a halt along the street next to my house. We got out and scanned the area, unable to see any sign of the girls. Seconds later, two cars pulled up at the house. Edoardo Genovese, consigliere of the Lucciano family, exited a vehicle with Javier in tow while four other men stood next to the second car.

"There's no sign of them, but we haven't gone around back," Santino updated Javier.

"Could they have gotten inside?" Edoardo asked.

I shook my head. "Not unless they broke in, and I haven't seen any signs of that. We could—" I stopped when Edoardo held up his hand.

"Let's make this easy." He pulled out his phone and tapped at it before gesturing toward the house. "They're one street over. Must have kept moving when they couldn't find you. Let's go."

Come on, Val. Where the fuck are you?

Back in Afghanistan, I'd participated in any number of dangerous missions. An undercurrent of adrenaline and a healthy dose of fear were to be expected, but I'd never experienced desperation like I did when trying to track down Val and Reyna. We continued to be one step behind them, and I was certain we weren't the only hunters on their trail.

We all hurried back to our cars. Santino and I jumped in with Edoardo since they were the ones with GPS on Valentina. Javi drove us one block over then parked on the curb with our backup behind us. At the exact same time, two cars coming from the opposite direction stopped along the same curb facing us some fifty feet down the road. Vargas. We'd found the girls, but so had he.

Stuck between the two factions, the girls peeked out from behind the large trunk of an oak tree in front of a white colonial house.

At first, no one moved. The trees swayed in the midday breeze, and small clouds passed overhead, but the rest of us were frozen in uncertainty until Juan Carlos Vargas opened the door of his car. Needing to stay ready, we all cracked open the doors on our vehicles. Men in all four cars hid behind open doors, weapons ready.

"Why don't we all calm down, yes?" Vargas called out. "I only want my daughter, and I'd say you want the same, Edoardo. Let's let the girls walk to their respective families, and no one gets harmed."

"There's no fucking way," Santino spat quietly. "We can't just let him have her."

"We can't endanger both of them to keep his own daughter from him." I respected Santino's feelings for Reyna, but I'd be damned if I was going to let Val be injured or worse to save someone else. It might have been selfish, but I had my priorities. Valentina was everything.

"Enough," Javier shot back with a stern glare.

Just then, Valentina's voice carried from behind the tree. "Reyna's staying with me. She's not going back to Mexico."

Fucking shit.

I understood her need to protect Reyna, but I didn't want her to be hurt trying to be a hero. Vargas was Reyna's father. Even under New York law, he'd have a right to his daughter unless those rights had been limited by a court.

"Edoardo," called Vargas, his voice growing tighter. "You need to talk some fucking sense into your daughter."

"I can call for backup," I quickly offered. "The locals could be here in minutes."

"No," Edoardo barked. "We handle this on our own. You have a problem with that, you can leave. Besides, I have an idea." He opened his phone and began to type.

CHAPTER 34
Valentina

"Valentina, *look* at me." Dad's voice resonated off the house behind me.

Edoardo Genovese had a strict side that could make grown men cry. The only person I'd ever known to be somewhat immune was Giada. Even in the middle of a shoot-out, I wasn't about to ignore him when he commanded my attention, no matter how much I hated to hear what he was about to say. I was terrified for Reyna. Adrenaline helped keep my mind focused, but every time I caught sight of my shaking friend, despair clutched tighter around my throat.

"I need to switch places with you, honey," I whispered to Rey.

She nodded jerkily, eyes vacantly staring at the white house behind us. I'd been keeping my eyes glued to the cartel since they were the only real threat to us. Peeking out from the other side of the tree, I could see where my dad was crouched behind the passenger door of a black sedan. He was parallel enough to me that I could see his hand extend behind him where he shook his phone. The men in the cartel cars wouldn't have been able to see his gesture. He was trying to tell me to look at my phone.

Motherfucker. I'd left the damn thing on silent.

"I know you care for your friend," Dad continued, "but it is not our place to keep her from her father."

I pulled my phone out of my back pocket, where I'd stashed it while we were running. There'd been little point in calling Kane to let him know we were coming, and he lived close enough to the school that asking him to come get us would have taken longer than simply running. When we discovered he wasn't home, I decided it would be safest to get to my house. We cut through Kane's backyard and the yard behind that, only making it two houses down before the cars converged on us. I'd been too preoccupied to even think of my phone.

"You hear me, Valentina? It's time to go home and let Reyna do the same." Dad continued with his speech, but I wasn't listening. His text was the real message.

Dad: Give Reyna your watch and tell her to keep it on at all times. We will get her back, but this is not the time. Trust me, please.

My watch? Holy shit! Had Dad put a tracking device in my watch?

I studied Reyna and prayed this was the right thing to do. I hated to turn her over, but I couldn't imagine another way out of the situation. Her father wasn't leaving without his daughter. And while my dad might have been stern, he was also a man of his word. If he said we'd get her back, I had to trust him.

"Okay, just give me a second!" I hollered, making sure Vargas could hear me as well. I unclasped the watch and grabbed Reyna's hand. "Rey, listen to me," I whispered. "My dad has a plan. You're going to go back with your dad, but this watch has a tracking device. You keep it on you no matter what, and we're going to come for you. I promise. I am *not* abandoning you. Okay?"

Rey's face crumpled, tears streaking down her cheeks as she nodded. Even in her darkest moment, her strength was unparalleled. My heart screamed and raged against the unfairness of her situation. How could such purity be subjected to such torment? I wanted to cry along with her, but I did my best to stay strong. Reyna needed to be enveloped in my confidence so that she'd have something to rely upon once I was no longer with her.

I wrapped her in my arms and squeezed. "Stay strong, honey, and remember you're not alone."

We pulled apart and gave one last lingering look before emerging from our hiding spot. Our backs to one another, we walked simultaneously to our respective families.

Please, God. Please don't let him hurt her before we can get her back.

With each step I took, the unbearable weight of sorrow compressed my chest until I could hardly breathe. When I realized Kane was tucked behind the back-seat door of my father's car, my feet stumbled forward in a rush to get to him. He somehow managed to swoop me in his arms while easing us inside the car to safety. I clung to him tightly as sobs emerged, the comfort I derived from his presence allowing my fear to surface.

"Please, Daddy. Please get her back," I cried, searching through my tears for the front seat.

"Shh, try to calm down." He spoke without taking his eyes from his enemy. "We can discuss everything back at the house."

Fifty feet away, Vargas scowled at Reyna as she slinked into the back of his car. He didn't even try to hide his fury.

More sobs wracked my body. Guilt and worry formed a putrid cocktail of remorse in my belly. I was headed home to a house full of people who loved me while Reyna was about to face a host of untold horrors. No matter how hard I'd tried, I hadn't been able to save her.

I sat helplessly on Kane's lap with Santino next to us on the silent ride home. When we reached our house, Kane tucked me protectively against his body on our walk from the car to the door. My mother met us at the entry, sweeping me into her open arms.

"My baby. I'm so glad you're safe." Her voice was breathless with emotion.

I gave her a moment to reassure herself I was whole, then sought out my father. "What are you going to do, Daddy? Please don't leave her with him for long. He hurts her. He's such a horrible man."

Dad nodded toward the living room. "Let's sit down and talk. We'll make our move on him tonight, but there's plenty to discuss first."

I nodded and started to walk before pausing to find Kane behind me.

He cradled my face gently and placed a kiss on my forehead. "You go talk to your dad. I need to make a call anyway."

It suddenly hit me that Kane was at my house. He'd come to my rescue with my father and just kissed me in front of my family. Had I entered some kind of alternate universe? Was this all a twisted dream I couldn't escape? My emotionally traumatized brain couldn't seem to process the situation. I opened my mouth, but no sound emerged as my eyes darted to my father's retreating form before returning to Kane.

"It surprised me too. Go talk to your dad; I'm sure he'll explain."

I followed Kane's instructions in a haze, sitting on the loveseat next to my mom. Seeing Kane with my dad triggered an avalanche of questions. How had my father known to come looking for us? Had he known about Reyna? How long? What was up with that watch? Was there anything my dad *didn't* already know?

"I see the questions darting around your head like machine-gun fire," my father mused. "Let's start from the beginning, though." He poured himself a drink before taking his usual place in the wingback armchair. "Back in December when we discovered that Juan Carlos was in the city and living so close to us, we learned everything we could about him and uncovered that his daughter was going to Xavier. I wasn't naïve enough to think that was a coincidence. We debated pulling you from school or having Principal Ruiz remove Reyna, but we held off for several reasons. For one, I knew you'd grown close, and the backlash I'd endure if we separated you would only make my problems more complicated. But even more importantly, keeping Reyna close provided us with a backup plan should Vargas continue to be a problem."

He'd known.

My dad had known about Reyna all along. Little gears in my head rattled and popped off their bearings, steam pouring from misfiring cranks. My brain was imploding.

"You *knew*? And you let me stay friends with her even though it was dangerous?" It wasn't an accusation. I simply couldn't comprehend how my overbearing father could be capable of such a risk.

The tiniest hint of a smirk teased the corner of my father's lips. "We hired security." Dad glanced at Javi. "Viper Operations has been tracking you night and day, ensuring your safety. If you left the house, their monitoring equipment alerted them. You were never without a set of eyes protecting you, aside from your time at school."

Viper 10k weekly.

The note in my father's desk. Viper was Javier. Dad had been paying them to keep me safe.

I gaped at Javier and Santino. "The party. You were there watching Reyna. And the dance..."

Santino's head moved side to side. "No, I was there watching *you*."

I sought out my dad, struggling to put all the pieces together. "And the watch?"

"In the past, I relied on the GPS from your phones to keep track of you girls. After Giada's and Camilla's incidents, I decided to get you each a piece of jewelry outfitted with

GPS so that if you were separated from your phones, I could still trace you."

"Why didn't you tell me?" The second the words were out, my lips thinned sheepishly. If I'd known I was being tracked, I would have made sure not to wear the watch when sneaking out—times when I would have been most vulnerable.

"We've tried very hard, despite how it may have felt, to let you three live your lives without us looking over your shoulders. It hasn't been easy to balance your safety with good parenting, let me tell you." Dad's eyes flitted to my mom's in an uncharacteristically touching moment. They didn't dote on each other around us, but I could feel their unity in the exchange of glances.

They'd known each time I'd snuck out. Mom had likely waited up for me to come home, worrying herself sick, but they'd let me do it anyway. They'd known about Reyna and our friendship. They'd known about everything.

"Did Javier tell you I was trying to help Reyna escape?" I glanced at Javi, but his face was inscrutable.

"Yes, and I'm afraid the delay in getting her papers was my fault. If we produced her documents and helped her get away, we'd still have been able to track her, but I was concerned we would need her here to finish things with Juan Carlos. That may seem selfish to you, but he was a threat to more people than just his daughter."

My gaze trailed back to Javier, who stared back at me in challenge as if to say, "Just try to be upset with me."

I rolled my eyes.

He never made me any promises of confidentiality, so I couldn't entirely blame him, but I would remember his duplicity. I'd also remember my father's generosity and the respect he showed me in letting me live my life. His actions gave me the confidence to consider being more forthright in the future. If I had faith in his ability not to overreact, maybe we could forge a bond worthy of a father-daughter relationship.

If there was anything that would test that theory, it was Kane.

My hands clutched each other in my lap. "How long have you known about Kane?"

Dad raised a brow. "Javier came to me after you gave him those plates to run. He kept me informed on your little ... charade." He glanced down momentarily before meeting my gaze. "I have to say, I'm not sure I've ever been so fucking proud." My dad, the consummate businessman, nearly lost his voice with emotion.

Tears flooded my eyes. "I wanted to tell you, but I was scared you'd hurt him."

Dad scoffed. "I wouldn't hurt a federal agent. He couldn't get any information from you, and he had the power to lock up Vargas and get him out of our hair. It was a win-win for us." His eyes darkened then, and his lips thinned. "But it seems there was one aspect of all of this we hadn't accounted for. You have feelings for Kane, don't you?"

The first time I opened my mouth, nothing came out. Images of my father's face contorted with rage, and disappointment filled my head, choking off my words. When I did finally get use of my throat, even I was surprised at my broken plea. "I think I love him, Daddy."

I peered over at my mom when her hand came down gently over my own. The love shining in her eyes sparked a flicker of hope that my relationship with Kane wasn't totally doomed, but my father would be the real test.

"It's not an easy situation," Dad offered cryptically. He hadn't exploded in anger, but he didn't look pleased either. "What I will say is that I do believe he also cares for you a great deal. Your safety was his only priority today."

"He's a good man. More like you than you could imagine." I tried to smile, but it came out shaky and lopsided.

Dad huffed. "Well, we can deal with that … situation after we take care of Vargas and rescue Reyna."

"I wasn't sure you'd help her and risk upsetting her father."

"I wouldn't have if we didn't have a lock on him. If we take him out while we rescue her, retribution won't be an issue. I wouldn't open my family up to the risk presented by hiding Reyna if Vargas was at large. Now, it's about time we put together a plan. I doubt he'll stay in the country long." He looked at Javier. "Call Filip and tell him to gather a dozen men. We need everyone here in the next hour but discreetly. If Vargas is monitoring my house, I don't want him to see us converging."

Kane joined us in the living room, but only briefly to inform my father he was going to gather supplies. I went up to my room to shower. When I came back down, my father and his men were sequestered in his office with the door closed. I desperately wanted to know what was going on, but my nosiness would have only gotten in their way. My father's unexpected leniency toward me wouldn't go so far as to allow me to participate in their raid. I was certain of that.

While they planned, I paced in my room or helped Mom in the kitchen. She asked me about Kane, which distracted me to a small degree. Mostly, I was a festering ball of anxiety, terrified for Reyna. Had her father beaten her? Was she even still alive? Would Dad be able to rescue her, or had her father seen the watch and made her remove it?

I lifted my teary eyes heavenward and said a silent prayer. *Hold on, Rey. We're coming for you.*

CHAPTER 35
Reyna

A SHARP PAIN IN MY FACE DREW ME HARSHLY FROM THE SOLACE of sleep. I touched my tender cheek as reality assaulted me in flashes—the terrifying car ride with my father; his demonic glare just before his fist cracked against my cheek; the feral hiss of his last words to me.

Get out of my sight before I slit your fucking throat.

Despite years of witnessing my father's heartlessness, I was stunned. I'd never heard the promise of such animalistic violence in his words before. He'd been genuinely close to killing me.

The truth of my situation brought on a suffocating despair.

I couldn't continue to live like this.

For the first time ever, the darkest of impulses whispered at the back of my mind. An option for escape that I'd never been low enough to truly consider, but now ... if Valentina couldn't rescue me, what choice did I have?

No.

I refused to give up hope for another solution. As long as I breathed, there was still hope.

I lay awake and stared at the moonlit ceiling of the room I occupied in an unknown house, miles from home. Miles from Val and her family. The only thing keeping me from feeling utterly alone was the watch silently ticking at my wrist. For once, it was a godsend that my father didn't know me well enough to keep track of my jewelry. He surely would have noticed the exquisite new accessory circling my wrist if he'd paid any attention at all.

As I lay in my borrowed bed, a visceral awareness crept along my skin—an ancient warning system telling me to stay alert. My heart jumped to a gallop in my chest as I peered around the room and discovered a silhouetted figure sitting in the chair by the window.

Panic surged through my veins like a flooded river.

"I've been sitting here for hours trying to comprehend how my own flesh and blood could betray me." My father's voice filled the room with an eerie menace.

I frantically debated whether to deny his claim because it would just make him angrier. My indecision paralyzed me, relieving me of the choice. Trying to strategize was impossible when fear dug its claws deep into my belly.

"I got word that you were talking to the feds. The *fucking feds.*" His anger spewed out in the form of disgusting spittle. "I had to leave important matters behind to race up here before you disappeared. After everything I've done for you. Tutors. A luxury lifestyle. I've given you *everything*, and you go and sink a knife in my fucking back." At the apex of his speech, he pounded his fist over his chest as his voice boomed with outrage.

Tears poured down my cheeks. In all my years, I'd never seen him this angry. Even when the mafia confronted him back in December, he'd been more inconvenienced than angry. This was something else. Juan Carlos Vargas was livid. He'd taken my actions personally, and deep down, I knew I wouldn't survive his wrath. Not when his eyes lit with such loathing and his words lashed with repugnance. My father had no tolerance for traitors. Had I known that he'd learned about Kane offering me federal protection, I never would have willingly returned to my father's custody.

Despite the dim lighting and the tears blurring my vision, I could see the gun my father clasped in his right hand as he stood.

This was it.

My usefulness to him had been nullified by my treachery. I was nothing to him but another enemy to put in the ground.

I tried to stifle my whimpering cries as I scooted off the bed away from him and plastered myself against the wall. My survival instincts had taken over, urging me to run. Logic dictated my chances of escape were zero, but I had to try. I wasn't ready to die.

"Please, Papá. Please don't do this." I hadn't called him Papá since I was a little girl. The word held no sentiment to me now—it was purely a tool I'd employed to keep myself alive. Something that poured from my lips out of desperate necessity.

"Why not? What use could I possibly have for a treacherous *whore*? Your mother may be worthless, but at least she's loyal."

"Because I'm your daughter—"

"You're nobody's daughter," he growled, hatred glowing in his eyes.

"I can get information about the Genoveses. I can ... I can still be useful. I can ..." My breathing hiccupped, cutting off my rambling plea. I detested my pathetic groveling, but I didn't want to die. I'd tell my father anything he wanted to hear if it kept me alive for a few minutes longer.

It didn't matter anyway. My tear-filled pleas meant nothing to him.

Juan Carlos Vargas aimed his gun at his only daughter without a trace of remorse.

My face crumpled with grief as I prayed for the bullet to take me quickly. *Please don't think this was your fault, Val. You did everything you could.* My thoughts wouldn't reach her, but it was all I had. Valentina was the one person who had tried to help me, and I didn't want her to carry the guilt of my death. I was just sorry I would never see her again.

As my eyes drifted shut, my heart lurched and seized when a sound tore through the silence blanketing the house, but it wasn't the blast of a gun. Lungs frozen in shock, I opened my eyes and ears to figure out what had happened.

My father still stood with his gun lifted, but it was now aimed at the empty doorway. He'd heard it too. A thump. The distinct sound of something heavy falling to the floor. Something like a body.

I slowly swiveled my gaze over to the dark doorway a handful of feet away from me.

Time stretched thin like a drip of molasses seeping from a tree.

Could this be my rescue? Was my father about to kill whoever was trying to save me? Was I willing to let someone die for my safety? Could I stop whatever was about to transpire even if I wanted to?

I had no time to answer the rapid-fire questions before a familiar form filled the doorway. How many times had I seen that figure watching me from the shadows? Not as many times as I'd seen him in my dreams. I would have recognized that iron stance anywhere.

Santino had come for me, and my father's bullet would be his only reward.

CHAPTER 36
Santino

ARMED WITH GEAR PROVIDED BY KANE AND OUR OWN unregistered weapons he pointedly ignored, we piled into cars and made the drive to the north side of Staten Island, where GPS indicated Reyna had been taken. I was surprised Kane had volunteered to be a part of the mission at all. What we were doing wasn't exactly legal, but then again, Vargas' treatment of his own daughter wasn't legal either. I respected that Kane was willing to put his life and career on the line for what was right, regardless of the red tape. His participation was appreciated by every one of us, especially since he had tactical experience as we'd learned through extensive questioning by Edoardo.

Kane devised a plan with little argument from the rest of us. We used Google Earth to assess the property, noting it was a two-story house about four thousand square feet in size. We formed three groups—one to hold the property at a distance and two others for covert entry of the premises. It was a safe assumption that Reyna would be stashed in an upstairs bedroom. I offered to lead entry to the front of the house with the intent of heading directly upstairs. Javier assumed command of the team entering from the back. Kane offered to follow one of us, but Edoardo suggested he stay outside with the backup to keep his hands clean. Kane didn't look thrilled with the assignment, but he didn't argue.

The worst part was the waiting. We needed the element of surprise to minimize our own risk, which meant striking late at night when Vargas and his men would be asleep. Each minute that ticked by while I sat helplessly stretched endlessly into eternity. My entire body twitched with the need to get to Reyna. If we got to that house and discovered she'd been hurt, I would spend my last breath making sure Vargas paid with his life. I didn't even care if I died in the process. Avenging her would be worth the price.

It took all my self-control to remain outwardly composed so Javier didn't strip me of my lead role. If he'd had any doubt in my ability to think clearly, he would have had no qualms leaving me behind, no matter how invested I was in the outcome.

If there was anything about the situation to be thankful for, it was that Vargas hadn't taken Reyna to his home, which was outfitted with stronger security. He had probably thought staying at a secret location would be safer, not anticipating that we could track his location. In theory, we would enter the premises undetected, take out the opposition before they had time to rally a defense, get Reyna and leave—all within a matter of minutes.

By the time we arrived in the neighborhood at just after midnight, I'd run through countless scenarios in my head and was ready for the real thing. We converged on the house from all directions, parking our vehicles on the surrounding blocks and moving on foot to decrease the risk of detection. The middle-class neighborhood was fast asleep. Streetlights gave the false assurance of safety to the hardworking families who were clueless that a ruthless animal had taken refuge among them.

I led my team of five through the shadows in well-kept yards until we reached the front steps of Vargas' safe house. Once we were in place, I used the earpiece provided by Kane to check in with the others and coordinate our entry.

We had decided it would be best to pick the locks and maintain our advantage for as long as possible. If an alarm was triggered, we'd charge in with guns raised, but if that wasn't necessary, we preferred stealth to chaos.

Luck was on our side. The damn house didn't even have an alarm.

Front and back doors penetrated, we moved in like locusts, laying siege to everything in our path. I directed one of my men to take care of a guard snoring on the living room sofa while I headed for the stairs. My heart pounded ruthlessly in my chest as I finally closed in on where I prayed I'd find Reyna safe and whole.

Just as I reached the top landing, a man popped his head around the corner as if to investigate a noise. I had my hand over his mouth and a knife across his throat before he ever made a sound. I allowed my knife to fall with him to the floor, taking my gun in hand and moving silently to the next doorway. Unlike the other rooms upstairs, this door was open.

I took a steadying breath and stepped into the doorway. What I found brought my mind into perfect focus, a purposeful sense of clarity settling over me.

Vargas stood across the room, his gun already raised in my direction, and madness rounding his eyes. A rumpled bed lay between us, and from the periphery of my vision, I detected Reyna standing just a few feet to my right.

We'd done it.

Reyna was still alive, and as long as her father's gun was pointed at me, she was safe.

"*No!*" Reyna cried when she saw me.

Vargas impaled her with a vicious glare. "No? This is all your fault, you fucking *cunt*," he hissed. "You can't cry about this when you're the reason we're in this situation."

The Vargas brothers had been twenty years apart in age and shared little in common except for their tempers. I'd been witness to the savage brutality inflicted by the elder Vargas when his anger flared. Juan Carlos was no different.

His rage was a sickness polluting his mind.

With no other warning, Vargas turned his aim at Reyna, his teeth gritted with mindless rage. His entire body telegraphed his need to kill her from his rabid snarl to the way he ignored my presence completely. All that mattered to him in that second was punishing the person he blamed for his downfall. An innocent woman whose only crime was seeking freedom from tyranny.

I didn't have to see him pull the trigger to know the bullet was coming.

I leapt into the air without reservation, flinging myself sideways. At the same moment, a shot exploded in the quiet night air. Pain barreled into my chest as I pulled the trigger of my own weapon, sending a second shot screaming through the air an instant after the first.

The force of Vargas' shot and my own gun's ricochet sent me flying backward into Reyna, but I didn't take my eyes from Vargas until I confirmed that my aim had been true.

Juan Carlos Vargas' head flew backward, his brains splattering across the window behind him. Only once I was sure he was dead did the agony in my chest register. My lungs were compressed tightly and unable to fill with needed oxygen. Darkness threatened to take me under, but the sight of Reyna above me gave me a reason to fight for consciousness.

She sobbed hysterically, her fear for me shredding her to pieces. "*Nonononono*..." she chanted over and over.

I clutched her shaking hand and drew her eyes to mine. "It's okay ... princesa," I wheezed. "I'm okay." I placed her hand flat against my chest where a Kevlar vest had stopped the bullet. It hurt like a son of a bitch, and I might have a broken rib or two, but I would survive.

Her breathing stalled as her hands flitted over the armor plating between us, then she lowered her face to the crook of my neck and sobbed tears of relief.

Wincing against the pain, I pulled her into my side and cradled her against me. Having her close helped me relax enough to coax air into my lungs.

"You're safe, princesa. I'll never let anyone take you from me again." They were words I meant to live by until my dying breath. I tapped my earpiece to activate communications. "Reyna is secure. Vargas is dead."

"Downstairs is secure," Javier's voice noted in my ear.

"No sign of life outside," added Kane. "Think you guys got them all."

"Thank fuck," I wheezed. "We're coming down." I met Reyna's eyes and tried my best at a thin smile. "If you'll help me up, we can get the hell out of here."

My beautiful princess grinned through her tears like a rainbow after the storm.

Getting to my feet hurt like a bitch. I held Reyna close, but that was more to reassure myself of her safety than out of my need for support. We eased down the stairs and made for the front door after briefly acknowledging Javier standing over a pair of bodies. Once the cool evening air brushed our faces, Reyna slowed and began to chew her bottom lip.

"What's wrong?" I asked.

Her eyes refused to meet mine. "I don't know where I'm supposed to go now. I don't have a home anymore."

"Tonight, you're staying with me. I'll sleep on the couch if it means I have you close and know you're safe. After that, we'll talk with the others and get you situated, but you don't ever have to worry about not having a place to go. I will *always* be your home if you need me." I shut my mind to the pain and leaned over to place my lips on hers. Our kiss was raw and vulnerable, a testament of devotion tinged with the salt of newly fallen tears. Tears of joy and relief and new beginnings.

CHAPTER 37
Kane

IF SOMEONE HAD TOLD ME BEFORE I'D STEPPED FOOT IN Xavier High that my life would be unrecognizable three months later, I never would have believed them. I certainly never would have imagined the upheaval would be a result of my own intentional actions or that I'd have zero regrets.

I'd done the right thing by helping rescue Reyna, which was what I told Rizzo when he called me on our way back to the Genovese house. The local police precinct I'd demanded supplies from had woken my boss at home when they called to verify my credentials after I'd left. Word had gotten to Rizzo, and he was beyond pissed.

"You walked into the 122nd precinct and implied you

were there under DEA instructions, pilfered their gear, then raided a cartel stronghold without prior approval?" His incredulity diluted his anger but only by a degree.

"I told you. He had a hostage, and her life was in danger."

I could almost hear his face turning a ripe shade of plum. "You fucking know that's not how we do things. I told you when you called earlier that you did *not* have authority to go after Vargas."

"I know, Riz." I sighed. "That's why I'm gonna make this easy for you. I'll hand in my badge in the morning." I had my own reasons for leaving the agency, the least of which was my firm belief that what we'd done had been necessary.

"Shit, Kane. You know I don't want you to quit." The anger drained from his voice.

"I appreciate that, but it's best for both of us. Trust me." I glanced up in the rearview when I sensed Javier's eyes on me while he drove. I would have preferred a private conversation, but maybe it was best Val's family heard where I stood.

"Whatever, kid. You come in tomorrow, and we'll talk."

"Sure, Rizzo. See you then." We'd talk, but nothing he could say would change my mind. I hung up and leaned my head back against the leather seat.

"You gonna follow through with that?" Edoardo asked from the front passenger seat. He'd come along on the mission in case he was needed but had stayed in the car.

"I am."

"My daughter have anything to do with that decision?" He turned and met my stare.

"She has everything to do with it."

His lips pursed. "You know my organization doesn't permit outsiders, right?"

Ah, so that was where this was going. "No need to worry. I hadn't planned to hit you up for a job."

"So, what exactly is your plan?"

My teeth ground together. "I don't have one at the moment, but that's never stopped me before."

Edoardo's eyes cut over to Javier, the two exchanging a look before he addressed me again. "You ever considered the security business?"

Javier put the car in park after pulling up at the Genovese house, then met my eyes again in the rearview. "If you're going to stick around, you'd be perfect for our line of work."

"I'm not going anywhere." I had considered security but hadn't wanted to get stuck working as a glorified bouncer. Working with Javier would be different. Something told me his brand of security would never be boring.

A glint flashed in his eyes. If I was any judge, I'd have said that was as close to a smile as I was going to get. I had a feeling Javier's approval was the best damn compliment I could get.

"If that's all sorted, I'm going to bed," grumbled Edoardo. "I'm getting too old for this shit." He stepped out of the car, and I quickly followed suit.

"Excuse me, Mr. Genovese," I called after him. "I was going to head home, but I'd like to let Valentina know Reyna is okay. Would it be alright if I went upstairs for a minute?"

He peered back at me, lifting his chin a fraction. "Five minutes, and you make sure you remember whose roof you're under."

I had to fight a grin.

Val was just like her father. I could only imagine the battles they'd probably had over the years.

I followed him inside and quietly made my way upstairs.

A soft patch of light filtered from the first door on the right. When I poked my head in, I found my girl asleep, propped up in her bed on a mountain of pillows. She hadn't changed her clothes and still had her phone clutched in her hand. I had no doubt she'd been worried sick and had fought to stay awake as long as she could. After her own traumatic scare earlier in the day, she'd been unable to withstand her body's need for rest.

Her eyes fluttered open the second I sat on the edge of the bed. "Oh, God. You're okay." Val flung herself at me, wrapping her arms tight around my neck. Her chest heaved against mine with broken breaths of relief.

"Shh, baby. It's okay. Reyna's safe, and everything's okay now." I rubbed my hand against her back until she relaxed her hold and her breathing evened.

When she pulled back, her face was still drawn in pain. "Did my dad send you up to say goodbye?" More tears filled her eyes.

I shook my head.

Her brows drew together in confusion. "Does he know you're up here?"

I nodded. "He sent me up, but just to say good night and let you know we were all safe." I ran my thumb under her eye to swipe at a tear. "I told my boss I was leaving."

Valentina's jaw hinged wide. "You what?"

"I'm done. You will always be more important than any job. I'd already come to that realization but seeing you in danger today and facing the fact that I could have lost you made it all that much more real. You're it for me, beautiful girl. You sucked me into your orbit, and now, I couldn't imagine a life without you. I love you, Valentina Genovese—from those quicksilver eyes of yours to the tips of your toes and every molecule between. I love every damn piece of you, forever and always."

Val flung herself at me all over again, but this time in a kiss that obliterated all others. She straddled my lap as if needing to fuse our bodies together and gave me her soul with the touch of her lips.

"I love you, too, baby." She continued to pepper me with kisses, smiling throughout.

I chuckled, squeezing her warmly in my lap. "We'll have to continue this later if you want me to survive the night. Your father gave strict instructions."

"Will I see you tomorrow?"

I slipped my hand around the back of her neck and pulled her in for one last lingering kiss. "Tomorrow and every day after. I'm yours, baby girl, and nothing's going to change that."

EPILOGUE
Valentina

TWO MONTHS LATER

"All ready?" I joined Rey in her room—the room that had been Giada's childhood bedroom before Reyna moved in—and plopped onto the bed. After Reyna's father was no longer an issue, my parents happily insisted that Rey stay with us while she finished school. I hadn't even realized how much I'd missed having my sisters around until I had Rey there with me every day. I adored having her so close. We'd even made plans to get an apartment together in the summer.

"Yeah, I just need to touch up my lipstick."

"That necklace is gorgeous. Have you worn it before?" A delicate pendant with three radiant emeralds hung from a thin gold chain around her neck.

She touched the pendant gently. "It's my mom's. She has a ton of jewelry, but this was one of the few things I remember her wearing back when I was little and we were close. It's my birthstone. I think my dad gave it to her, but I don't care so much about that. Mostly, it's a reminder of the good times."

"I'm sorry she couldn't be with us tonight."

"It's okay. I'd much rather her stay where she is and get healthy." Reyna was cautiously optimistic for her mom, who had been admitted into a ninety-day rehab facility. My dad and his men had gone to the Vargas house the day after the raid and retrieved Reyna's belongings, including a teddy bear stuffed with thousands of dollars. While they were there, they gave her mother the choice of rehab or going back to Mexico. She'd chosen rehab, much to Reyna's relief. The two had started talking over the phone early into the program. Her mom had done well, but years of mistrust would be difficult to overcome. Reyna wasn't about to forget how her mother had abandoned her to an alcoholic haze.

"Well, the necklace looks perfect on you. And I love what you did with your hair."

"I'm not sure why I spent time on it. The cap will just smoosh it."

A giddy grin spread across my face. "Graduating is *totally* worth a bad hair day." Now that I'd been accepted into the NYU music program, I had a new enthusiasm for college. Kane spent weeks wearing me down about pursuing my music. First, he had me read about music programs, then he tricked me into touring the facility. While performances were a part of the curriculum, there weren't as many as I'd expected. It turned out, not everyone who studied music planned to play on a stage. Before I knew it, he'd convinced me to ask my NYU advisor if my acceptance to the school of business could be transferred to a different program. I'd had to do an interview and play for a panel of professors, but it was worth it when I received word that my transfer had been approved. I would never have had the courage without Kane supporting me. He'd even helped my stage fright by insisting I play for him frequently. He adored listening to me play, boosting my confidence more than I imagined possible.

"Yeah, yeah. Easy for you to say," Reyna teased. "You'd look good in tin foil and flip-flops."

I burst out laughing. "Come on, I'm sure the guys are already downstairs."

"Now that Kane is working with Javi and Santino, the three are practically inseparable." She was right. The guys had quickly become family, which worked great for double dates. Javier was a touch older and spent his free time in the city with Giada, but the rest of us spent almost every weekend together.

As suspected, we found the three guys in the living room with my father, each holding a crystal glass of scotch. Dad's face warmed when we appeared, the creases in the corners of his eyes deepening with pride.

"You two look absolutely beautiful," he said, walking over to kiss our cheeks. His hand traced over the watch I'd gotten back from Reyna and kept on at all times. I was happy to wear it and loved seeing the peace of mind it gave him. Not long after she came to live with us, Reyna had been given a similar watch of her own.

"Thanks, Daddy. You guys ready to head to the school?" Xavier's graduation was small enough to be hosted in the school auditorium. It wasn't fancy but considering it might be the last time I ever had reason to walk those halls, I was glad graduation would be in the same building where I'd grown up.

Santino put his arm around Reyna proudly. "Let's do this. I'm ready to see my girl cross that stage."

Reyna's grin filled my chest with happiness. Without the burdens she'd carried for so long, she'd spread her wings in the past months. I was getting used to the more lighthearted version of her but still paused to appreciate each of her unguarded smiles.

Mom took a thousand pictures of us. Together. Apart. With my sisters and then our boyfriends. We took pictures until my cheeks ached, then took a couple more. I was her last kid to fly the coop, so I dredged up all the patience I could muster, knowing she would be especially emotional.

Kane wore the suit he'd worn to the Valentine's dance. He was utterly delectable, only this time, he was all mine. His golden stare followed me throughout our photo shoot. The possessive touch of his gaze set my skin on fire and stirred a seductive heat deep in my belly. The form-fitting white dress I'd bought for the occasion made me feel confident, but it was Kane's molten desire that gave me wings.

Our cheering section rocked the building when we crossed the stage.

I felt so damn blessed.

The school hosted a small beer and wine celebration following the ceremony. After so many years of having kids at the school, my parents were friends with most of the faculty and fell into easy conversation. I found myself looking for Kane but couldn't spot him in the crowd. As my eyes scanned the room, I happened to catch Chloe snag Gio's tie and pull his lips to her in a scorching kiss.

My jaw dropped to the floor.

Where had that come from? I'd had no idea Chloe was even interested in Gio—they seemed so contradictory. She was feisty, even bordering on the demanding side, while he was chill to a fault. Judging by the panty-melting grin he gave her when they pulled apart, their differences weren't an issue for him. Maybe a better word for them was complementary.

The unusual flush coloring Chloe's cheeks indicated I was right. Graduation might be the start of more than one new adventure for those two.

Gio's gaze collided with mine. I grinned and shook my head playfully. He returned my grin with a wink, then focused back on his newest pursuit.

Wondering what had happened to my own date, I pulled out my phone to text Kane and discovered he'd already reached out.

Kane: Meet me in the music room.

A shiver danced down the length of my spine.

Me: On my way.

After ensuring my family was busy enough not to notice my absence, I slipped out of the auditorium. My heels echoed off the vacant hallway, so I took them off and silently walked down the main hall, shoes in hand. When I reached the music room, the door was cracked. I pushed it the rest of the way open to find Kane leaning against the grand piano, carnal desire dripping from his perfect form.

"How did you get in here?" I murmured, only half aware of the words tumbling from my tongue.

"Does it matter?" he mused. "Shut the door behind you." I did as he ordered, knowing the classroom doors locked automatically when shut. The small window was covered as always, ensuring our privacy, and Kane had cracked the supply closet door to allow a thin stream of light to filter into the room.

I dropped my shoes without taking my eyes from Kane and gave in to the seductive pull coaxing me toward him. "The others will come looking for us if we're gone for long."

"Then we'll be quick." He tugged me flush against him, drawing a gasp from between my lips.

In a heartbeat, he had my legs wrapped around his middle. He walked us around to the front of the instrument, where he set my bottom down on the keyboard cover. "This is how it should have been the last time we were here. This is how it always should have been and how it always will be." His lust-soaked voice was a velvet caress against my skin.

I answered with a kiss—my tongue sweeping over his as my heart was tenderly placed in his protective grasp.

Kane's hands slid between us and shredded the crotch of my silk thong.

I gasped, then giggled. "You know I didn't bring an extra pair."

He grinned. "I suppose you'll have to go to dinner without." His lids grew hooded as he undid his belt. "Are you ready for me, beautiful? Because all I could think about seeing you walk across that stage was pushing deep inside you."

All humor fled. I adored when Kane talked dirty. All it took was one filthy whisper, and my core wept for him. He'd been seducing me daily since our first time together. I'd gotten on birth control at the earliest opportunity and been an avid student of all his lessons.

When his thick cock pressed inside me, I drowned in pure bliss. My jaw dropped. My breathing shuddered. My clit throbbed. With just one touch from Kane, my body writhed.

"*God, yessss,*" I breathed.

Kane groaned, then launched himself into a punishing rhythm. Normally, he teased me incessantly, drawing out my orgasm until I was mindless with need, but today we were on a time crunch. Lucky for me, he knew just how to make my body sing. He slid two fingers on either side of my clit, gently pinching the bundle of nerves. The sudden intensity of his touch drove me quickly to the edge, but it was his words that tipped the scale.

"If I could, I'd fuck you night and day. My cock was made to be inside you." His deliciously dirty words brought my orgasm to a crescendo—a clattering, apocalyptic explosion of sensation. Kane grunted his release, his arms squeezing me as my inner muscles did the same to him. I reveled in the intoxicating release that transformed me into a gelatinous blob.

A lazy chuckle bubbled from my chest. "How am I supposed to make it through dinner now?"

Kane lifted his head from my neck and grinned. "You can thank me with a blow job later." There was the Kane I knew and loved.

I rolled my eyes with a smile. "Come on, stud. Let's go celebrate."

Dinner was fabulous. My parents rented out the back room of a small Italian place where we gathered with my cousins, their men, and my aunt and uncle. We drank wine and talked until almost midnight. The night was utterly perfect.

ONE WEEK LATER, I gathered with my parents and sisters for another family dinner with an entirely different dynamic. This time, the boyfriends stayed home, and we were all infinitely more nervous.

It was time to meet Connor.

Several schedule conflicts had prevented us from meeting sooner. The weeks of anticipation had built up to a manic state of anxiety, at least for me. Dad had grown increasingly withdrawn over the last week as the date drew closer. I couldn't blame him. Meeting Connor would forever change our family, even if only on a subconscious level.

I rode with Mom and Dad to the city where we met Camilla and Giada outside a restaurant called Neary's. Mom had said Connor suggested the place when my dad grimaced at its mention. It looked charming to me. A long green awning welcomed diners from the street, and the small brick front was well kept with little lanterns on either side of a pub-style window.

Once we were all together, we stepped inside as a family. The interior didn't look all that different from the mom-and-pop Italian places Dad loved to frequent, so I wasn't sure what his complaint was until my eyes landed on the large Irish flag on the side wall. I rolled my eyes, irritation crawling at my skin.

We are meeting a long-lost member of this family, and Dad is fussing about eating at an Irish pub?

Good grief.

Mom talked to the hostess, who led us to a table set up in the back corner. A red vinyl banquette extended the length of the wall, but a large chunk of space had been left between our table and the next. More space than there was between any of the other tables in the place. The separation gave the illusion of privacy, which was a welcome relief. We didn't need eavesdroppers on an already awkward evening.

Just as we took our seats, a tall man in a gray suit strolled over to our table and placed his hand on the back of the empty chair. He was fair-skinned with neatly trimmed black hair and the most radiant blue eyes I'd ever seen peeking beneath a deep-set brow. The stark contrast of his bright stare against the backdrop of such harsh features was an unsettling juxtaposition. Control warring with passion. Beauty marred by ferocity. The man was utterly captivating.

"I suppose this one's for me." He nodded stoically. "Connor Reid, and you must be the Geneveses."

My father rose swiftly, followed by my dumbfounded mother, whose trembling hand clutched at her chest.

"Connor," she breathed. The breadth of emotion contained in that one exalted word brought tears to my eyes. She was finally getting to meet the child she'd missed for so many years.

My brother's face softened when his eyes fell on her. "Mia, it's good to finally meet you."

Mom choked on a laugh mixed with a sob. "Yes, um, you can't imagine how happy I am to be here. Let me introduce you to everyone. This is Edoardo and the girls—Giada, Camilla, and Valentina."

Dad shook Connor's hand, and we girls smiled and waved in turn.

"Have a seat," Dad said before returning to his own chair. "Do you eat at Neary's often?"

My eyes bulged. Was he really going to bring up the restaurant? Connor was never going to give us a chance if Dad scared him off during the first meeting.

"I think it's lovely," I chirped. "I don't get to eat in town often, so trying something new is a treat."

Connor's eyes flitted briefly to me before rebounding straight back to my dad. "I do come here often. It's family-owned. That's actually why I wanted you to see the place." His tone was businesslike. Confident. He didn't seem affected by my father at all, which said a lot about him. Dad's intensity was often more than most could bear.

Dad lifted his chin. "I'm aware of its ownership, but I wasn't aware of your connection to the family."

"I suspected as much. The Byrnes' are my godparents."

As the two men spoke, the rest of us looked back and forth between them as if we were watching a strange tennis match, the rules of which were undefined. What was going on? Dad and Connor seemed to be having a coded conversation the rest of us couldn't follow.

My father leaned back in his chair. "And how does your godfather feel about this little family reunion?"

"He thinks it's fate."

"And you?"

Connor lifted a shoulder. "What else could it be when the long-lost son of the Italian mafia is raised at the table of the Byrne Brothers?"

Our small corner of the pub went eerily still.

No wonder Dad had been so wary about our dinner. Neary's was owned by the Irish mob. I didn't know much about them, but I'd heard whispers of the Byrnes. Had Dad told Mom his suspicions? Just how thoroughly had he investigated Connor before tonight?

Giada, being Giada, was the first to break the spell. "First the cartel, then a federal agent, now the Irish. We're like Rudolph's Island of Misfit Toys."

One by one, we all tumbled into a fit of nervous laughter. Even Connor couldn't fight off a glimmer of amusement. As though we'd passed some sort of test, he motioned to a waitress and eased us into the start of dinner. From that point on, our conversation flowed, and new alliances were forged. Dad even partook in Connor's chosen brand of whiskey instead of his usual dinner wine.

I could see hints of my mother in Connor's profile, but he had to have taken strongly after his father. I wondered who the man had been. I couldn't imagine not knowing my past. Had that uncertainty molded Connor into the guarded man sitting at our table, or had his newfound Irish family been at the root? While he'd relaxed enough to converse, he was by no means at ease. Connor was a fortress of a man.

I could only hope he'd let us in one day because he was our blood—our family—no matter who had raised him. Getting to know him might not be easy, but it would be worth it. And if the Irish became a part of our world, I had a feeling life would never be dull. Although, we Genoveses never had a problem keeping things lively. Yeah, I had a feeling Connor was going to fit right in.

Thank you so much for reading PERFECT ENEMIES!

Bonus Chapter

While Santino and Reyna's relationship may have been a side plot, the evolution of their love was still a paramount part of the *Five Families* saga. I wanted to give them a satisfying resolution but felt like it would take the spotlight away from our leads, so I wrote a bonus chapter where the two could solidify their feelings for one another. Senior prom can be a very momentous evening—a night full of firsts—and it's no less magical for our couple.

Flip the page and read about every delicious detail!

A Note from Jill

The Five Families is a series of interconnected standalones, and while *Perfect Enemies* is the final installment of the series, I'm thrilled to announce that I will be doing a three-book spin-off series called *The Byrne Brothers* about Connor and his brothers in the Irish underworld. Those will kick off in 2022 after the duet I've got planned for my next release. So many exciting things to come!!!

***

Didn't catch the beginning of The Five Families Series?
Check out book 1, Forever Lies,
to learn about Alessia and the chance elevator encounter that changed her life forever.

***

Make sure to join my Facebook reader group and keep in touch!

Jill's Ravenous Readers

BONUS CHAPTER
Reyna

"Pardon the interruption, but your limo is here."

Edoardo Genovese stood in the doorway to my room, where Val and I had gathered to finish getting ready. Her dad had black hair and dark eyes like my father, but the two men were nothing alike. When Edoardo looked at his youngest daughter, the cunning in his sharp gaze softened with the gentle crinkle in the corners of his eyes, not regaining any of that hard edge after shifting his focus to me. My father would have seen the daughter of his dead rival as a tool to instill fear in anyone else who might challenge him. I couldn't fathom the hell Valentina would have experienced had the tables been turned.

I had to remind myself regularly that Juan Carlos Vargas was dead whenever the anxiety he triggered started to close in around me.

My father was dead, and I was free.

I'd never been so happy in my life.

"You ladies look absolutely stunning. In fact…" Creases formed on Edoardo's forehead as he looked back at his daughter. "You two look a little *too* beautiful. Maybe I should tell the two gentlemen in my living room that they need to head home."

"Daddy!" Val called to him playfully.

Edoardo grunted. "You have your watch on?"

She lifted her wrist to display the elegant platinum timepiece. "Always. I don't even take it off to shower."

He dropped his chin and frowned. "That only leaves us with one problem." When his eyes lifted to me, my stomach knotted with worry. "I need all my girls to be safe, including you, Reyna." Edoardo handed me a small box I hadn't noticed he was carrying.

My hand had the slightest tremor when I took the package from him and removed the silver gift wrap. Inside was a watch identical to Valentina's. I slipped it from its container and admired the extravagant gift with a ball of emotion lodge in my throat. On the back was an engraving.

Family 03.30.20

The day my father was killed, and I became a part of the Genovese family.

I'd never received a more precious gift. Tears blurred my vision as I stood and wrapped my arms around Edoardo's middle.

"Thank you … for everything."

He placed his hand gently on the back of my head so as

not to disturb my styled hair and held me close. "Wear it in good health, my dear."

"We're going to ruin our makeup," Val sniffled. She snagged a tissue for herself and handed me one. We both laughed as we dabbed at our eyes.

"What on earth is going on?" Val's mom stepped into the room. "I leave you two for five minutes, and you're suddenly in tears. Come on, it's time to get some pictures. Then it'll be my turn to cry." She didn't ask about the watch, but I got the sense she knew. She was very involved in her family, which was a welcome change in my world. She'd been so excited to go to the salon with us and take part in getting us ready. Maybe one day, I would have that again with my mom, but it was still too early in her recovery for me to emotionally invest in that possibility. For now, I would just be grateful I had Val's parents in my life.

Edoardo excused himself as we made our last adjustments before heading downstairs. We'd both gone with updos as a more formal look for prom. Val had chosen a sultry red floor-length dress, mentioning that red was Kane's favorite color. I had found an emerald-green satin gown that I adored. The bodice was snug, accentuating my modest curves, and the full skirt made me feel like royalty. Val and I had collapsed in a fit of giggles at the dress shop when we realized we'd look like a Christmas tree together. We quickly agreed that neither of us cared and bought our dresses without a single regret.

Everything about prom was like a dream. Instead of going to the dance out of fear that my life would soon be over, I was totally unencumbered. My heart was full of joy and gratitude for the blessings in my life. That and ... anticipation for a little surprise I'd arranged for that night.

When we stepped into the doorway of the living room, Kane and Santino simultaneously rose to their feet with matching looks of awe on their faces. Kane wore an all-black suit—his shirt, tie, and vest all in the same shade of midnight. It wasn't a tux, but the monochromatic style with vest was plenty dressy and unquestionably handsome. The style suited his complicated personality and would be a striking backdrop next to Valentina's crimson form.

Kane shook his stupor first and coasted to Val, but I paid no mind because I only had eyes for Santino. My date wore a somewhat more traditional tuxedo, the thin lapel made with rich velvet, and a stark white pocket square with three sharp peaks on his chest. It was the only adornment for the modern look, giving Santino a sophisticated, classic vibe that I found absolutely bewitching. He was the most gorgeous, captivating man I'd ever met, and his eyes drank me in like a dying man at the fountain of youth.

One measured step at a time, he drew closer until the green satin of my dress brushed against his thighs. "Princesa, you are the most enchanting thing I've ever seen." He lifted my hand to his lips and pressed a kiss to the back of my fingers.

Heat blossomed across my cheeks. "You might not say that if you could see yourself. You're too handsome to be real." But he was real. And he was mine.

We'd spent every opportunity getting to know one another over the past month since my father had been removed as a threat. He came to the house in the evenings and took me out on weekends. I'd learned about his background and how Javier had helped him off the streets. His mother had been killed in a car accident early in his life, and he'd never known his father. He'd taken me into town to see a Broadway show—something neither of us had ever done. We'd hung out with Val and Kane on a number of occasions. Gone out to eat and watched movies at the house. It was the most magical month I could ever remember having.

It didn't take much thought for me to realize I was in love.

I had doubted I'd ever have the luxury of romance, but now that I'd found the man of my dreams, I wanted him to know how I felt. Tonight would be the night.

"You two ready?" Val called to us. "We need to get pictures done if we're going to get to the restaurant on time."

I nodded, my cheeks now radiating heat like a supernova from embarrassment over where my thoughts had taken me.

"Just one more thing first," Santino said before retrieving two clear boxes from an end table. He handed one to Kane, then opened the lid of the remaining box and removed a gorgeous white rose corsage. He slipped the delicate arrangement over my wrist, stepping back but keeping my hands clasped in his. "Absolutely stunning."

Unable to help myself, I swept forward and placed a kiss on his cheek. Fortunately, Val had made sure we were both wearing smudge-proof lipstick.

Santino grinned proudly, then squeezed my hand.

"Okay, it's photo time! And I don't want to hear any complaints." Mrs. Genovese clapped her hands together and ushered us out to the back patio. We spent a full thirty minutes on photos without the hint of a grimace from anyone. When we wrapped up, Val and I made one more pit stop to freshen up before we met the limo out front.

Despite growing up wealthy, I'd never ridden in a limo before. My father had always insisted on using his armored cars for fear of an attack, no matter the occasion. Tonight, fear was a distant memory. The Genoveses had provided a limousine outfitted with the finest luxury finishes. Val and I sat across from the guys, giggling and singing to the pop music filling the cavernous seating area.

The limo ride was invigorating and only the beginning of a night full of firsts.

We had a delectable dinner at a local steakhouse where the homemade rolls basted in butter melted on our tongues. I guessed Mr. Genovese had made arrangements for us because a check never arrived at our table. The guys exchanged a knowing look before helping us from our seats and summoning the limo driver.

On our ride to the dance, I wondered if a person could die from happiness. My heart was so full of gratitude that I thought it might split wide open.

From the minute we got back into the limo until an hour into the dance when Val and I excused ourselves to the restroom, Santino maintained constant contact with me. Whether it was the brush of our thighs while we sat next to one another or the gentle support of his hand at the small of my back, his strength and warmth were my constant companion. I adored knowing he wanted me near him just as much as I craved his presence.

We took silly pictures together in the photo booth, danced without a care in the middle of the crowd, and laughed until my belly ached in the very best way. I'd been doubled over laughing at a group of guys showing off their prowess at doing the worm when the music transitioned to the first slow song of the night.

Santino sobered and stepped close, taking my hand in his. My breathing hitched.

"May I have this dance, princesa?" he murmured just over the music.

"Of course."

He pulled me securely against him, our bodies flush as the strains of Taylor Swift's "Lover" filled the air around us. Gently swaying to the soft melody, we soaked in the perfection of the moment.

I hadn't been sure how I'd unveil my surprise that night, but that song had been the perfect segue to my plans. When the music began to bleed into another more fast-paced song, I took Santino's hand and pulled him toward the table where Val and I had left our clutch bags. Unclasping the white satin, I pulled out a plastic key card and held it between us.

"What's this?" he asked.

I gnawed on my bottom lip, suddenly self-conscious. "I had kind of hoped we could end our night upstairs. This day has been incredible, but one thing would make it absolutely perfect."

Santino's piercing stare held me captive. Ignoring the card, he pulled me in close, one hand encircling the side of my neck. "Are you saying what I think you're saying?" His voice was abraded down to coarse gravel, scraping sensually across my skin.

I nodded.

"You know I love you enough to wait. You don't need to do this for me."

My nerves melted to a pool of liquid elation at the sound of those words on his lips. Santino loved me. It was the first time he'd said it. I'd felt it in every caress and stare, yet hearing it was different. It was concrete and tangible and all the affirmation I needed.

"Nothing would make me happier. I love you, too, Santino."

Our lips found one another in a lingering kiss full of promise.

I may not have had much experience with boyfriends, but I knew the difference between bad and good. I'd seen every form of unsavory man through my father's business dealings. I knew exactly what I didn't want, and in defining that, I also knew what I did want, and Santino was everything I could have asked for. I didn't need a collection of conquests to know when I had a good thing.

"This is your last high school dance. You sure you don't want to stay a bit longer?" The corner of his mouth crooked upward.

"No, thank you. I know exactly what I want."

His beautiful lips spread into a full grin.

"I just need to let Val know we're headed up."

"Lead the way." He motioned toward the dance floor with one hand and kept his other clasped in mine.

I managed to catch her eye at a distance. She did an exaggerated motion pointing up, and when I nodded, she jumped up and down and shot me a giddy thumbs-up. I could only laugh. She'd driven us here earlier in the day so we could check in to our reserved rooms. I wasn't the only one with a key card in her purse. Edoardo expected us home by two a.m., but the night was ours until then.

The close confines of an elevator ride amplified the anticipation to an intoxicating degree. We rode to the ninth floor with an older couple, necessitating a degree of decorum. I managed to keep a lid on my hyperactive nerves until we reached our room. Once the key card clicked into place and the door swung wide, reality was its own sobering force.

This was it.

I was going to share my body with this man. A man I loved to the depths of my soul. My savior saint.

He slipped my clutch from my hand and absently set it on a bureau before kissing me deeply. I relaxed into the kiss, but my fingers were anxious for more. We'd done plenty of kissing over the past month, and I'd been thinking about this night for ages. Imagining the feel of his skin. Dreaming about the first sight of him bare before me.

I pushed his jacket over his broad shoulders. While he slid it the rest of the way down his arms, I made quick work of his bowtie, then focused my attention on his buttons.

"You in a rush?" he teased gently, stilling my hands in his.

"I've been imagining you naked for weeks. If I don't see more of you soon, I might explode."

He chuckled before breezing through the buttons and pulling his shirt loose, giving me a glimpse of his golden skin beneath while he worked at his cuffs. Instead of discarding his shirt with his jacket, he lifted a finger and swirled it, instructing me to turn around.

I exhaled shakily and complied.

His warm hands ghosted up my arms. As they slid from my shoulders down to the zipper at the back of my dress, his lips trailed kisses along my neck.

"You are incredible, Reyna Vargas. Your courage and kindness are only matched by your breathtaking beauty. I'm not sure how I could have earned such a precious treasure but know that I will never take you for granted. You are *everything* to me." His words wrapped protectively around my heart while his hands eased my dress toward the floor.

I took a shuddering breath and turned to face him. His eyes held mine, despite the temptation of my exposed breasts. He helped me step out from the pile of my skirt, then shrugged off his shirt. I'd expected to be awestruck by the sight of him, but I could never have imagined how I'd feel when he revealed a newly inked crown tattoo over his heart with my name scribed on the inside of the back rim.

It was simple yet elegant. The only artwork gracing his copper-skinned chest.

A crown for his princesa.

My hand was instantly drawn to the smooth lines, still healing. "You've marked yourself with my name." Saying the words didn't make it any more real. It felt like a dream. I meant so much to him that he was willing to put a permanent reminder of me on his body. "When? Why didn't you tell me?" The words tumbled out of my mouth without thought. I was too dumbfounded to think clearly.

"Last week. I didn't say anything because I didn't want to scare you."

"Scare me?"

"With the intensity of my feelings. I didn't want to overwhelm you."

I leaned in and placed a delicate kiss at the center of the crown. "I can't think of anything more beautiful than to be overwhelmed with love. Feel free to overwhelm me anytime."

Santino pulled me hungrily against him, ravishing my mouth with his. The heat of his chest blistered against mine, stirring an erotic warmth deep in my belly. It was a sensation he'd conjured time and again, but this time, I would follow it to its end. See what delights my body could produce.

I pulled at his belt to release the buckle, my hands exploring his washboard abs when he took over and freed himself from his slacks. Once we were both left in our underwear, he walked me to the bed, easing me onto my back, then hovered over me. His kisses lowered down to my breasts where he lavished each modest peak with dedicated attention. Every caress of his tongue and graze of his teeth spurred on the molten pleasure building deep in my core as if a system of nerves ran directly between the two locations. I couldn't believe I could feel such aching arousal without him ever touching me down there.

I'd thought about exploring my own body in the past, but when my every movement was on camera, I was too scared I'd be caught on film and end up entertaining my father's guards. It had been too risky. All I'd known was the few times my fingers had explored my folds over the past month while I was safe in my own bed at the Genovese house where I wouldn't be exploited.

Santino knew how to coax my body into mindlessness better than I had imagined possible.

When he slid my panties down past my ankles and brought his mouth to the apex of my thighs, I thought my mind would shatter. I gasped, sucking in a lungful of air before releasing it on a wanton moan that would have embarrassed me beyond measure if I'd been remotely conscious of my actions.

"It feels … so good," I breathed shakily. "Please, don't stop."

"I wouldn't stop if the world ended outside our door. I'm going to give this perfect body of yours so much pleasure, you'll never want to leave my side." He nipped at the inside of my thigh, startling me. Before I could respond, he licked the length of my slit, sending me back to an ocean of disoriented bliss.

He nudged a single finger inside me, continuing his ministrations to my throbbing clit. I was stunned at how the pressure from his intrusion intensified the pleasure. When his other hand came up to flick one of my nipples, the sensation building inside me threatened to drag me under.

I gasped and writhed.

"Let it happen, princesa. Don't fight it."

I tried to obey, but my muscles squeezed without any permission from me. I thought maybe I was doing something wrong when my legs began to twitch on either side of his head. When I glanced down, Santino's eyes were already trained on me victoriously. His tongue switched its motion just as his fingers flicked at my other nipple, and I tumbled over a cliff I'd never known existed.

I cried out as pleasure lanced through my body like pure rays of sunshine piercing the dark. Every molecule. Every nerve. Every fiber. Alive with electric energy. The pleasure flowed through me, pulsing and ebbing from one extremity to another until my mind eventually drifted back into the confines of my body.

My eyes drifted open to find Santino above me, staring as if memorizing my every feature.

"That was ... there aren't words," I rasped.

"That was only the beginning." My beautiful man smiled warmly down at me.

My body felt utterly spent, and while I was thrilled with what we'd done, I wanted more. Sensing his hard length pressed against my thigh, I rolled on my side and cupped him over the gray briefs he still wore.

His breathing hitched. "That's not exactly what I meant. We don't have to do that tonight."

"I want to. I want to feel you inside me, and I want it tonight."

His forehead dropped humbly to mine. "I love you, princesa."

"I love you, too."

His lips gently touched mine before he lifted himself up and slid off his underwear. The sight of his cock drew all moisture from my mouth. Thick and ridged with veins, his dark shaft bobbed heavily with a slight lean to one side. His body was incredible, even with the gnarly scar on his right shoulder where my uncle had shot and nearly killed him months earlier. The skin was still pink and newly healed, but it only added to his perfection. He was a survivor, like me.

"I didn't exactly know this was on the menu tonight, so I didn't bring protection."

I grinned impishly. "There are a couple of condoms in my purse."

He retrieved the small bag and fished out a foil packet. I watched intently as he rolled the clear latex onto himself in one smooth motion. "This will hurt some. I can't promise it will feel good this time." He settled back over me, and I lifted my legs to draw him closer to me.

"I'm glad. That means you're my first, and it's something special we'll always share."

He grunted. "First and *only*."

I bit my lip on a giggle that morphed to a gasp when his tip began to press at my opening.

"Breathe, princesa. Breathe and keep your eyes on mine." He rocked gently, allowing my body to adjust and stretch. After a minute, once he was an inch or so inside me, he paused to bring his lips back to my breasts. His teasing licks coaxed a renewed coil of desire to unfurl in my belly.

It was time.

He brought his gaze back to mine, ensuring I had no second thoughts, then surged inside me, pushing past the barrier of my virginity. I gasped at the brief sting but was surprised that it hurt less than I'd anticipated. Maybe the course of my perfect day had helped. Or maybe the pain was less because the man I was with made me so deliriously happy that he chased it away. What I felt was a fullness that mirrored the swell of love in my heart.

Santino trembled above me. "Are you okay?"

"Yes, you?"

He chuckled, making us both moan. "With you naked beneath me, I will always be more than okay."

When he began to gently thrust, I stiffened a tad before relaxing and welcoming the feel of him moving inside me. His body arched and flexed with each movement as though he clasped his own reins with infinite control. I began to move with him as though dancing to a song I'd known all my life. In a matter of minutes, Santino seized me tightly, hissing as his cock seemed to grow even larger inside me with his release.

Never letting me go, he rolled to my side and nuzzled his face against my neck. "I kept it quick so you wouldn't be too sore. Next time, we can go slow and explore."

Next time. I grinned.

Who would have thought life could be so good.

A Note from Jill

The first time Reyna appeared in *The Five Families* world was back in book 4, *Impossible Odds*. She's one of those side characters that grows a voice and begs to have her story told. I knew I wanted a happy ending for Santino, and when I developed Reyna further to write *Perfect Enemies*, I knew the two characters were destined for one another. Santino was the perfect man to give Reyna the worthy, honorable love she so deserved.

I considered writing a separate novella for the two, but their story fit so well within the Valentina's book that I decided to weave the two together in the hope that they compliment the overall story rather than distract. Hopefully you enjoyed reading their bonus romance as much as I loved crafting it. Bringing two enemies together is fun, but sometimes a pure, gentle love is just what the soul needs.

Know that the saint will cherish his princess, always.
And the princess will love her saint till the end of time.

***

Intrigued by Conner Reid?
Check out Silent Vows, the first book in The Byrne Brothers spin-off series.
Noemi Mancini has been promised to a ruthless Irishman. He represents everything she hates in the world yet summons her darkest cravings. She wants nothing to do with him, but if she tries to refuse him, her father will kill her. There is no escape, and the worse part is, a part of her doesn't want to.

***

Didn't catch the beginning of The Five Families Series?
Check out book 1, Forever Lies,
to learn about Alessia and the chance elevator encounter that changed her life forever.

***

Make sure to head to my website at www.jillramsower.com
to join my newsletter and keep in touch!

ACKNOWLEDGMENTS

I wanted to take this chance to give a heartfelt thanks to the ladies of Shameless Book Con. As you may or may not know, the romance book market is rather flooded. Getting books to readers isn't always easy, and it's hard for a reader to know what books to choose from the plethora of options. A successful publishing career requires tons of hard work, a little luck, and some priceless help from those already entrenched in the business. In the past, I've thanked the individuals who have played a role in helping me—my incredible author friends, dedicated readers, family, editors and PR team—but the ladies behind Shameless deserve a hardy thanks as well.

As the 2021 event approaches, and I reminisce about 2019's shenanigans, I feel enormous gratitude that I was invited to be a part of such a spectacular gathering of book lovers. With the release of *Perfect Enemies*, I will celebrate my third anniversary as an author and have twelve published books to my name. However, the ladies of Shameless scooped me up from a vast sea full of authors and put a spotlight on me when I'd only published my *Fae Games* series of five books. They believed in me enough to give me a coveted spot in their lineup of Showcase Authors, and that meant the world to me.

Angie Lynch, Christine Ferrelli, and Angela Spencer,

thank you, from the bottom of my heart. All the dedication and energy you pour into hosting a weekend of spectacular events is appreciated on so many levels. While I'm excited to head to Orlando this year, I'm also incredibly humbled and grateful. I'm living my dream, and it couldn't have happened without the generosity of people like you.

ABOUT THE AUTHOR

Jill Ramsower is a life-long Texan—born in Houston, raised in Austin, and currently residing in West Texas. She attended Baylor University and subsequently Baylor Law School to obtain her BA and JD degrees. She spent the next fourteen years practicing law and raising her three children until one fateful day, she strayed from the well-trod path she had been walking and sat down to write a book. An addict with a pen, she set to writing like a woman possessed and discovered that telling stories is her passion in life.

Social Media & Website
Official Website: www.jillramsower.com
Jill's Facebook Page: www.facebook.com/jillramsowerauthor
Facebook Reader Group: Jill's Ravenous Readers
Instagram: @jillramsowerauthor
Twitter: @JRamsower

Made in United States
North Haven, CT
07 January 2023